T0149671

HIDDEN

HIDDEN

SACRED/SECRET

ATHLENE MACLEOD

HIDDEN
SACRED/SECRET

iUniverse books may be ordered through booksellers or by contacting:

iUniverse
1663 Liberty Drive
Bloomington, IN 47403
www.iuniverse.com
1-800-Authors (1-800-288-4677)

ISBN: 978-1-5320-6449-4 (sc)
ISBN: 978-1-5320-6450-0 (e)

Print information available on the last page.

iUniverse rev. date: 05/18/2019

"No people has ever insisted more firmly than the Jews
that history has a purpose and humanity a destiny."
— Paul Johnson

"No people has ever insisted more firmly than the
fundamentalist Mormon that the purpose of humanity is to
become like God and that to become as God one must find
his spiritual calling and become his human destiny."
— Anonymous

The question is: Has the Fundamentalist changed his ways and
given up? Or has he sociologically survived long enough and
adapted for so long that he is still here surviving in secret among
us? And ever a part of our environment the same way our brains
are distant from our souls and is he using silence and evolution
to reinvent with society its hidden outcomes and agendas?
What is a Fundamentalist?

Dedicated to
my mother Fern
my daughters SaMaria, Mary, Adona, Angela,
Eliza, Heidi, Ariel, Michal, Maryland

CONTENTS

PREFACE

December 31st, 2010 I met with four very amazing people and was asked to take a good look at writing a book, about the positive and hidden effects of polygamy in the United States. It didn't seem like a lofty idea to me, at the time but I seriously questioned who the audience would be?

Over the next few days, my mind zipped through old memories and stored journals from my grand-cesters!

Extensive research and a plot that would get someone interested... 'oh really'

Where did I start?

The reason we were entertaining a story about the effects of polygamy in the world was because we had a common respect for my daughter and several other people these friends had known over the years.

People they had lived next to, who had integrity and affinity for their communities and a deep love for their families; who were the proud and profound descendants of the polygamous culture.

In 2010 I was working with a young woman who had been searching for five years for her biological parents. She believed that she had already met her mother but for some "reason" the secret was being kept from her. As she did further research, she found a cousin who knew about her adoption and was informed that "it would be very dangerous" if she pursued the search any further!

However, after some fear and tears, she realized that her suspicion would not be satisfied by the answers she had found. Instead of the power of interest and love she previously had felt she was experiencing an astonishing concern that she was either stolen or sold as a child from the underground era of polygamous reform.

So, this young lady and I went to work looking for all the foster homes she had lived in. There was a repeat in these homes...a pattern occurred. She finally met her mother and to her sad and horrific surprise she found out that her mother had sold her not once but twice... At least that's how her mother saw it...

The bishopric where her mother resided had convinced her that the only way for "her or her baby" to receive salvation was for a holy adoption to go through, inside the temple. They told her, "this would cause a moral shift in their history". Her mother was so convinced that the only possible way for her to be "forgiven" and receive Eternal Life was to denounce the father of her child and allow a "worthy" set of parents to seal the baby to them in the House of God when it was eight days old! The first sale, she explained, had taken place before she had given birth!

The interesting thing is the mother never received any money. However, the adoptive parents paid the hospital bills, her rent for nine months and $50,000 to the Church adoption agency.

The young woman and I spent hundreds of hours looking for the records of foster children she knew who were related to her by blood lines. We found many children who had been ripped from their homes and placed in LDS Foster Care because their "immoral" parents were practicing a religion that was socially unacceptable? At the time, she still didn't know who her father was...an infamous polygamous, she thought.

The number of children that have been taken and hidden hasn't been addressed because it's "unheard of", astonishing and blasphemous to the LDS people.

The young woman found her adoption papers finally after seven years of intense research after questioning her mother repeatedly. The young lady's mother then told her daughter that not once, but twice she had been sold. The reasons became increasingly apparent as she and I looked further and further into: this outrageous idea of confiscating babies before they are born and impounding their bodies for research on the polygamous genes. (A story told to her by her mother after she had finally found her.) A research that will cause you to shutter.

Questioning Mormon officials about enacting such a heinous crime was one of my hidden intents, and I asked several bishops and stake presidents how they felt regarding the wellbeing of the innocent children whom were born to unmarried young people and polygamists and their reaction to this was unanimous! They all had the same belief that babies and children are far better off with a father and mother who has been sealed in the temple where they have a "chance" to serve the Lord and follow the "Living Prophet"! Without a previous briefing of any kind each of them simply said and almost word for word, "Polygamy is not ordained of God and is unrighteous and an abomination to the Lord and young women who get pregnant out of wedlock are considered irresponsible and counseled to give the child to parents who have been unfortunate at conceiving their own but willing to sacrifice for a child's future and faith."

When I asked, "Did not our Prophet Joseph Smith establish this Celestial Marriage law when he was here?"

"Oh, yes, but that was done away with long ago. It was only to take care of the widows and orphans." They would come back with a hundred reasons that Joseph was still a prophet of God and worthy of 'ushering in the last dispensation of time', but, but, but.' Is it really possible that the souls of these precious babies and the salvation of the parents are at such a risk that they can be "taken, hidden and given away! Is it real?

YES, it is!!

My intention is not to prove Joseph Smith an imposter. Neither is it to prove that all polygamous people are bad people or good people. My intention is to bring out into the light the icons in history so that honor can be restored to some of the hidden ones.

One of my friends had worked at the DA's office in Salt Lake City for 35 years. And she had proof from the court trials that took place that they removed the children from their safe and loving homes because of 'technical errors' that occurred in the courtroom which were overlooked by attorneys working for the polygamous or defendants: proff that <u>they</u> would lose, and the Church would win. She also had proof that would aid our research.

She was so touched and inspired that we would actually attempt to challenge the Church on behalf of the mothers who had been robbed of loving and raising their own babies. Her heart and mind was actively looking for a way to get the innocent and the willing back to their families and she had helped several children find their way back home…

Who would believe that polygamous children fear being taken out of their homes because they are hated, not for who they are but because of the acts of their parents?

The fundamentalist parents of these polygamous children teach them that they are above the law of the land. They are taught to believe that the government of the religious body is above the legal laws in their jurisdiction because the laws of God are higher, more righteous, (not much different from the LDS Church) but the laws of man are evil and are created to protect the criminals.

They are taught that the innocent need no recourse and that only the criminal would beg for pardon against a crime they have not yet paid. The children are taught to pay every day for their wrong doings and to repent and seek forgiveness even if they are uncertain of their shame or guilt.

They are taught that they are bound by a higher law that gives them __no__ room for error in their personal lives and therefore they could not break the lesser laws of man.

Just like all other societies where the rules get broken by the few it is the whole-body that reaps the benefits or the consequences of the rebellious.

"Jesus was a rebel." They are taught, but his law was not for the week it is for the meek.

When Jesus said, "And the meek shall inherit the earth. (That word that did not exist in Jesus' day).

Polygamous' are not the only fundamentalists…

The Lost Books of The Bible teaches that Jesus said, "And the innocent shall inherit the earth."

These children are trained to follow orders until they have a mind of their own and can make decisions that are good for "all."

But there are always those whose job it is in every society to challenge the "way". They are the Orin Porter Rockwell's and the Martin Harris's in every culture and in this history, it is John W. Young the son of Brigham Young!

It seems that Utah took on the right to condemn any and all who embarrasses the Authorities. The same thing that the Pharisees and Sadducees were doing in Jesus's time.

It seems Utah has taken on the scapegoat effect: killing one goat for the law and letting the others go free for the purpose of glorifying the policymaker. Scandalous!

The way we see it is that Utah is still using "polygamy" as a term in the court system to condemn those they want convicted and to exonerate those they want to expunge.

Examples will be made for this opinion, by way of controversy and enlightenment and by way of historical evidence...And the bold term "adoption" is the largest course of rancor and a counterfeit course of salvation for the indentured servants of the Lord or otherwise...

Known as wayward and insubordinate followers: the polygamous who choose to live the law they have been taught instead of following the living prophet are excommunicated and their "life works" are expunged from the records of the church.

And that is what happened to John W Young.

INTRODUCTION

I was twelve years old when I went to care for my great-grandmother. I was muscular and tall for my age so I thought that was why she had requested my assistance. The year I went to her home was 1946. I could be with her for only ninety days. School would start again, and I could not afford to miss any school. Besides I had a boyfriend no one knew about, and I wasn't going to let anyone know how precious he had become to me. I often felt homesick after separating from him on the path coming home from school.

My great-grandmother was 106 years old at the time I went to care for her. She lived exactly one more year, to the date, from when I arrived to care for her. On June 5th, 1947, she passed into the next life…I am now looking back into my stay with her and getting the facts, and my feelings sorted out. She was an amazing woman and had a rich and dramatic history.

Thank the Good Lord I kept an elaborate journal of my time with her and the vibrant and resilient stories she told me.

I am 68 years old now. It is the year of our Lord 2002, and I have been amazed abundantly in my life by the challenges given to the "children of men" and the "saints" …I have suffered my share of indecencies and heartbreak in my life, but I don't see myself as less fortunate than my fellows. I have had my share of exotic and elaborate experiences as well. Sometimes I see myself a continuation of my great-grandmother's story and sometimes I feel like there's a breach in the contract I might have had with her amazing and passionate Lord.

CHAPTER 1

May Constance Alexandria Davis

Born in London, England on May 30ᵗʰ, 1840 in a small hamlet called Honeybrooke, where May lived until she was ten years old.

She ferried across the Cambridge River and "swam the vast waters of the Atlantic", in 1850. Her ship docked in Port James on October 25ᵗʰ, 1850. The whole adventure across the ocean took 21 days and 14 hours 22 minutes and 15 seconds.

After a short stay and a winter of heartbreak in Jersey City with her uncle, she made a long and arduous trip to Salt Lake Valley. She arrived in Salt Lake City on the 24ᵗʰ of July 1851 with her sister Annie and her Aunt Millie. She was eleven years old, and the huge party, she felt, had been set up just for her personal liking. Upon arrival in the great new city of Zion, she and her companions went directly to the President's house and were immediately put to work as per the terms of their agreements and contract with her father.

May's, Aunt Millie was nineteen and built like a princess and her sister Annie was seventeen and built like a workhorse. The combination was perfect for May, my great-grandmother, who was neither shy nor awkward, but young for an immigrant and apprentice.

The President, and also a prophet, Brigham Young gave them room and board and two days to recover the long journey to Zion. On Monday morning at 3: AM they altogether attended morning prayers and began the long life of pioneering the new frontier.

My great-grandmother called the President and his associates "brothers." As "God would have it," it turned out to be a blessing in general for my great-grandmother, which by terms of her own vocabulary she married her "brother" and no one, would have known the difference. And strange as it was, her children were accustomed to calling their own father "uncle" until they were old enough to figure it out for themselves.

Because of the age difference in my great-grandmother and my great-grandfather, it was easy to understand the almost silent way they lived their life. My great-grandmother's love for her husband was bound by a reverence that took my breath away when she spoke of him. But still, she kept her maiden name and was known all her life as "Sister May Davis."

She fell in love in 1845, when she was five years old and smitten with the deepest love. She told my great-grandfather in 1854 of her love for him, at that time great-grandmother was only 14 years old. As fate, would have it, she was separated from him for almost two years. As he served a mission, in Britain. They married on the 28th of July, 1856 in the Lion House. Then later when the endowment house was finished, they took their endowments together.

She gave birth to 6 children in 8 years' time. During the first 7 years of her marriage 2 of her children died in her arms and 1 year later so, also did her husband.

At 36, she delivered her granddaughter, and 11 years later she watched as her youngest daughter, only 17 years old, slip away; dying in childbirth.

Her first and oldest living son, Hyram was crippled, like her father, from a fever caused by a bullet wound given to him when he was 13 years old, which often reminded her of her father's crippling from the fever of the Spanish Influenza.

She was the third wife of Joseph Fielding. Then my Great-grandmother gave him three more wives during the first six years of their marriage...

There was an explosion on their anniversary in 1862, that took his life, in 1863.

Twenty-six months after her marriage to Joseph she gave her best friend, Libby to him as a wife. Libby died in my great-grandmother's house of milk fever three years later, leaving her six-month-old son, Heber, for my great-grandmother to breastfeed and nurture. She said it was as if she had triplets...

CHAPTER 2

England

Tuesday morning after cleaning the hen house I came in for morning milk and cheese to find great-grandmother with a stack of black and white pictures. The edges were crumpled, and the images were fading slightly, but I could tell she had not shared these pictures very often. I felt a sense of deep respect and reverence by the way she sat in her chair, so upright and elegant. Her view of me took me by surprise. I very quietly pulled the hardwood chair away from the cold stainless steel table and sat waiting for her to say prayers. With my head bowed and my hands folded neatly in my lap she started instead with such a surprise she said...

"When I was a small child I went with my elder brother Henry, my Father and my Mother to visit my grandparents in Manchester. My sister Annie was sick at home with the flu and in those days, we seldom took any more risks than absolutely necessary. We stayed at your great-great-grandparents for about a month, I believe. I was given a chance to meet and enjoy my cousins, Aunties, and Uncles, my blessed family, as only a young child can experience. My mother's father had met a powerful man that he wanted my parents to meet with and have long conversations about the gospel and to look at the business and how it was leading the industry in Manchester."

I reached to touch the photo on top. That had caught my eye. Great-grandmother tapped my hand, and I recoiled it back to my lap.

"Please wash and dry up first, my dear." She requested.

Great-grandmother then paused and said a simple and clever prayer for our bread and milk and cheese, ending with, "I declare in the name of Jesus our friend, AMEN!" Then she started her story again with,

"My introduction to the gospel was sure-footed from the beginning. I had my first acquaintance with Joseph Smith the "Prophet" in a way that was bound to influence anyone.

"Only five years old, I was one of the delights of that era. Somehow, I had survived the cholera, Spanish Influenza, and the plague that hit the surrounding area and so had my parents. The major destruction of the cholera and epidemics of the time had taken many of my aunts and uncles, father's mother, and cousins I never had a chance to know. I was a shining hope for my family. My mother lost two of her children to the flu and three others born after me. They probably died due to mother's frailties and malnutrition, which was very common for women who wore corsets in those days. She nearly died herself as she cared for my father when he caught the Spanish Influenza. Mother's father, William, recovered but was left with a gait that was embarrassing to him for years afterward. When he was on the mend and working hard, my father's business became highly useful, and he grew to great status in the community. Many prominent men sought him out for his services. He owned and operated a printing company and was brilliant in the art of print and designs.

"My father inherited his printing knowledge from his father. In those days having a family business was such a powerful means to an end…the end being wealth in the next generation…unlike what happened in America most recently.

"There is little respect today for the old common goals and achievements. That I am sorry for. Back then we all expected the value of our parents work to carry on, making life more reliable and friendly for our children's children."

That was how it would begin with my great-grandmother, the way it started, to unravel; Her story. I watched over her for 90 days. I did little jobs, washed walls, cleaned cabinets and crystal pieces. I took walks with her and helped pull countless weeds, and more and more; An unreasonable list of things. The beginning was beautiful and eerie; the end was passionate and eternal.

I think every child should have a chance to know the great people who helped them get their roots: the foundation of their existence.

My father and mother hardly knew great-grandmother. They spoke of her seldom. While I was spending the summer with my great-grandmother, I would often wonder how my parents were surviving without her love and her inherited grace and understanding about the world… When they had shared their memories, with me, it was more like a lost idea than an embracing one. My mother had spent some time collecting family genealogy from great-grandmother. She gathered a few poems and prose, some military documents, a playwright, church records and such that she had used to prove relationships to members of our family. But the little book my mother put together squelched the intangible worth of the five generations of history packed into the layers of society great-grandmother embodied.

My mother's keen interest in family history was probably my ticket to the convalescence of my great-grandmother. What a blessing to have my life wrapped into my great-grandmothers.

It is more of a blessing to me now though than I felt it was then. Having Great-Grandmother memories and my mind working together now is much more helpful in the challenges I must face today. I love to reminisce that special time we spent together.

CHAPTER 3

The Long Road to Great-Grandma

There was a long dirt road to great-grandma's house. As we bumped along from gravel to sand and back to gravel again, I felt like I was on a rollercoaster ride. My tummy would go up and then down making me laugh out-loud and giggle as we went along.

My parents were proud of their beautiful and durable, blue 1945 convertible. I loved going fast. I kept saying to Daddy "go faster, go faster." My brother was annoyed by me, but he was just as eager as I was.

'Daddy's little girl,' I got whatever I wanted, that's what Jonny always said to me.

Mother had a hard time handling the jarring of the car and was competing with me on the other end of the spectrum asking daddy to slow down, or she would hurl. I sensed he was having a good time making her uncomfortable. He said we were late and in a hurry now, but slowed down a little just to speed up again. I will never forget that ride. I still feel the warm summer air on my face, and the tug on my scalp as the wind tore at my hair. Neither will I forget the mess I had to brush out when we got to great-grandmas.

Great-grandmother had asked if I could spend the summer with her. My mother and father had several discussions about me going and decided it couldn't hurt for me to spend time with her and it would be useful for my personal development. So, they said. I sensed my age a difficult factor for my dad and my independence for my mom. Mom was concerned that I would not take the responsibility seriously, and my dad was concerned that I wasn't big enough. I kept saying over and over again, "I'll show you, I will show you."

The big trees and the smell of the stream running in front of the property were what caught my attention first. I saw the trees long before we reached them and the water along the side of the road came right up to great-grandmothers driveway and looked so inviting. It was hot, so hot; I swear you could see the moisture evaporating over the ditch. I saw asparagus at the corner of the long driveway, and I saw cattails and pussy willows by the bank of trees that ran the whole distance of Great-Grandmothers yard. I was dying to check out the barn and old sheds and the path that lead to an abrupt stop across the lake. And before the car came to a stop, I got my first warning, "Don't you dare run off now! Until you see your great-grandmother and have been invited to go off, do you hear me?" My mom nearly shouted.

My father opened the door, and mom grunted out of the car carrying her big belly out in front like a water ball and cradling the side of her belly with her hand.

We knew she would be having the baby soon and one of my family's concerns was me not being around when she delivered. Oh, well I said to myself, it's not like she had me to help-out when she had Johnny.

My mom was beautiful, shining, and glorious to me. My dad helped her out of the car and carefully helped her from the dirt driveway to the long sidewalk that ran the distance of the lawn. There was a little bridge of concrete that covered a small part of the stream, which was full of fresh irrigation water. I watched them cross over the concrete bridge with care and grace, my brother right behind them...like a stupid ritual. I took off and jumped the distance from the driveway to the sidewalk clearing the stream and long patch of grass...coming in for a landing about twenty feet in front of my family. I was cool! But my mom thought otherwise, "Are you going to make a show before you even get to the door!" She chided.

"Come on Nessy! She's just excited to be here." My dad returned. Mom rolled her eyes at him with that look that says, "You are going to be the death of me!"

I inherited my mother first name, Vanessa. My dad called mom Nessy when he was coddling her, but he called her Vanessa when he needed her attention or was demanding the attention of her.

"Behave yourself, please." She begged me...and I became the cute little princess in the darling little petticoat and chiffon dress, my mother made me out to be...

"Well, hello, there you are, come in, come in." My great-grandmother met us at the door looking like a goddess in a satin dress with an unpainted face and small flowers in her beautiful hair.

How can something so old be up and about, my mind was screaming? By the looks of my family, I wasn't the only one questioning it either.

Hugs were exchanged and then tea. They talked, and I looked around.

Great-grandma said, "I can tell you are just dying to go check things out. Your room is that one right off the bathroom in the hall and when you get to the barn and the chicken coop remember you are in a dress; I saw your stunt in the front yard. Little escapes my notice dear. John dear, help your sister get her things from the car…Is that ok Henry? We have things to talk about and the children have discoveries to make." She smiled at my father and he excused us.

My dad just shrugged his shoulders, and looked like he was about to ask, "Is there any other possibility?" My mother smiled in her disapproving, "approval in a way." Her smile warned me again to take notice of my behavior…she was about to be embarrassed again and she just knew it.

But I left gracefully and helped my brother unpack my things. Until last month he was my best friend in the whole wide world and nothing could compare to how I enjoyed his company. He was always so thoughtful and generous. He didn't seem to be older than me; we got along like we were the same age. But when he went to high school things began to change and for the whole school year I was trying to work things out in my head. What happened? I figured it out last month finally. He grew up, and I wasn't ready to lose him yet. So, I was making life difficult on every level. Somehow, I had to make him hate me so I could make the separation without getting hurt. At the same time, I was challenging new feelings about my newly recovered old best friend, who was now the object of all my spare time and imagined affections.

Johnny and I went and saw the barn and the chicken coop…I counted twenty-six hens and one rooster, five white turkeys and two black and white striped ones. One of the striped ones was a Tom. He looked like he weighed 100lbs. There were seven ducks; six probably were ducklings this year. There were four geese, playing tuff-tuff and barking at us. I wanted the big one to either bite me or shut up. I walked up to her and put my hand out. Johnny slapped my hand back and said, "You are always looking for a fight!"

"No, I am not! I'm looking to make a friend." The goose barked at me again and then when we walked by her I coaxed her to follow, and she did. I needed my jeans to climb the fruit trees so that would have to wait. The hills were too far away to hike, but there was a lake not very far away, I was excited to go see.

When we thought, they had enough time to do all their adult talking we started back again. I saw a fox and some ravens along the way, and when we came back into the yard, I saw a water snake. I wanted to pick it up, but Johnny said that it would stink and make mom sick…he was right, so I didn't.

We said good-by to each other, and my family left me there…in heaven I thought, with an angel, or a muse, I wasn't sure yet. "Who would be willing to teach me a billion things." I thought.

I was so excited. Mom and Dad and Johnny needed to hurry on their way, or they wouldn't make it back before midnight. Mom had already wearied. I felt my love for them and a tug at my heart as we stood in the doorway and I watched them drive away.

Great-grandmother asked me if I wanted to help her gather eggs. I said I did, and we went to get two dozen eggs from the hen house and close the door for the night. At 8:30 Mr. Rogers came over with his wife to check on great-grandma and they took the eggs we had gathered.

They left a meatloaf and some salad for dinner and so great-grandma, and I sat down and ate our first meal together. She said a very long prayer and we ate slowly. She poured us a glass of milk from the refrigerator, and I noticed that the fridge smelled funny. She went to her room and got into her night clothes as I did mine and then she knelt beside her bed and asked me if I would like to pray with her.

Her hands so soft, her power and grace were so compelling. She was a masterpiece, a divine instrument in my young life.

As I am writing this I am 68 years old. I continue to marvel at how strong she was at 106 years of age. Great-grandmother said she was strong because she never missed her prayers on her knees, and that we would know when her time is up because she would not be able to kneel anymore. I have never felt as strong as she appeared to me then.

The next morning and every morning after that she started on her knees again. It took her a few attempts to get up, and she had a special little bench-pillow that she used to kneel on, but she was there faithful at 6 AM every morning.

After lunch that day we started a ritual of prophetic expression. I asked a question then she would answer. "Grandmother, did you know your grandparents?" And off we went on this incredible journey into her life… The next day I asked a new question sometimes she would answer me short and leave me thinking and sometimes she could carry the story clear into the night.

Great-grandmother was a marvelous storyteller. With such perfect attention to facts and details. It would be as if I was living her memories.

CHAPTER 4

Manchester England

"I was born in England in 1840. My parents, your great-great-grandparents were well known in England for their business and economic class. We were in the printing business. I came to America before them with my Aunt Millie and my sister Annie. My parents came over later, leaving my brother to manage the printing over there and my father brought his printing expertise to Zion. Here we were with the Saints. By the time, my parents made the long trip here I was married to my sweetheart. My grandparents never made the journey here to Zion by ship, but in their hearts, they were among the "Saints".

"But to answer your question; I was five years old when I went to Manchester to visit my Grandfather and Grandmother. We took a buggy as was common then, from our home which was a modest two-bedroom home, to my grandparent's home in Manchester. It was an eight-hour ride. Their home was far fancier than ours; at least that's how I saw it. The entry was right off the main street with an iron gate and a garden in front, the balcony was so large they could have dances on it. Their house was surrounded by buildings on both the East and the West sides. The steps going up to the house made it feel like I was going into a museum and the entry was a massive marble encasement with stairs leading upward and curving to ascend the balcony above. The foyer was built to have refreshments in, and the chairs and benches were of excellent construction. All rooms for sleeping were on the upper level, and the eating and entertainment rooms were on the main level. It had a basement and lower chambers for servants and cooking.

"My grandmother met us at the bottom part of the stairs and ushered us into the parlor where we took off our cloaks and put on our shawls. We were served tea and crumpets. She was dressed in an ordinary evening dress with her hair finely wrapped into a French bun and a beautiful pearl hair pin that went from the tip of the hair bun to the end. There was a square emerald surrounded by mother of pearl and then by diamonds at the top of her neck tie. She was the most beautiful thing I had ever encountered. I saw immediately where my own beloved mother received her beauty. I was overcome, and my mother's fan tapped me gently on the shoulder for gawking."

Great-grandmother paused when she told me this and her eyes trailed off into space as if she had gone back there to relive it...

She then said, "That is when I saw "him" for the first time. He came down the stairwell as charming and as debonair as a man could be. My mother raised her fan to her eyes and tilted it to me, a custom to let me know that I must divert my stair again...Then I was ushered out of the room and taken to bed by what you would call a nanny. We called her Na. She was our nursemaid. I did not want to leave, but in my family first you did as you were expected and then if there was any room for doubt you could express it in private. I was far too young for the adult meeting that would be held shortly after my parent's arrival.

"I figured it out the next day; "he" was a "missionary" in the company of Heber C. Kimball. His name was Joseph Fielding. The brother-in-law to the Prophet Joseph Smith, he was forty-eight years old but to me, he looked like he was a kid. He was light on his feet and had no reserve or meekness when addressing my other cousins and me. He was always asking the questions as if we all had the answers. The very most important question he asked us was, "Would you not like to know that you can spend the rest of eternity with your family and the ones you love so dearly?" And then he looked right at me, I was certain he saw into my soul, I could only nod my head, and shaking it in answer to a no, instead of a yes; which caused everyone to smile and laugh at me. Then he said, "That is right my dear it is unthinkable not to have your dear family forever, isn't it?"

"I should have been embarrassed like your mother was when you jumped the ditch", great-grandmother said to me…looking me right in the eye.

'Yes, my mother was embarrassed, but I was not embarrassed," great-grandmother continued, "I was overcome that such a man would even consider talking to me. I felt blessed and warm all over. And when I went to bed that night I asked our nurse to tell me all about the visitors from America. When she finished with her stories, I prophesied that I would go to America and see for myself if there was an eternity. Her laughter took me by surprise, "Yes, you shall, I believe!" she said.

Later that day great-grandmother told me a list of things she would like me to accomplish before she would give me any more bits of her memory. She called it encouragement when she chastened me and said that the "Good Lord" chastens those he loves. She hoped that I would be sufficiently humbled and encouraged by the time I had to go back to Babylon, her description of Salt Lake City, for school.

She left me little time to reflect on my own condition with my new boyfriend. She hustled and bustled me around like we were in training for some big event.

She styled her own hair every day and on Sunday she gave it a break and let it hang freely. She said that even a woman's hair deserved a Sabbath day, a day off. She was quiet and very appropriate in all her manors and soon I found myself desiring to be like her, in expression and wit.

We went to church in the evening the second night, and she was very polite to introduce me to everyone. We rode in Brother Kay's station wagon with his wife and daughter. On the way returning home, Sister Kay commented on how polite I was and asked if it was more because I was shy. I remember being, slow to answer...like... what was she asking me anyway? I replied, "I enjoyed the meeting and the sermons very much, thank you. At home I am very outspoken, so I thought it better to practice some reserve."

My great-grandmother seemed to be grateful for my answer, and I wondered how long I would be able to stand up to my new reputation of shy.

But my education with my great-grandmother was pivotal in my upbringing and when I returned to the city I was a changed person. A person I was honored to be, by adults. My peers despised me. My grandmother said, "You have to choose your audience and know why they are your choice. If you leap without choosing, you could fall for anything. It is not your heritage or your gifts that make you who you are; but your choices!"

My next question at lunch on Wednesday surprised me as much as it did her. It sorta just burst out. She was cautious as if she was aware I wasn't clear about the question and then she chose to answer it as if I had intended it just that way;

"Grandmother, how did you "know", I chocked on the word, that you would go to America?"

She gave me a description of a fire that "burns" in the heart and whispers at the same time answers to questions that are hanging in the balance of our mind:

"I was five, and I just knew. It was the same kind of knowing that I have had many times in my life that expressly gave me directions to follow.

"I had met Heber C. Kimball and Brother Joseph Fielding, spokesmen for the church and Jesus Christ our Lord. I was young and impressionable to be sure, but I was also wise for my age and eager to know the power that I felt when I was in the presence of those men and my parents…my family changed that evening when we met with the Brethren. My Aunt Millie, only 12, was there, and my brother Henry was 8. I watched as they felt and experienced the same amazing emotions I did. And as I balanced my emotions, I watched my family be converted by the same process I was. The feeling, the burning, became familiar and more acceptable to my young mind and heart. I was too young to know how absolute my devotion would become, but it has never been shattered.

"My whole life's commitment is rooted in that time with my family in England. I was not afraid to come to America without my parent's because I would see them again and I knew it would be sooner than later in my life. If I could have walked to America, I would have started immediately. I wanted to meet all the saints. When it was time to go back to Honeybrooke I didn't want to say good-bye to our new friends; Brother Kimball and Brother Fielding. I was probably feeling like a niece would, who was saying farewell to an uncle. I felt less sadness from saying goodbye to my grandparents.

"In the buggy on the way back north of Cambridge, I watched the landscape and listened to all the sounds in the atmosphere when it rained I let the drops of water cleanse my face, and I pretended they were washing my heart as they fell. I remember crying. My mother asked me, "why the tears?" I told her I was sad because I wasn't old enough to be baptized. She marveled that it meant so much to me. She reminded me that it was only a short wait of two years and seven months. But in my heart, I was already a member of my mother and father's new church.

"I watched Brother Fielding baptize them, and brother Kimball confirm them as members, I watched my grandfather be ordained a priest and my father a deacon and each of my family received a blessing and a promise that they would see the promised land, all of them except me...I was too young. My brother, Henry was also baptized, and he was promised in his confirmation that he would be a priest in the house of David. I didn't understand any of that then...I just heard and felt the power behind it.

"My grandparents were the reason we found the gospel of Jesus Christ. I worshiped them and felt my little prayers ending up like promises to show them how good I could be so I could be with them forever and ever. Each day I was there with them I learned more about perfect love.

"The last day before we left to go back home to Honeybrooke my mother and grandmother got into a very tight situation. My mother left hurt, and my grandmother would not come down to say goodbye to us. I went to her room to say good-bye. I tapped on her door, it was open, and she stood and asked me to come in. I asked, "What made you sad, grandmother?"

"She looked deep into my eyes. I thought she was reading something in them she looked for so long. Then she picked me up in her arms and she said, "Someday you will understand that not all the things we do make perfect sense, and that we have many lessons on forgiveness to learn. I love you dear, that is all that really matters. Be a good little girl and you will grow into a fine woman. Promise?"

"I promise, grandmother, I will miss you…I love you, grandmother." I whispered to her and left quietly down the hall. I had my hands folded in my front with my head bowed, my bonnet mostly covering my eyes as I walked, and I passed the door to Brother Fielding's room. As I passed the door very quietly, as quiet as a mouse, I saw he was praying. I only paused to question, why would someone pray before bedtime? I moved quickly but silently down the hall, and when I got to the bottom of the stairs, I turned and in the dining room and against the fire mantel two of the helpers were praying as well.

"My sensitive nature was caught in a flurry. What was going on to make everyone so tentative?

CHAPTER 5

99 Questions

Monday night before I went to sleep I started a list of questions. About four days into my stay, realizing my list was getting out of hand, I decided I would stop at 99 questions.

Over the following days, I spent with great-grandmother I was careful to ask my questions in a way that would keep us in conversation. Only once did she say she was unwilling to answer one of my questions… It was the one about my parents, "Why do you suppose, grandmother that my parents would stay embarrassed about the principle of celestial marriage when they knew that it was no longer required for them to live it?" She would not answer for them…but she replied for the *principle* of celestial marriage, she said it was hidden, sacred and secret from the world. When something precious is shared with those who would mock it, the value is not just diminished for the one receiving the share, but also by the one who has not been careful with whom they have shared. She called it "casting pearls before swine." Not a pretty picture for my little mind. Then I asked, "how do you tell a swine from a regular person?" She laughed…

My great-grandmother's laugh was like, what I imagined the tinkling of angel's bells to be, it was mesmerizing… She said that was usually the problem. It is very hard to tell before you say something important if the person who is listening to you will be sensitive or resigned. It takes years and years of sharing the message before you sense the likeness of someone who is eager to hear and convert or someone whose curiosity has caused them to be in judgment about things. She said it is easier to just "give up" and most people do. But a few hung on to the original message and played out the full cycle of their commitment to their marriages…there was a huge loss and a martyr's gain.

I asked her, "Who held on… to the principle, I mean?"

She answered abstractly. Trying to avoid letting me know of all the ones she really knew about.

She said, "there is so much pain involved in the processing of the struggles around living in a world where most of the community opposes the original idea… Many people do not know the difference between doing what is right and doing what they are told. These people fear that they will be controlled by the stronger forces around them and instead of being genuinely involved they are only invested in other lives as much as the 'others' prove to them that they are right. When something happens to make life difficult, many people just give up. Staying faithful to a cause or a dream is hard for people who do not know their own mind…Joseph the Prophet said, 'without vision, the people perish.' it is so easy to be persuaded to do hurtful and evil things when an outside source is leading you…However, it is also easy to be lead astray by your own thoughts when you are not close to the Lord. Evil has no particular entry into our minds except when we give up…do not ever give up…

"You will know when you are giving up because you will tell yourself things like, 'I don't care, they are the ones responsible for this, not me. I hate my life. I wish I wish, I wish. Also, I need, I need, I need. If you have something nice, and you don't want to share it, being greedy, being mean, being right all the time, being lazy, being deceitful, being vengeful, taking what doesn't belong to you, wasting time; time is the only thing you have that is actually yours. Besides the beautiful body Heavenly Father gave you. Your mind is the tool that helps you control both of them. Time and your body; never, never, never let anyone be completely in charge of your time or your body. This life is a gift to you from your Heavenly Father and your expressions ought to show how important you believe you are to him. After all, He created you. Everything he makes is imperative. He wastes no time! Consider your thoughts and you will know if you are giving up or standing for what is important to you.

The next morning, I asked her, "What happened that caused everyone, including your mother, to be so concerned, in Manchester when you were there with your grandparents?"

She answered, "I didn't finish that story because the details so intertwined with my future in the Gospel and I'm not sure how much you really want to know about that."

I told her I was trying to keep my mind straight. That I wanted to see the things happening in my life my own way and before they make trouble for me. I said I wanted to judge for myself what is right and what is wrong.

"It wasn't like that she said. It wasn't a right or wrong thing that put pressure on my parents or grandparents. It wasn't troubling to my parents or the way they were in their own lives. The terrible news that arrived came to us like an awful shock that startled all of them. I was too young to be involved.

In England, you must have a license to preach. The brethren had come to us because Brother Brigham Young had sent them. Brigham Young had made his way to England early in1840. There was no need for them to get a license to visit. But someone reported that there was preaching in grandfather's home, and so there would have to be an arrest. My wonderful grandfather decided to turn himself in and pay the price of the mistake. My mother did not see that her father "turning himself in" was an appropriate way to deal with the authorities. Grand-mother saw that the only thing for her to do was to support her husband. My mother wanted to argue the whole affair and Grandmother told her be still and pray.

"Brother George Albert Smith was a great friend of my family. The problem was that the Prophet Joseph had been deceased for little over a year. Rumors were that Sister Emma Smith was so upset about the "plural wife" thing, (that's what she called it), that she had engaged with other men to control and demolish the church even in England. The love the people all had for the Prophet was so deep we could not bear that the rumors could be true. But Emma never denied it. Many felt that she had been the ultimate cost that took the Prophets life.

"There was another rumor that the government was going to round up the Mormons and put them on a reservation like the Natives, in the Territory of Huron known as Pineries. They would call it Mormon Relief and the Mormon Reserve. I remember it was a bad winter that year so much sadness and broken hearts… sickness too, that just took its toll on all the saints everywhere.

"The next few years of my young life, before I could make it to Zion, I spent growing up. I did not have the same kind of freedom or worries that my friends had. I was very busy learning the relevant arts to be useful as a handmaiden of the Lord and a pioneer in the new world.

"There were many unprincipled enemies of the Lord making havoc on the Saint's, and their circumstances were grave. Some starving, some unfortunate homeless Saints were giving up, yes, going into the darkness of their own hearts. Thousands of Saints were still pouring into Nauvoo even though the grief and sadness and havoc of the day were causing such a horrible test. Some of the Saints were having a terrible time accepting President Brigham Young as the rightful leader of the Church. News had come that the Saints were leaving to the Great Salt Valley. It was a powerful and passionate time. People were making choices and facing challenges like the ones people suffered during the Holocaust. My family arranged relief packages and support for the wives of the deceased Prophets, and the suffering Saints. Weldon Creek later called Garden Grove was in desperate need of supplies and reinforcements for the Saints as they would pass on their way to the Great Salt Valley. We were very, very busy.

"Winter Quarters in Platte Nebraska was another place which was destitute of supplies. Most of the Saints just stayed on the Missouri River. It has become a belief that it was all wilderness between Nauvoo and the Great Basin, but I had a chance to see Winter Quarters, and it was lovely.

"There was a petition sent to the Queen of England to help with the relief of the Saints, in it contained 13,000 names. England denied the saints help. We were the publishing company in Cambridge so my grandfather was always informed. He contributed to publishing 5000 Book of Mormon's and the "Millennial Star." I remember when grandfather published them, and it was considered acceptable to the Lord to dance and sing and be merry in the name of the Lord for the blessings and abundance that the Saints received and that they had survived. We had a marvelous dance at my father's place in Honeybrooke, and we went to a ball in Manchester at my grandfathers.

CHAPTER 6

Dreaming of Zion

"In Honeybrooke, for seven years I spent every waking minute chasing life...I was so compelled to become a member of the church and to get to America. I made myself grow up. I would pray as if God could remove one more day without notice, making my journey to Zion sooner than later.

"Honeybrooke was a veritable *Secret Garden*. The ride from Manchester to Honeybrooke was eight hours long. We started as soon as breakfast had been served. The day we left from Manchester to Honeybrooke my grandmother did not come down to say goodbye and I wanted so badly to see her beauty standing on the balcony looking out at me, claiming me as her possession.

"About 3: pm that day my sadness was interrupted with a drizzled of rain. At first, I let it run down my face and into my eyes and hair. Then my brother Henry warned me that soon I would be freezing if I didn't cover myself. So, I reluctantly lifted my parasol.

"We road, in a two horse-drawn buggy, Made of hard cedar wood. I could smell the rain as it sprinkled on backs of the horses and the warm cedar wood the buggy was crafted from.

"I was a bit disturbed by the interruption the rain made to my sad thoughts of leaving Brother Smith and Brother Fielding at Grandfather's house, I still wanted to brood some more. I was by no means cheerful as the random drops descended from the sky, but soon I could not ignore the nature of our condition. Just as Henry had predicted that: I would get wet and cold sure enough the countryside began to disappear in mist and rainfall. Father and Henry quickly put the canvas cover over the wire rims of our convertible buggy and on we went. Mother tucked me in with an extra blanket and the world around me began to disappear.

"I dreamed I was floating across a great body of water and the land that had to be "somewhere" was hiding from me, I started pawing rapidly then swimming through the water looking for the land, then I was drowning, because of my stupid dress. I remembered my dream because it was so real to me. When I finally woke the *Secret Garden* of Honeybrooke was back on the map again. I could see little garden plots and rooftops beckoning us forward, but my hands and feet were cold, and my dress was a prison of fabric tangling me up and making me feel like I was drowning, it was damp and cumbersome.

"The countryside of Honeybrooke was charming…I am an old, old woman today remembering my lovely birthplace. This home is big and safe but nothing like the cottages that had been crafted and designed in a culture built by hundreds of years of care. My hometown met me that day with climbing roses and stucco siding that was catching the last rays of the evening sun and the air was filled with the smell of aspen and cedar fires…along the roadside, the wheels of our buggy would echo against the sides of beautiful mansions and eloquent cobble walks that led to the front doors, behind wooden fences and herb garden buttresses. Window coverings would move as some child or curious eye peered out to see who was passing through.

"For the first time in my little life, I felt different from them. I had a secret that they were looking for as they connected the evening hour with the haste we were making to get home before nightfall. Dogs barked, and roosters crowed! Everything that had been so pleasant before now seemed upset. My precious Honeybrooke would never hold me like it did before I left for Grandfathers house.

"When my wobbly little legs and toes hung to the sidewalk, my Nanny and Butler were graciously standing at the buggy to help bring treasures and travel luggage into our home.

"The thatched roof and ivy that had welcomed me back were soon disappearing as from my dreams… we had always been best friends, but now they stood in the way of me getting older and on to America, my character was showing up, and I sure wanted to throw a tantrum, but of course if I did it would prove the fated truth: I was still just a baby.

"My Sister Angelina had been ill before we left and could not make the journey with us to Manchester. When she saw me, she picked me right up and said, "What creature is this and how is she so sad?" I buried my head in her shoulder and whispered, "They took away my friends and now I have to be here, waiting for so long before I can see them again."

"Well, butterball, when we wake up in the morning I will take you to the schoolyard, and we can have a few rounds on the whirling-dervish and a couple of pushes on the swing while you tell me all about it, okay? I missed you, and I'm so glad you are back. Come now let's get you out of those wraps and into some warm nightwear."

"K," I whispered as we passed all the lovely furniture and smells of baking bread as the kitchen disappeared as well. My little heart was recovering, but my mind was determined to grow up.

"In our room, there was a big doll with glass eyes and long black hair, and a pinafore sitting in her very own rocking chair. I ran over to her and knelt down where she sat, putting my head in her lap and started to cry. "Oh, Rosemary," I asked, "what magic do I need to grow up?"

"My sister chuckled at me and said, "Must I remind you that only good little girls get to grow up?"

"She then moved Rosemary from her spot and sat down in the rocking chair, pulling me in on top her lap and tucking Rosemary into mine...Annie wanted to know everything, but she was so willing to wait until morning.

CHAPTER 7

ANNIE and SEVEN YEARS in LONDON

"Angelina Rose Anna Davis was born in a small cottage on the edge of the Sherwood Forest in the fall of 1834. Her birth was anticipated by parents and grandparents from both her father and her mother's side of the family. Henry her big brother just a year older was being charmed and whipped about like a cannon ball by his uncles in the cottage kitchen. Henry's giggles were contagious and often he had everyone laughing.

"The Davis families had met at the cottage to celebrate the blessings of freedom from the war of England's aggressor Scotland and King Edmunds rule. The huge town celebration took place every year in the Little Morton Hall and then weddings and christenings took place in the Chester Cathedral the next day. People came from every borough and hamlet around. A few magistrates and dignitaries came and stayed in the Hotel d'le Wood. Servants, maids, waiters, and maître D's alike were bustling about making a swarm of tangible excitement.

"Upstairs on the third level in a mural painted room with elaborate window coverings and tapestries was a serious collection of opposites. David Alexander Davis, my father is being hushed and scurried out the side door of the beautiful bedroom and forbidden to return until further notice. Margarethe Antonietta Sharriez-Davis is having her baby. The housekeeper and her quorum of maids are preparing for the doctor's every needful thing. The chamber pot already has the markings of "broken waters" and the smell of blood distilling in the room. Mother had requested to stay standing until she will need to "bear down" upon her contractions, and the doctor a well-seasoned midwife and blood drawer had agreed to her terms.

"Without proper warning, however, Angelina Rose Anna's head crowns and comes into the hands of the housekeeper. With a screech of delight the baby, the housekeeper and my mother, all at once announced the new arrival. Mother was scarce to the edge of the bed when her proud and tormented husband commanded he be let back into the room. As ornate and lovely as the room and accommodations were and as lively as the house had been previous; nothing compared to the pleasure and thrill that permeated every square inch of the house. The walls were busting at the seams, and the uncles and other guests ran into the street shouting, "it's a girl! It's a girl! Angelina Rose Anna... hallelujah!!"

"And then nearly 12 years later, my sister Annie didn't appear to me, before I went to Grandfather's house in Manchester, as a 'beauty' but the next morning when she woke me up I could see in her the features of my Grandmother Sofia. And I asked her if she were an angel?"

"She replied, 'I am a water monster, come to eat you alive if you don't move, move, and move!'

"I think you are the most beautiful person in the world." I squeaked as she slipped on my under-slip and pulled the strings tight.

"Come on,' she encouraged, 'or we won't get through our adventure before someone notices we have escaped.'

"We tip-toed down two flights of stairs and passed the kitchen staff, who all turned a blind eye, and ran quietly out the back door. My clothes and my bonnet and my hair were all but a veritable prison…In the past, I would have made a fuss and pulled at them and tampered until they were a mess, but today was the first day of my "growing into a fine lady" and "getting ready for Zion."

"Many times, in my youth and at family gatherings mother would retell the birth of Angelina, and throughout Annie's life, she proved to be as stunning and brilliant and sudden in every way.

"Several young men in the borough would stay at a distance and stare at her. Some men would generate enough curiosity to inquire of her. Often, we had calling cards at the front table requesting an audience with her. Father insisted that she not entertain the idea of courting in Honeybrooke because someday she would be going to America and seek an honorable mate in the house of the Lord. She was strong, and smart and deliciously sweet, with the voice of a muse. She loved to read me stories and turn me into her puppeteer or little drama-queen.

"On Annie's 16th birthday Father allowed a "coming out" ball and dinner in her behalf, but what was very curious about that is everyone knew that my Aunt Millie, Annie and I would be leaving for America in just under five weeks.

"Three days before the ball Father threatened to use his gun if one more young man came to woo and request a dance at the ball. Her dish was full of cards, some of them were repeats. She would correctly say, 'This young man is too eager,' in Fathers' voice, or 'this young man is not…young at all…hummm!! Much to do about nothing!'

"The truth is Annie had met her "love" on a trip we took to General Conference in Manchester in 1849. We met with a group of immigrants leaving for Zion in a beautiful garden on the river. There was a potluck, games and close to 100 baptisms. Among the Elders was a charming and entrancing gentleman.

"Annie had converted to Mormonism the day she took me to the school park; the day after we came home from Grandfather's house in Manchester. She never doubted anything. It was as if she born already knowing and just waiting for the Gospel to be sent.

"Annie was not yet 14 when her heart and soul gave way to the most handsome man she had ever seen. He was so dynamic, and she was so smitten.

CHAPTER 8

Dreaming of America

Great-grandmother what is a convert and what is smitten, I mean really…how does one know that they are converted? And how do you know that the person you love is the ONE?

"Heber C. Kimball and Joseph Fielding had been given the profound responsibility to proclaim the Gospel and open the door of salvation to the British Isles. Brother Heber felt his inadequacies and was given a blessing by the hand of the Prophet Joseph Smith. Brother Kimball requested the company of Brigham Young for his companion, but the Prophet had other work for Brigham to do…so he sent John Young a brother of Brigham to go with Brother Heber to England. It was 1837 when Brother Kimball and Brother Fielding came to teach the Gospel in London England. I wasn't even born yet, but the distilling of the Spirit of God was surging through most of the British countryside.

"The very same day that the Brother Kimball and Brother Young preached in Manchester and got their foothold in Rev. James Fielding's' chapel. The Prophet Joseph and Brother Thomas B. Marsh in Missouri;

thousands of miles and oceans apart, had a Revelation, and they were commanded by the Lord to "gird up their loins"…meaning don't be discouraged by rumors and haters of truth. They were promised that the truth would prevail.

"That very year the brethren requested my grandfather's help in printing the necessary literature. Shipping the Book of Mormon, a Testament of Christ, would cost more than having the book published locally.

"A convert is the recipient of conversion. Conversion is what happens to something when the outsides of it don't match the insides of it and a major adjustment occurs,

I'm sure my face was eschewed. She went on…

"In life, we have first the chance to learn the limits of our body. As the body grows it converts all the energy of chemicals and fluids necessary to change it from a baby to an adult…this is a physical conversion. The ideas in the brain are translated into physical mass.

"A mind is a place where information about possible and historical events are stored. In the storage process, there is something we call memory. It allows us to use the information stored by accessing it through conversion…one idea is allowed to assist the other idea, and a conversion occurs.

Great grandmother, then trailed off to, "I believe 14 steps are going up to the attic… If my memory serves me correctly on the number of steps. After the first climb, the steps (whether I'm thinking about it or not) are converted into a distance that becomes real in the mind even when I'm not near the steps.

I studied her face wondering about the attic and questioning if there was one here or was there one in Honeybrooke?

"The mind is said to be stronger than the body, however, what we actually experience is tangible only through touch, sight, sound, taste, smell and another experience of spirit. Learning the limits of the mind is enormous. I believe that the combination of these senses in high proportions causes the 'still small voice and the burning in the bosom.' So, to be converted one must have a combination of these realities mix.

"The other lesson we learn is in the way we experience the presence of things not seen, heard, smelt, felt, or tasted. We call this *emotional*. It comes from the Greek word "emote": to move one thing through something else. This emotional learning is said to be the most difficult and to take the most time to learn for some because it is the combination of so many different probabilities in our life...When someone is converted into the gospel they have no fear or doubt left, no condition will block their way. The Gospel provides many opportunities to learn and transform our body, mind, and emotions into powerful human tools...

"When my sister dreamed of America the conversion wasn't just to the land, it was to the feelings that drove her there in body and mind. When she saw Brother Heber the first time, she was smitten by a condition she had no real power over, and the feeling dominated her disciplined mind and body because the experience was like taking the steps to the attic the first time. Once she had seen him the connection in her body and mind created a conversion and she was left with a change of heart and mind which could support her beliefs: that it is actually possible; to know the will of God.

"Annie was converted to Brother Heber before she even knew who he was or the conditions and circumstances of his life. She was converted to Brother Heber like I was to Zion before we had even taken the steps to get there. In her mind, she had "seen" him.

"By April 1841 with the help of only nine apostles there were over 7500 converts, The Perpetual Immigration Fund was in full procession.

Grandfather had printed 5000 copies of the Book of Mormon Testament of Christ, *The Millennial Star,* had been published, and over 2500 were in circulation. I was one and Annie was seven.

"My sister Annie saw President Heber C. Kimball at the General Conference in Manchester in 1850. The morning Annie saw Brother Heber pitching a ball for a young boy to bat, she nearly lost footing, and I caught her elbow before she would have plunged into the river. Her hat loosened from her head, and as she reached to adjust it, the ribbons found her mouth, and she stopped dead still and stared at me like I was a ghost. When she could breathe again, she said, "We must! find father, we must!"

"Annie lifted her fan to keep her blushing from being a melee and slowly and carefully continued her stare from behind the fan until we were several yards away.

"She met with father and later that evening around a campfire hundreds of people came and gave their testimony of their conversion. Sitting at the head of the meeting were the Presidents of the British Mission, and one of them was the handsome young man who bedazzled her earlier. After the meeting was over my sister and I were escorted, by a gentleman father had picked, back to our hotel. Annie paced and paced until finally at about 2:AM Father tapped at the door and entered very discreetly. He hugged my sister and told her she would have a chance to meet and visit with Brother Heber at Grandfather's on Tuesday where he would be coming for dinner and the dance.

"Annie was 14 she would be turning 15 in September, but she had seen Brother Heber in a dream when she was 9 or 10. Father had said she had the dream because she had seen Brother Heber before when she came to Manchester with father four years before. But Annie insisted that she could not have forgotten that face, the face of her future husband. Father informed her that Brother Kimball was betrothed, and she only said, "So…" Father chuckled and kissed her on the cheek as he was leaving the room he whispered, 'So the Lord is preparing your heart along with your mind, goodnight dear. Love you both'…in a whisper he left.

"Father told me later that as he had stood in the hall and allowed himself to feel the tears run down his cheek and into his beard, he permitted the facts he knew of the Church to run over his mind and into his heart where he coveted the protection of his daughters. He then went to his room and gently woke mother and prophesied, 'It won't be long before our daughters are leading the church and the world.' He told me that mother grunted her approval and slipped back into slumber, but he did not sleep the whole night, there was a fire burning in him, and the heat was stirring up energy that he had suppressed. His youth and his eagerness to serve the Lord were embellishing his mind the only future he could see were far across the ocean in a dirty, uninhabited, wasteland called *the Great Salt Valley.*

'Annie didn't sleep either, and I heard her ring for a cup of chamomile tea and a bag of ice. She sat, and she wondered, and I dozed in and out… My mind was expecting with each wake to be in the New World with all my lovely things left far behind. I was nearly 10, and I could hardly tell anyone my weird, selfish reasons for agitation. I thought it rather odd that God would confine an age limit to a testimony of the Truth. He said after all, 'By the mouth of babes ye shall hear my truth and it shall set you free.' Why then couldn't someone be a member of the Church if I was requesting my own accountability at five?

"I was baptized, by my father on my birthday when I had turned eight. I was confirmed a member of the Church by Brother Fielding. He blessed me with the strength to know the will of the Lord and to choose for myself whom I would serve in my life. That I would know as sure as the sun rises in the east that the Lord was my Savior and that He had chosen with me the man who would be my husband, and that I would be sealed for time and all eternity to him in the House of the Lord. He promised me that I would never doubt or be confused by the challenges that women have with jealousy or greed and that my heart was pure and unadulterated and if I stayed faithful I would see the Savior and know that He has always loved me. He promised me that I would have a chance to visit with the Three Nephites and hear for myself the stories of the Saviors coming to the American Continent. He promised me that the pride my father and mother felt for me would be a source of strength during the hard times I would experience as a messenger and handmaiden of the Lord. He promised me that other women would call on me for guidance because of the strong connection I had with the Lord and that when I was mature I would lead congregations to believe in the Lord and to seek the blessings of freedom and wealth that were their inheritance. He promised me that my children would call me 'blessed' and speak my name from the house tops to remind the world of the truth of the Gospel of Jesus Christ and the Principle of Celestial Marriage. He promised me that I would find it a delight to live the Law of Celestial Marriage and would never suffer from the insecurities of a lesser thought or concern of my husband's devotion to the Lord or his love for my being. He promised me that I would love all of my sister-wives! And I believed every word he spoke. Two years later I was anxious to be in those blessings and participating in those promises.

'During the Conference, I had my share of tummy butterflies and bump-ins with emotions. At the campfire, I could smell the sweet pine and aspen wafting through the air and sitting on the log benches in front of father I was nearly an arms-length from Brother Fielding. I wanted so desperately to call him uncle and follow him around like some other children did. But I had sworn myself to growing up and instead of behaving as the children did I watched the ladies and attempted to be discreet and untouchable. I soon realized that the 'act' the ladies had didn't fit my character either, and I began to act like the younger men whom I felt were more interested in the Gospel and more devoted to the Presidents. Every single word they spoke would replay itself back through my head with voice and amplitude. They could stand and lean into each other as they debated the things they had heard and they could raise their hand a bit and get the attention of the speaker and ask a clarifying question. But the women sat as if they were frozen and not supposed to be there.

"I felt the warm sensation of grace and warmth that surrounded my beating heart and when I looked at Brother Fielding that feeling would grow and to my astonishment when he looked at me I would relax instead of freeze up like the stiff-bodied creatures around me.

'My grandmother and my mother stayed mostly at the Hotel the first two days of the conference. Father promised not to let Annie and I stray and then made Annie swear to keep close to me. Father looked at me with no discord at all. I knew he knew me…I wasn't even the least inclined to step out of line. I was on a mission to grow up. To take a step out of perfect alignment could challenge eternity for me. Father was touched and inspired by my devout and tentative understanding. His pride in his daughters was apparent. But my mother was not ready to have her daughters out in the new Church unescorted and without class refinement.

"My brother Henry was fathers pride and joy. I saw why father enjoyed Henry. Henry chopped wood, fed the fire, said, "Yes, sir… or… Yes, Brother Young, Yes, Father. He was like an extra arm and an extension of Fathers mind.

'Henry was sooo handsome and shy and proper. He was the perfect example. He studied the Brethren and watched their every move. I studied him and watched his every move. Soon I could see where his intentions were leading him, and soon I had cultivated the perfect question for him. 'Brother Henry,' I asked, 'what do you intend to do with all the power you feel from being accepted by the authorities of the Church?'

"Well, little sister, I plan to travel with all that energy to every corner of the earth and proclaim that Jesus is the Christ and that the Book of

Mormon is a New Testament of His Almighty Power. That is what I intend to do..."

"I want to come with," I pouted...To which a whole congregation chuckled except Annie, she was beaming from ear-to-ear that her little sister dared in a meeting to raise her hand and confront the arrogance of the speaker. She was delighted that I had dared to ask the very question that had been disturbing her for hours... 'What happens to all these new hot-headed young men when they get a little power to push around?'

"President Joseph Fielding then stood and asked if he could address my question...He gave a very lovely and long persuasive sermon. I was convinced that if one hair of Henry's head got out of place, he would be burned to crisp, and he better manage his ego and his attitude committedly or else he could not magnify his calling.

CHAPTER 9

Joseph Fielding

"Restoration of the Gospel" was a cloudy term in New England...
and so was the 'New England' title', great-grandmother began. "Causing
some to turn their heads for scorn and some would turn their heads
with respect..."

"Didn't the pilgrims come across the sea to find a land to worship
freely?" I asked great-grandmother. "And wasn't freedom of worship one
of the primary points in the charter for Independence from England?
Then why would they call it the New England?"

"Those are several questions, my dear...Let's start with: many of the
ships coming to America carried soldiers, to keep the peace here while
America was establishing territory and gaining land for crops. Others
brought immigrants for labor. Defending the land and working the
land was too much for a plantation owner. So protection was granted
to owners of large parcels of land, and laborers were bought and then
given room and board for the privilege of being in America. Freedom of
worship was not separate in ideology from commerce and trade. Even

moving to America didn't stop the common Englishman. It was his duty to control happiness and wealth in the name of Christ. Women were arm candy and children still represented men's power through blood. England still held America in servitude because England 'outfitted' us with all our economic and military needs. And even though we had gained our Independence more than half a century before Joseph had his first vision, England's laws, and mindset was sound in our culture. Some people hated England and some still considered her the 'Motherland.' The ones who considered her the "motherland" would tip their hat with respect and the ones who harbored rancor and descent would turn up their noses.

"My wonderful, handsome husband, your great-grandfather was born in Honiden, Bedfordshire, England a community fast growing in wealth and beauty. At the time of his birth, the newly established American Pioneering Spirit was in high demand. American soil had become the refuge of the Old World, and streamline ships were dumping their cargo at every port. America had to look at the cost of freedom for the price of murder. Sometimes half of the steerage of a new ship would be filled with convicts released from the prisons and penitentiaries of Europe and Britain.

By 1852, Brother Fielding was 55 years old, and I had seen him in Manchester, Honeybrooke, and Lancashire several times. I knew what I was looking for when I saw him in a crowd, on the street or in Grandfathers printing shop. I was looking for a certain expression that comes from only one soul that knows the other… 'oh there you are my beloved'…He was destined to be the President of the British Mission and the church in England. His kindness and devotion to the Word of God were very particular, he was profoundly devoted to the Prophet Joseph Smith and considered him immediate family.

"From the beginning of my 5-year-old acquaintance with him, there was a destiny in his hands waiting for me. While I was creating a miraculous maturation, he was helping defend the Prophet he loved and to move the Work of the Lord along.

"I had no boyfriends and like my sister who was courting Brother Kimball without others knowing it I was courting Brother Fielding without anyone knowing it. It was not a secret to me it was a sacred right. I knew he was a married man, and I knew that the first time he met my family I was in a carriage promenade with my father and mother. But I saw the same things other people saw in him but I experienced the light of Christ. I saw the light of love and cheer of the Savior. I wanted him to want me. So, I stayed my distance and did nothing to provoke or lead him or my parents or even Annie to know my heart. There were times in my young life where the sound of his voice would carry my conviction of the Church with such strong tenor that it was as if he was speaking the words right into my ear."

Great-grandmother leaned very close to the table and searched my eyes, "I never stopped believing that he would find me someday and know I was the one he was waiting for, to love him and to join him in the development of the Zion he spoke of."

"When he was young, he was strikingly lean and handsome. His wife and his sisters loved to share their memories of the dances and evenings where he would be chased around by a group or several groups of girls and young women who were curious about his preference and his taste in girls… His brother and uncle were of the clergy. His brother James was a very prominent minister and his sisters, and the girlfriends were fretfully worried he would take up the "cloth" instead of marrying and have a family. His Father and the family moved to Canada where they were joined by Martin Harris and Orson Pratt and learned of the Restored Gospel.

"The very day he heard of the Prophet Joseph, Brother Fielding took out on foot to find the Prophet and know for himself the will of God. And so it is that the Prophet Joseph met two of his other future wives upon meeting with your great-grandfather. The prophet married two of Brother Fielding's younger sisters, and Brother Hyrum married his youngest.

"The seven years I spent getting ready to come to America were rich with excitement. Wars, rumors of wars and the economic revolution were critical gossip and news flashes. The poor Red Indian was being driven off their land and persecuted just as the saints were, but the Fathers of our country had little or no regard for the "Red and Black" man's soul.

"Gold fever had hit the west. There was a shortage of women on the west coast and a lack of men on the east coast, so it was said that they gave women money, and a possibility of shared land and shipped them by way of Cape Horn or drove them by wagon train...women went crazy! Out there in that desolate world without father, mother, sister, brother and upon the first sight of oasis they would clamor for safety or affection...all suddenly it would be lost by an Indian raid or a buffalo stampede. And then the gold rush came and nearly drove the nation to recklessness.

"Brother Parley P Pratt had established a "paper" called the 'Millennial Star.' It was used to circulate information about the church and the world for the Saints.

'The Potato Famine was driving the population of urban England to catastrophic proportions. The Saints were harvesting converts in such extraordinary proportions that the Governor of Missouri was conspiring with the President of the States to exterminate the Mormons; due to an "infestation of gigantic proportions". Fear of starvation and apostasy was the concern of the Saints, and Governor Boggs was afraid they wouldn't die. Governor Boggs had been sent false affidavits of the "Mormons" being in alliance with the Indians.

"Was Governor Boggs a good man?" I asked Great-grandma.

"It was believed, and rumors circulated that he had been elected to the highest office available in the state because of the expulsion of the Saints from Jackson County and he was very much responsible for that. Rumors circulated that the Saints were going to 'declare violence against the other citizens' when this news came back to Governor Boggs he sent a warrant for Brother Joseph and Brother Lyman Wright's arrest. After that it was a series of beatings, tarring and feathering, one recurrent nightmare. Many saints were so heartsick by the rage and hatred of the citizens and that they left the church to seek a calmer domain. So many horrible things were done to drive the Saints away. I had a girlfriend who survived the Haun's Mill Massacre, Kathryn Johnson, she helped me put up fences to keep the rabbits out when we homesteaded the land in Marysville.

"The death of the Prophet Joseph was expected to calm the crashing waves of Mormon infiltration and the famine was surely going to send the common people back to the field to work the land and cut the timber. And Governor Boggs was not the only Evil man working overtime to destroy the Lords Work. But the Lord had other plans for the Saints.

"I was barely born when the new City Nauvoo was incorporated and dedicated to the beautification of the saints. Nauvoo could have its military protection from within the Church. The Nauvoo Legion was established, and Dr. John C Bennett was the first mayor. It was from Nauvoo that the first missionaries were sent to meet my parents and grandparents. And even though ambassadors and the Prophet Joseph were sent to Washington, and President VanBuren expressed sympathy and a solemn regard for the persecution of the saints, still the papers of expulsion were never lifted. The Saints are still to this day, in 1946, fearing for their lives, if they live in Missouri. We always pray for that law to be lifted so we can go back and rebuild Zion.

"The Prophet Joseph had a vision and prophesied on August 6, 1842, that the Saints would continue to suffer and that they would be driven as far as the Rocky Mountains. But that they would also build cities and become a mighty people. At the conference in April of 1843, he told the Saints that angel's dwell with God and that they live on a sphere that is like a planet, a globe like a sea of glass and fire where all things in glory are manifest. He also told the saints that our spirits are fine matter and that though we cannot see the spirit "It" is real and can be measured. He said that the valley they were in was the "Garden of Eden" and that it was where our Father Adam and his families began.

"The prophet also prophesied that William Clayton one of the Governor's he met with, would be president of the United States.

"There were newspapers created called "anti-Mormon" papers. Even against all the slander and the odds the Prophet was nominated and sustained as a candidate for President of the United States, and it was published in the *Times and Seasons* in May of 1844. More and more talk was made about moving the Saints before persecutions started getting worse again. The plotting and conspiracy continued, and mobbing began again. The Prophet became the Mayor of Nauvoo just before they murdered him. The Governor demanded all firearms be turned in, and the Prophet was taken for "his own protection" that is what he was told; off to Carthage Jail. I was barely four years old, and the History of my people was graphically witnessed and rewritten every single day.

"Where was great-grandpa while all this was going on?" I pleaded.

"Well you know, he was the President of the British Isles, and his work was there converting new members and managing the affairs of the Church in England. His brother, the Reverend James Fielding, was embarrassed by some of the teachings of the church, and though James had mercy for the Saints and allowed his brother to preach in the Cathedral after a short time, the Reverend would not let Brother Fielding back in the Cathedral again.

"How old was he?" I queried. And then, "Did you get to see him very often in your seven years in England? When we cleaned the cabinet in your room, I loved your little beaded purse, Was it from England too? Is it a child's purse?"

Great-grandmother gracefully and very slowly lifted herself from the little, wooden dining table and walked to the cache of trinkets on the shelf of the glass case in the living room.

Days ago, when I jumped the ditch in the front yard, I had a brother a father and mother and a new sibling on the way. Today as I watched great-grandmother 'May' I was being filled with an imaginary and very real world of my hidden history.

I saw her lift the elegant little purse and an old fan that was spread carefully. She closed the fan and opened it with her right hand and held the purse with her left hand gently at the ribcage under her breasts. She began the return to our table, and I stood to watch her come over. Then I heard her voice change a bit somehow it became the voice of a muse, a mystical enchantress. I felt my cheekbones rise, and my face began to soften, and moisture came to my eyes, she had such a gift of story and majesty, "Etui, my child." Then as if the world in Kaysville disappeared and I became a resident of Manchester I was transported into her world as a child.

"This is my mother's needles clutch, an etui. I was handed this on the first baby parade my mother and grandmother took me on. I was one-year-old, and the story was given to me by my father over and over again.

"It was the fashion to show-off your child in an expensive walking cradle in the park on Saturdays and Sundays in the afternoon. The weather was perfect, and my wealthy grandparents had indulged in the finest carriage so they had to participate in the newfangled prams parade. Father said that when mother handed me her etui, I became the new owner. He said my eyes lit up like I had just been given an ounce of gold. She let me carry it proudly on the stroll but after that, she had to hide it from me.

"Mother brought it to America when she came here and gave it to me with pride as she retold the story again. I coveted this little purse, and when she finally gave it to me, I put it away not to use it again. It reminds me of the value of gold. That is why it remains in such excellent condition. What is precious to one could be trash for another.

"What is a pram, great-grandma?" I interrupted.

She looked over at me finishing the walk back to the table and handed me the little clutch with caution in her beautiful blue eyes. "It is an elaborate push cart for pets and babies. Mr. Whitney was a talented craftsman and very soon the carriage industry was bustling in America as well. Oh, no! American women would not be denied the passion of showing off as the British did.

"It was on just such a prams parade that my parents walked and talked to Brother Fielding and became acquainted with the Restored Gospel of Christ. While I was being entertained and rocked into my childhood. The Saints were being torn from their homes in Nauvoo and threatened by the demons that look like civilians.

As the Gospel of Jesus Christ was being presented to my parents, in the park and at firesides in Manchester and Cambridge in England the prophet Joseph was being prepared for his execution.

"Brother Fielding was old enough to be my father, he was actually older than my father, but there was a fountain of youth in Brother Fielding. Brother Fielding was 48 when I met him, and then when I married him, he was 55 but not a day older did he look. It seemed to me that he had gotten younger and more sensibly attractive. His charm would spread over a whole village and wrap itself into every heart. He was a prankster and a beloved storyteller. Brother Heber C Kimball later became my brother-in-law, and I was often aware that Brother Fielding and Brother Kimball had a great love for each other. They ruff-housed and chided each other like the best of friends. One day in this very house in the company of your grandfather John Willard Young I heard your great-grandfather say."As did David, the apple of God's eye swear to Jonathan, 'brothers for eternity' so I declare that you Heber shall be the love of my bloodline and inherit all the glory of my family. I am your brother eternally, and our children's children will have brotherly love for each other while sharing the Kingdom of God. I love you, Heber!" He raised his glass, and it was the final sacrament he had taken before he passed into the next life. He was 66 years old. He came here to visit me I was his third wife. By choice, I moved down here to what became Kaysville and left the matters of the church to his first wives. Sarah, Joseph's second wife, saved my life and was an angel of mercy. The clock was ticking to a halt when Sarah saved my soul.

"Great-grandma what is 'the apple of God's eye,' I braved?

"Come here, now and first look at this finely and perfectly knitted etui…"

So, I moved very close and gently touched the soft beaded surface. As I looked my face and eyes were drawn into the pattern sewn with care, and I was considering that her little teeth must have married it somewhere when she so kindly commanded, "Now with that same gaze look up here at me."

I was feeling a bit uncomfortable when she asked, "What do you see in my eye? Look very, very carefully…What is the picture you see in my eye?… Can you see yourself?"

I suddenly got goosebumps and started to be overwhelmed when there in her smile and the mirror of her beautiful blue eyes was the perfect "ME"!

I took a sudden deep breath that I didn't know was coming and crawled into her arms. "Oh, great-grandma I think you love me."

"Well, I most certainly do, my dear, and you are the apple of my eye. When King Solomon was in the temple with the priest, he was told that even though David had sinned with the death of Bathsheba's husband that in all the other things of David's life he had pleased God, and that the Savior of the world would be born through the lineage of Bathsheba and David. 'The apple of my eye' means to favor not as in favoring, like wanting, but it means 'being-like' like resembling…God was declaring that David was like Him."

It was late. We had dinner, then said prayers and went to bed. I slept like a princess in a fine castle, looking around, wondering where all the marvelous experiences would take me. I dreamed I was in a house with a winding staircase. And when I finally stopped looking at everything and started at the first step the staircase began to turn, and as it twisted I saw different rooms with the future in each of them. I saw happiness and thunderstorms, a wedding, a courtroom, one had been created for huge arguments which screaming was coming out of the room. I saw a bomb go off in the distance, and I lifted my hand to cover my eyes. I came all-the-way to the top of the staircase, and there were huge open portholes in the turrets of the building that I could see around the world. There was no damage from my view and the sun and gardens looked like heaven.

I wanted to wake up that morning. In my journal before bed, I had written, or rather scribbled, *please, please dear Lord let my great-grandma live long enough so that I can be a part of her memories. I want her to remember me when she gets home to you.*

The 99 questions now looked stupid and unimportant. There was a compelling love for my great-grandfather that hid behind my great-grandmother's interpretations of things and even though I knew she loved God more than anything there was something about the way she transformed when she considered him as her husband. I felt like he was often there with her coaching her and living side-by-side with her.

As soon as prayers were over in the morning, I told her of my dream, and I asked her if there was a time in all her life that she had missed great-grandfather.

She said, "My life has been just like your dream. One room, one choice, one change after the other, and in each step of my life I have looked to him for guidance."

"Do you pray to him?" I asked, carefully.

"I guess in a way I do. I know that Our Savior hears and answers my prayers but in a particular kind of loving memory, I talk to him and ask him if he still remembers me. I know that he will come for me soon and that when he comes, he will be young and graceful as I remember him. I know that he is the part of my soul that belongs over there with our Father-in-Heaven. I love that about my life. I know that through all of my experiences someone has been at the throne of God looking out for me. I have never felt chastised or ridiculed or berated by his presence." Then she leaned over very close to me and whispered, "He loved me the first time he met me in that buggy in England, long ago.

CHAPTER 10

The Hidden Room

The ceiling in great-grandmother's closet was so high that if I stood on the highest shelf, my head still would not touch the ceiling. There was a beautiful light with a dangling cord hanging almost to the shelf. I saw it and tried to image myself getting up there to check it out. On the wall was a switch for the light in the corner that shed light on the rail of clothes. In the far end of the closet, near the ceiling, there was another light socket with a large bright light bulb. When I flipped the switch, the overhead light did not come on. Great-grandmother had requested a group of small boxes that were on the shelf. She showed me a lever that was at the back on the side of the closet that folded down into a set of hidden stairs. It was built with beautiful architecture, the wood was polished and robust. As I traversed the steps and ascended to the top one, there was a handle on the wall near my head I considered it for several seconds when great-grandmother asked, "Are you quite ok? Now I know you are not afraid of heights, my little tree climber." "No," I answered, "just checking out the second set of stairs...I would like to go up further but why, where would it go?"

"I will let you check it out later. For now, bring me the pink-papered box and the blue denim one with the brown wallet. Be attentive and you can go with me to pick cherries at Brother Kimball's home after lunch."

I quickly brought the items she had requested and set them on the stainless-steel table and washed my hands. The running water was so warm as if it had been sitting outside in the sunshine. There was little dust on my hands, but the lesson of fingerprints was a lesson I did not want to repeat. I slowly came back over to the table, and as I was about to sit with Great-grandmother she said, "Don't bother sitting sweetheart go check out the attic and while you are up there, do a little inventory for me...will you? I haven't been up there for ages. I know it is just the same, but I miss it, just the same."

I didn't run, but my heart was racing. In my mind, I could see my great-grandmothers smile following me, checking me out and taking in every little noise I made. I pulled the shelf down again and climbed up respecting the steps, but it was so hard I could almost feel myself swear! I just wanted to fly! I got to the last step and at my hands level was another handle and on the other side of the closet wall a brace. I pulled the handle and as graceful as a swan, a second set of steps came down exactly like the one below and only a step distance from the shelf, all the way across the shelf, leaving me a landing and a new set of stairs to climb. When I reached the second to last step, there was another handle for me to grab with no lever to pull. Quick as a whip my mind conceived the cord that would turn on the light, and I pulled. I was transfixed, and let out a sigh. A music box chimed and the sound of *Skaters Waltz* was playing. I was still considering what the heck, when on the second stanza the upper ceiling began to lower and a new set of stairs came in right behind me with the last step turning into a small landing and braced by both sides of the closet walls. This set of stairs like the others did not squeak or make any sound. As I nearly flew up them at the third or fourth step, I remembered Great-grandmother telling me that she could imagine that fourteen steps were going up to the upper floor but that it wasn't until she had actually done the climb that she would remember. It was there that another handrail was available on my left, and it was made from the same precious wood and polished to the same perfection as the stairs. "Oh, Great-grandmother," I whispered, "Oh, Daddy!" There was a little bench at the top of the stairs, and I sat down.

This room…this treasure…Inventory? Are you kidding me? I felt like I had gone from my twelfth year to twenty in a Nano-second. I was bewildered, bedazzled, and befuddled all at once. Along the west wall were two doors exactly alike, and rather close to each other. The polished hardwood floors did not squeak! You could not hear my feet echo! The first door, when opened, had a permanent wall behind it, it was no longer used for sure. The other lead into a bed chamber. I nearly cried walking in and going to the round, stained glass window to look out between the perfect inlaid bluebirds and the vines, which my fingers automatically reached up to touch. What kind of sadness was this or intrigue? I vaguely remember these windows driving up the driveway? Are they too high, and small, against the plastered sides of the house? My mind was already working on the perfect copy of this room on the other side of the wall which you could get to from the hall downstairs. No worries I will check it out later.

What was happening to my mind? I paused, closed my eyes, and I touched my head down against my chest, I could smell the linens on the bed…it was so comfortable here. I could feel a soft breeze. I looked up, and there was an old transom holding the fan that was slowly turning and the roof fan that was spinning rapidly. I could see the hot air on the ceiling lifting out of the room and the cooler air running in from the corners of the room to catch up…a calm essence of air catching me by surprise and creating a breeze of perfect luxury.

In the corner, beside the armoire was a chamber pot that had been covered with a silver plate and on top was a collection of dry flowers. Instantly I saw a romantic arrangement of elegance leading my mind to my dear, great-grandfather's betrothal and the times they spent together when could he see his beautiful girl again. She was so much younger than him. She was such a charming addition to his mischievous eyes…I crumpled to the bed and sat on it and even risked jumping on it. It was a masterpiece it did not squeak either. The floors had the most beautiful tapestries, the pictures hanging were of my Great-grandmother with my Great-grandfather in various expensive frames and beautifully crafted. There were pictures of what I am sure was her mother and father, my great-aunt Annie and my great-great-aunt Millie. The dollies and the chest of the drawer were inlaid with gold and elaborately crafted; probably worth a million dollars. The comforter and the feather tick were made from the finest French linen, I could tell that this was where my blessed great-grandmother had hidden every detailed memory of that man she worshiped like she did. The rest of the house was the faux. The rest of the house was now the mystery. My great-grandmother had been a wealthy lady and had been given the glory of the Gospel to replace it, but her husband had given it back in honor and reverence for her silence, I assumed. The candles and lamps were of Tiffany origins, and the tray and tall vase of dry flowers were of the purest crystal. The tray had a selection of jewels which I dared not touch, some stones some nuggets that looked like pure gold. The rough stone that was blue lapis, an emerald, maybe a ruby and some topaz? I had to pick up a piece of what looked like gold to bite on it, and then I saw teeth marks already there…gold…like real gold…in a hidden room…I wondered was I in a dream? And then the flowers in the vase brought me to my senses because they looked as if they had been picked from the prairie and still smelled of minty-rose. My dream…the rooms in my dream… untouchable and delicate…preserved like magic.

I rushed to the outer room and shut the door behind me, it made no noise. I then took in all I could of the upper chamber. There were a wooden table and four elegant chairs, a telescope at the end of the room by one of the windows that faced east, which window I could tell opened. There was a small door that when I turned the key in the lock, it opened on its own accord, onto a patio large enough for two chairs or the telescope stand and a chair. I had to tip my head to get back in but not by much. I stood straight up in the door with my shoes off, and the frame barely pushed down on my head. I was five feet tall, I knew that.

There were two stained glass windows, one at either end of the north and south walls and another transom with a duplicate of the fans that were in the bedchamber. Once my eyes had adjusted it was plenty light up there but there were only four crescent-shaped, stained-glass-windows and a fake door at least as it would appear from outside, and the stained-glass windows in the bedchamber.

There was a chest, like a pirate's chest. I walked over and knelt down beside it and touched the latch, the lid came right up, again not a noise. Inside there were some more precious things and an emerald green ballroom gown, with satin slippers to match, a tiara on the shelf of the chest and two white baby blessing dresses.

Near the bookcase, there was a rocking horse, of polished wood, and a rocking chair with a beautiful long-hair doll sitting in it...'Oh, My Heck! RoseMary?' I questioned.

The bookshelves were beautiful and the books all collectibles. I recognized the McGuffey's Readers and some of the church books. The lamps in this room were less expensive but still very beautiful and very tastefully set. Some were kerosene lamps, and some were candle lamps. There was no visible electricity in these rooms. There was no way to heat the room.

I had lost the sense of time, and I was preparing my apologies for great-grandmother when I realized that if our ride had come surely, I would have been called down. I stepped from the last of the ladders and gently swung it up, then took a long slow turn to find great-grandmother, sleeping atop the blanketed bed as if napping.

I walked still as a mouse to the kitchen and looked at the clock to my amusement I had only been upstairs for 30 minutes. It was only

10:35. I moseyed over to the things laid out on the table and was thrown into another world entirely different than the one upstairs.

One box, the big papered one, surely had contained only pictures. Old crimped corners and an occasional bend were the only things that even indicated that they had ever even been looked at. I carried these into the kitchen; I knew they were not full because it wasn't heavy. I went immediately to the sink and scrubbed my hands again before I even looked at the other two piles.

The denim box apparently had held some love letters and programs for plays and operas and even the ballet; entertainment in Washington DC and Texas, in London! England's Play House, the home of Shakespeare, a key with a red, satin ribbon tied to it; Room Number 53 engraved in the iron on the ribbon embroidered Grand Hotel, Spain.

On top of the leather wallet was a watch, tickets from London to New York, a train ticket to Jersey City and a coin with an American eagle on it and 1840 minted into it.

It was all circulating my energy, it was like a garden hose turned on at full capacity hitting the edge of a big iron tub and going round and round, fast but to slow to tell the tub was filling up. Circling round and around, small words hitting with impact as I breathed in and out. London, New York, Jersey City, Texas, Salt Lake, Washington DC, Spain and gold in a dish upstairs!...

I very carefully made sure every single item was exactly as I had found it and walked, I felt like I crawled, into the front room. I walked to the big west picture-window. Placed my twelve-year-old hands on the windowsill. And shut my eyes. I knew I was not sleepy, nor hungry for food. I was not worried. I knew my own father had not seen or knew of the attic room, I was completely unaware of what my family was capable of or where we came from really. I was a poor child with a spoiled attitude and my father and mother both struggled every day of their life to keep me in shoes and school books.

Down here in my great grandmother's world she was surviving by selling chicken eggs and an acre of land at a time, to pay her taxes. I had uncles and cousins that were filthy rich, but I had never left the country, neither had my mother or my father for that matter. Now I was curious who was my Grandmother, Delories? I mean who was she? Where did she go? And why did I not know her?

Would I know my father when I saw him again at the end of summer vacation? How did I not know my own mother, or did I? Would I get to know my baby when I got back home? Was there something wrong with my mom…or was great-grandmother a witch of some kind and all this made up.

I hurried back to my room and ripped my journal off the shelf. The first thing I wrote was, 'Does my mother know who she is? Does she know her heritage?' I had scribbled for maybe 20 minutes as fast as possible when I heard the tires coming up the drive. Shortly Brother Kimball came in, and I rushed to the kitchen. Great-grandmother had set a cheese sandwich on a napkin for me and poured a half glass of milk. I noticed a towel neatly set atop the papers and pictures on the table and between rapid bites I said I was writing in my journal, and I asked if there was anything I should do and if I had missed something important before we left? Great-grandmother replied, "This is your great-uncle Samuel Kimball. He will be our escort today. And a fine one he is at that. Thank-you Little Vanessa for being so quiet and letting me rest for a whole two hours."

I just shook my head yes…what was she talking about? I looked at the clock, and it had turned 1:00. How long had I stood in the front room at the picture window?

I had no!!!! Interest in picking cherries. Fast as a whip I looked at my great-grandmother and with all the possible power I could find I said, "Let's go get them cherries!"

"Those cherries," she corrected. I suddenly realized we had no need to pick cherries we were on a power outing of some kind. But I was wrong, pick cherries we did. And after I was exhausted and she had picked through all of them carefully she was exhausted too. Uncle Samuel carefully wrapped his loving arm through the crook of hers and led her like a belle-donna from the orchard, her long gown covering the grass in the shade like a feather and reminding me she was a matriarch, a queen. Who was this uncle? I have never heard of him before.

It was 6 pm when we were sitting at the table again. Great-grandmother was dozing and softly breathing. Uncle Samuel's wife Rachel had sent some warm casserole home with us. I had dished her portion first and was sitting down with mine when she began, "I remember the fancy tux and correctly set tie, a contrast of becoming gestures and correlating words...he had: the maître'd. He was the second person I had met in my life who had a clairvoyance that was nearly palpable. I felt him read my mind in every thought. His attentiveness to detail was almost frightening. My husband was just as aware as I that this young gentleman, serving us had a spirit that seemed to hang in our presence. His eyes neither met mine or my husbands, but he shared his love for the art of service with such expertise, that my husband requested an audience with him after he was relieved from his work.

"I didn't intend to tell you about the Gran Hotel before I told you about my trip across the Great Atlantic Ocean, but the key...it always calls to me.

"Oh, excuse me, please, great-grandmother, you know I am starving for every morsel you could possibly give me considering the afternoon I had in paradise..." was she really laughing at me? Shocked, I sat dumb-founded.

"But," I continued, interrupting her humor, "I find it curious that there are two sides of a continent at this very residence in Kaysville, and I get it that you will only be sharing what you think I am capable of handling...but I have hormones too! I had to keep my head about me or faint twice today... So laugh,"

She reached over and caressed my hand with her soft leathery hands. And whispered, "You are so perfect for this job."

I just wanted to cry.

She began gently, "The family, what's left in my life, came together last month and decided they wouldn't have me found three days dead in the 'old mansion.' In keeping with my own agenda and helping them keep from declaring me 'incompetent' I joyfully accepted their request for a 'handmaid', but I refused one from outside of the family. It was your father who asked if you were too young for the job. I had met you one time at a family reunion six years before."

I stood up, "pardon me?", I apologized and sat back down, "I remember, now." I took a new look at my companion and started to cry...

"Yes, that is the only time you ever met your grandmother, Delories, and she passed just last year. She was 97 years old and had lived in Colonial Juarez since 1908 when the new driving force of politics started assaulting the children of the "Promise".

"I have so many, questions great-grandmother. The fantasy upstairs keeps whispering, to me. You asked me for an inventory of the attic. And the way I see my parents now...is a source of heartache. I know who I am, I am all of this..." I had stood up at some point and was pacing the kitchen, "but I am still so much more than, than, than...what.

"If I apologize one more time to you it is not because I think I have let you down or because I am not enough to handle this it is because my mind is organizing and stretching and pulling and pushing and mixing me up! I hate, I love, I miss my Dad. He always balanced everything." I finished with a blow of soft air through my teeth."

Again she began gently with, "And he is the one who requested the pardon from your mother so you could spend this time with me, and he is the one who had taken the time to forgive your grandmother Delories for letting your mother make her own choices when she was not ready to pay the consequences of them. We can thank him over and over again, and you don't need to know everything. I did not keep a journal. I kept a few records and an exceptional memory. I had promised Brother Fielding before he went to meet the Lord that I would live to tell the tale of our life and our love for the Prophet Joseph and the Principal of Celestial Marriage as was given by the Lord to the Prophet Joseph. And before Brother Fielding left he constructed a plan that would keep me very much alive until now. So I'm counting on you, my dear, to have an open mind and be fearless. I'm counting on your questions."

It was 6:55 usually, this was our story time. Tomorrow would be the church. I was yearning to take a walk, and I was eager to have all the stories I had made up in my head figured out. I wanted to watch her comb out her long silver hair and ask her more about the Gran Hotel and the ballet, etc.

"It's ok," she said, "we have 62 days left, together, and I believe that what you need to know and want to know will all be sorted out. I am going to take a very long hot soak now. Would you like to take that walk? She paused and paused, "Trust me, I'm not going to drown or catch pneumonia while you are out. Let me make a suggestion; just promise *you* won't drown or get pneumonia," we both smiled at each other.

"On the far end of the lake, there is an uncertain path leading to what looks like *nowhere*...take it and this." She handed me a towel. The phone rang as it always did at 7: pm on Saturday night, she lifted the receiver and before she said hello, she brushed me off. Then she said, "Hi, sweetheart, Nessie took a walk to the lake she is doing very well. We get along great, thank you so much." Great-grandmother wisped me away with the flick of her finger as I was walking out the door I heard her say, "I believe that you are right about that, she is so much more than a child…she is a beautiful soulmate."

Because of the way great-grandmother had arranged the items on the table. I could tell that the watch was going to be her first real story for me, and I was anxious to hear them all. But the lake and that path, that suddenly disappeared into nowhere, had been calling me since the day Johnny, and I had seen it and avoided getting punished for pursuing it. Yep there it was now stretching out before me, it had my name on it. I could see it now again from my mind's eye between the bluebirds in the stained-glass window upstairs…I turned casually and looked up at those identical windows, then kicked up dust from the road and as I went screaming down the grass path on the east side of the lake…'My real name…Scavenger…that's my name, and here I come,' was bouncing out of my mouth between footsteps.

CHAPTER 11

The Atlantic Ocean and Jersey City

The path around the lake was old and worn down by many different tracks, of which the deer, rabbit, and muskrat were the most abundant. It was evening, but the sun would not be setting for at least two and a half more hours. I was tired from the day's adventures and my mind kept racing back to the possible conversations that my great-grandmother was having with my father. The bulrushes and the cattails were high enough at the head of the lake that I could barely see the farm house, (little mansion) and there hadn't been a car on the dirt road since Uncle Samuel had left. He was a very lovely man, happy, kind, fatherly; such a gentleman I liked to think there was a story coming there as well. The path began an incline not very steep but black volcanic gravel was loose, and I was too tired to fight its need to make me slip. There were patches of the black lava under the pebbles and sometimes it sounded like the loose tiles in my bathroom at home. I watched as the rocks bounced against the souls of my feet and I picked up a larger rock to tap the lava. I could hear the sound of the tapping from underneath. Suddenly an eerie new feeling swept over me, and I considered getting off the path, but there were cow droppings, and defiantly horses with shoes and a rider had been here not too long ago. I moved on now much more excited than before. As the path abruptly came to an end in front of an enormous boulder, I could choose left or right either way. Behind the large stone were two sets of stairs going down and into a cave. I could feel the warm air and the moisture from the water below. Of course, it would be too dark in there for me to see. I thought why didn't she suggest a flashlight? Down I descended slowly, brushing the pebbles off as I went…I giggled I bet everyone who comes here does the same thing. The stairs came together on a platform about six feet down and the cave expanded in every direction. I could see the reflection of light on the water in the cave, as I put my hand on the right side of the entrance, there was a shelf, on the left side was the twin shelf…both were supplied with numerous flashlights and each shelf had a Tupperware container with, of course, extra batteries. There were two gradients about 3 ½ or 4 feet wide on the north and west and south side, and each sloped very gradually down about 5 inches. I had not picked up a light, but by now my eyes had adjusted, and I could see the black sand and the cavern to the east that was most likely that echo I heard while tapping the lava outside. It was perfectly warm and exciting.

I immediately took off all my clothes and hopped into the water. The descent was sudden, and I was aware that it was getting cooler at the bottom. I could hear the streamlets dropping their current contributions as I bounced up and down to see how deep it was. Was there no lower portion? And then I took off towards the cavern. "This place is fantastic," I said, out loud, "and I can't believe it! Johnny is going to crap when I tell him."

I listened to the water, I listened to the walls, to the air, and I could hear my heart. It became so apparent to me that this place had been loved and cared for by everyone who ever entered it. I believe this is what a temple felt like. I heard myself ask, "Great-grandfather, thank-you for my blessed grandmother, but can you tell me why her life was such a secret?" I heard him answer, in a loving and gentle voice, "It is the very most sacred things in life that are shared and spoken of least…in that way they are protected from being violated. Please tell the love of my life I miss her, will you?"

I dried myself off and literally sprinted all the way back to the house. I came bursting through the back door like a cannonball. I saw great-grandmother drying off her hair, and as she turned to look at me, I could see the passion and pride of a million visits light up in her eyes. I expected myself to be out of breath, but as I unlaced my shoes and set them on my shoe spot, I could hardly wait to crumple her in my hugs.

"What an adventure, what an amazing, amazing…uh, wow… wow…when did you last visit their great-grandmother?" I squelched her a hug, and she set me back a bit and said, "Why I'd say about 10 minutes ago!" We both laughed. She was so young, and I was so old.

"That is where I lived and became alive.

So many times, I wondered up the hill to talk to your great-grandfather after he passed. I drug the kids up there over and over again. He and I started carving the stairs the first year we found it. There were natives here who came and went and eventually didn't come back again. We bought all the property from Nephi to Santaquin on the west side of the lake so we would never have to worry about intruders. I invited my sisters and family to go there with me, and some of our neighbors found it, but we never put up "No Trespassing" signs because first, it belongs to Mother Earth. I recently sold most of the Santaquin side to. And about 60 years ago I sold most of the land on the east side of the lake ascending to the road to Brother Young. His family owns most of the property from the road east to Highway 89. There are still hundreds of acres left for us to hike and use, there is still one home on the east side of the lake and west of the road that belongs to me. Sister Kay lives there. We will visit her before you leave here. She has a beautiful grand-daughter I'd love you to meet. Her name is Wendy you will be best friends. She is dashing and a daredevil like you.

"You are surely interested in the phone call." I nodded my approval, and she told me that my mother had been having contractions off and on for a week. That the doctor said she could deliver any day. She had seen Dr. Allred in Murray, and she was very happy that I was having such a great time. She said I could call tomorrow sometime after church and talk to them about all my adventures.

"When can I go back upstairs?" I ventured the risk of being told, 'never.'

"We shall see, and perhaps I can give you some more details tomorrow…she looked towards her desk, where she had moved the boxes and wallet from the kitchen table.

"I know it's time to sleep, I have plenty to write in my journal…but before we say prayers can I ask you one question? "When you visit, the cave does Great-grandfather talk to you? He told me to tell 'the love of his life' that he misses you, and he said the reason the room upstairs is a secret is because it is sacred. The fewer people know, and the less they know, the longer it will be safe there."

"Thank-you, I miss him too. Yes, I get to hear his melodic and vibrant voice when I go there and when he gets my attention I usually get flushed with love and admiration even still."

We said prayers. I wrote in my journal. I wanted to know how to ask my mother if her heart would mend and she could forgive her mother. I knew I had a sibling on the way, and wanted to tell my mother I love her before she went into labor.

After prayers in the morning, I asked if I could call mom. But I realized before I even finished my question that if she hadn't slept waking her would be a mistake. So as soon as we got home from church, I called…Dad answered the phone and said they were putting things together for a trip to Grandma Vera's. That would be where mom would deliver and recover. I asked if I could talk to her, he said to make it quick and between contractions. He then asked mom if she wanted to talk now and she was instantly on the phone. "Hi. Baby," she said. "Are you having a good time? Are you staying put? I miss you so much, just a minute." I heard her squeak and breath and knocked the phone around a bit, and then she was back, panting… "I probably need to go so I can get in the car now."

"Ok, Mom, I love you…I love you, good luck…See you soon, bye." She was crying, "I love you too, honey see you soon. Bye." Dad came back on and said if things went well the baby would be born this evening and that he would call us with the details. I told him I loved him and hung up. I took a minute to compose my feeling. I wondered where Johnny was?

We had chicken salad sandwiches, and I informed great-grandmother, "its June 30th I have 61 days left. I miss my family especially Johnny and Dad, but I don't want to leave here. This feels more like home than anywhere I've ever lived." The new place we moved into in Millcreek was an old, old house much like this one. We had moved from the Uintah Basin nearer to the city so mom could be near father's mother during the end of her pregnancy.

We went to the yard and sat in white lawn chairs. The trees shaded us and it was sweltering in the sunshine but the breeze was refreshing, I knew great-grandmother was extra tired today. She would sleep for a few minutes then wake, then sleep again. I went inside and got my book, *The Wonderful Wizard of Oz,* by L. Frank Baum and began to read where I had left off. In about half a page I saw a movement in the yard and over the top of my book I could see a mother cat carrying one of her brood into the barn. I watched her take the kittens one at a time to the barn, drop them off then make another trip I counted six trips but wasn't sure I hadn't seen her first trip…I set my book down and quietly snuck in to see how many babies she had. There were ten kittens all black ring-tail tabbies. They started crying when they detected me, the mother came running back to protect them from the new intruder. I made my apology and wanted to split before she decided to move them again. As I was leaving she cried at me and I hunkered down to her level and asked what was bothering her…She looked me up and down and cried again. I promised to bring her some milk and left quickly. On the far west side of the lawn, I walked quietly to the house. I got a little milk for her in a tuna can and hurried back as fast as I possibly could without disturbing Great-grandmothers rest. As I came back in the barn, I whisper that I was back. She was sprawled out with 20 front paws kneading her teats as the kittens sucked so loud that I could hear them. "Wow," I cooed, "You guys are starving. What's up mommy cat, too many kittens for you?" She stood up dragging a couple of them with her as she came and cried her disbelief that I had come back and crammed her nose into the milk purring at top volume. "Well," I said, "I guess dinner on the town isn't reason enough for us to be friends?" She kept purring but didn't resist me so I kept up my flattery. When she was done, and the sharp barbs on her tongue were scratching the sides of the can, I asked her if I could hold one of her babies. She came over and wrapped her body around my leg so I reached down to pet her. Oh dear, she was a stray, and I had fed her. Now she would follow me, and I was in big trouble.

Great-grandmother changed her pose as I walked back to the lawn chairs. She looked out from under her beautiful summer hat and smiled at me. I see you found Madam Moselle. I wondered if she had birthed her brood yet. She's a fine mouser and very sweet. How many kittens did she have this batch?" She requested.

"I counted 10. I saw her nursing that many as well. But the kittens were not all in the barn at first. She brought the kittens from over there." I pointed to the corner of the house.

"She usually has them under the house and lets them get old enough to start hunting for food on their own before she moves them to the barn. I'm sure that is all she had. She is an excellent mother.

"Will you get me a cushion from the chair in the living room, my shawl and the leather wallet from my desk in my room? Thank-you, also get two glasses so that we can have some of this sun-tea." I smiled and nearly ran to gather the things she needed. The tea was from the peppermint in her garden, I watched her as she put about half a cup of honey and a tablespoon of sugar in it.

Every evening except Sunday about 6 pm a young man came over and worked in her yard. He took great care in the grounds as if it was Great-grandmother doing the work. But I saw her pay the young man every Saturday.

I felt so welcome and at peace. Everything she asked me to do was considerate. I was anxious now for the call about my new sibling, but very much more excited about the chapter of Great-grandmothers life that tied her to the Church and her husband, Brother Fielding.

I handed her the wallet and shawl, put the cushion behind her back and took her glass to fill it. On the little white, wicker table were some wooden coasters and a ring that held napkins.

"You must be nervous about your mother," she inquired.

"Yes, I am," I said too fast. "But as you can see I can hardly wait to hear about the watch and the tickets and the coin...please, let me pressure you, ok." I smiled as much as I could, and I felt the unnatural strain of my smile muscles blocking my eyes.

She chirped, "Well I have to say first, it's a pleasure to have such a tentative audience. Shall we begin?

"The watch was the last thing my father had given me before I left him in England. I had coveted it for years as I watched him prepare and in perfect timing attend all his church and business functions in England. Mother made a little pocket just inside the waist of my dress and told me always to make sure the chain was inside, or it would be easy for someone to steal it from me.

"As we docked I had the watch in my hand. And I stopped the time with this little button." She showed me the button, "it was exactly, from the time I put my foot on the ship in London, to the time I put my foot on the dock in Port James: 21 days, 14 hours, 22 minutes and 15 seconds.

"My sister Annie had the tickets, and as we left the dock, she handed me mine and said, 'This is the most precious gift you have received since you were born. Remember that now you are in Babylon, a city full of corruption. Do not leave my side; we need to travel to Uncle Seymour's still today and get something to eat.' She and my Aunt Millie were exhausted from the Ocean and all the screaming sailors. There were other Saints on the same passage we took, but father made sure we had a first-class ride. Being on the Ocean the first day was beautiful we left the Port Water Loo at 5: AM and by the time the sun had come up, porpoises were swimming alongside the ship. There were a couple of other ships that passed but no pirates or sea traders. We took a lot of embroidery for the hours and days we would have to eliminate, one at a time. I was very lucky that I didn't get sea-sick my sister was sick for the second and third days, but my Aunt Millie was sick almost half the time. The food was distasteful and smelled like fish even when it wasn't fish. When it was fish served, I preferred fasting.

"I was very grateful to be so close to the City of Zion and eager to do anything to help out. Annie bought train tickets to Jersey City, and when we arrived there, Uncle Seymour was delighted to see us. He helped get our luggage and took us to dinner at a very nice restaurant. All I wanted was mashed potatoes and turkey gravy, and real water. Annie handed me my train ticket after dinner, I tucked it in the Book of Mormon I was carrying.

"At Uncle Seymour's we spent days getting ready for the trek across the wilderness. I learned how to roll my clothes so they would unfold and with the least number of wrinkles. We practiced washing our clothes by hand and hanging them to dry in the freezing cold, then bringing them in stiff as a board and warming them up by the stove.

"We were receiving instructions from the women who had been sent from the beginning era of the Perpetual Emigration Fund. It seemed very practical to have some experience before heading out.

"Father had been given the report of the 'iron-rails' that would be laid. But the big concern was how far into the future would that be. The new rails 'idea' was huge and on every newspaper front.

"We left London on September 3rd and arrived on September 24th at 5:22 pm. If we had not stopped at an earlier port, we would have been earlier, but we could not dock and set out carefully in the dark.

"Uncle Seymour was my mother's older brother. He had a very nice house and a good bankroll. He helped us when he could, between all the other chores he had. His wife was the daughter of a merchant and dressed very richly and was at a charity event or ball of some kind nearly every day. A few times I felt like we were in the way. Our journey to Salt Lake didn't allow us to bring many lovely items and father promised as soon as he could secure passage mother would get as much together as she could, and he would send it to us. We didn't have much money. I was 11, my sister, Annie was 16, and my Aunt Millie would soon be 19. I didn't want to go to the Christmas ball. But Annie and Millie did so Aunt Ginger laid out every possible dress for them to try on and she was so jubilant to take them as they were to go.

"It had snowed heavily that morning and though some of it had melted it was still cold and icy on the roads. Uncle Seymour's bell-man prepared and drove them to the ball. On the way home, they hit the embankment and rolled the carriage. No one was seriously injured, but

Ginger had been trying for ten years to have a baby. In the summer, Uncle Seymour had taken her to Paris and to Spain to comfort her and see doctors for her condition. When they got back, she had promised that if by (September 23rd) which is the first day of fall, she wasn't pregnant then, she said she would quit trying, and complaining about it. When we arrived on the 24th of September in Jersey City, she was three weeks pregnant. The day of the ball was Christmas day; she was over three months pregnant. She didn't miscarry, but the complications of her maternity and confinement were difficult, she delivered the baby almost seven weeks early, the baby did very well, but Aunt Ginger died three days after from complications of the delivery. It nearly killed Uncle Seymour. He hired a wet nurse and then made arrangements to go to Salt Lake as soon as the baby turned a year old. It was a dark time for my Uncle. All of us tried so hard to make things work out. Ginger was such a beautiful and lovely woman. There was so much heartache and loss. I began to feel a profound responsibility, for the people around me. I wrote to my father and mother often, but I was lonely.

"We were supposed to leave for the Great Salt Lake Valley on the 1st of May, from Nauvoo. We would take a train to Chicago and then catch a ride to Nauvoo with some travelers heading there. From there we would travel by wagon with the Saints, across the plains. It had been done many times by now this being the sixth year of the Saints experience crossing the wilderness. Thousands of people saints and foreigners were settling all over the west now. They had a real science of traveling by wagon and the railroads in the inner cities figured out. I wasn't worried about it myself, but as it got closer, I was concerned about my frail Aunt Millie. She was much like my mother, and I worried she would get ill and not recovery quickly.

CHAPTER 12

The Very Long Walk

Great-grandmother and I had drank our tea. She had gone to the house to relieve herself in the bathroom. We had a sacrament meeting to go to in 20 minutes, so I cleaned things up and took the leather wallet back to her desk. On the way to her room I asked loudly, "Great-grandmother, when did you get your gold coin?"

"It came in an envelope from Uncle in Nauvoo just before we headed out on our wagon train. He had found one minted in my birth year and sent it to me he said that it was his token in the promise that as soon as his baby turned one or my father and mother came to rescue him and go with him he would come to us. I wanted to use it to help cover the expense of the move, but Annie refused. She said I had sacrificed enough giving up my bed and my school and all the things she missed about home. She said if I used it to keep happiness alive it would stay with me until I die, and she would never let anyone talk me out of it."

We went to the sacrament meeting, and we arrived back in time for dinner which was spaghetti and meatballs with garlic bread from Sister

Kay. Soon as we got through the door, the phone rang. Of course, it was my dad. Great-grandmother asked me to answer the call, and she went to freshen up. I was so sad, so excited, and so alone all wrapped up in one. The first thing I asked is, "Where was Johnny?" Dad laughed. Johnny had taken an extra job for the summer he was delivering a large newspaper route, also taken up a lucrative job weeding and mowing lawns. He was actually, mowing our lawn when Dad called last. Mom delivered a 6 pound, 6 ounce baby boy David Clinton, and Mom was sleeping; she did splendidly and she was happy the baby came early.

I was relieved, and suddenly, I was exhausted. I said, "I love you. I miss you so much, kiss mamma and the new baby boy for me, tell Johnny I'm doing good, and I have a secret I want to share, so call me sometimes. Love you, bye." And I handed the phone to Great-grandmother and went to my room. It was only 7 pm, but I felt like it was midnight. Sundays were like that.

Monday morning, I was going to hear about the wagon train and her first day in Zion. I wanted to go to sleep and dream, about my new baby brother.

I dreamed I held him: he was so small and weightless, and then a stranger came in through the front door of our house and took him right out of my arms! It left me stunned and afraid of what was next. Momma and Daddy were crying, and Johnny was pacing back and forth. The stranger was in a uniform, and it seemed like no one was fighting for him. When I woke up in the middle of the night it was so hot I was sweating all over, and hurried to the bathroom I felt my bladder would burst. I washed my face and realized I had been crying in my sleep.

After prayers in the morning, Great-grandmother asked me what I had dreamed of that had caused me to cry in my sleep. I told her my dream. She explained that torture, is experienced by separation from what we love even if we have agreed to the separation.

She described the journey by wagon…the hot days were sweltering days when it rained the wheels of the wagons would get stuck…and after so many trips the Saints had become wise to some of mother nature's tricks and didn't fight her as much. They had violins and guitars, banjos and tambourines, flutes and harmonicas in their camp's and every single night there was singing of gospel hymns and waltzes played. Husbands would dance with their wives and girls would teach each other how to dance. Boys would behave very shy and then be encouraged by an aunt or uncle. After that, they would dance until they mastered the step.

"She was bold in declaring, "I loved Garden Grove it felt like all the ancient spirits of the Apostles were there just lingering in the trees and the breeze. Even before my best friend Libby told me of her trek across the wilderness, I felt the connection to the spirits that helped the Saints on the trek. Libby was a survivor of the Haun's Mill Massacre and when the opportunity came for her mother to leave Missouri she was one of the first to go and one of the first to have her baby after crossing the river. There were nine babies delivered that night. Libby was only three years older than me. She and her mother were bold and driven women.

When Brother Brigham told the brethren, they could either join the Mormon Battalion, or they could haul the poor folk from Nauvoo, or they could go on the scouting party that was heading for the Rocky Mountains to find the mountain called Timpanogos, with its corresponding lake, her brother left them and went to join the Mormon Battalion. He was only fifteen."

"She said that every day they prayed that he would find his way home. Libby was lovely. She said that the night before the Battalion left they had a grand-old-ball, and she waved bells that jingled in rhythm to the music at her 15-year-old brother, and she cried and prayed over and over again that she would see him again someday.

"She said she heard Brother Brigham say that not one hair nor one soul would be lost of the Mormon Battalion, and that they would triumph over the adversary and that the Lord would send other guardians just as he did for the 'Stripling Warriors' and to help with their families as they traveled to the New Land without the blessings of their sons and husbands company.

Great-grandmother said, "We didn't have to worry about another Mormon Battalion being called; the war with Mexico had been resigned since the signing of the Treaty of Guadalupe Hidalgo on February 2, 1848. It had been two years since the treaty. But the Saints seemed apprehensive because they had been deceived so many times before.

"News came that the brethren had been called back from the British mission because Brother Brigham was very ill and there was a fright that he might not live through, what they thought was food poisoning."

Great-grandmother told me that they encountered the Indians three different times who came to trade with the wagon train. She said that the bonnets the women wore were very different from the English summer hats she was used to. She said that she could watch the Indians from under the brim of her bonnet, and they couldn't tell if she was looking at them. She said some of them were so handsome in their nude dress with their ribs showing. Their eyes exaggerated by their painted faces. Some of them spoke broken English and tried to get them to give up buttons or jewelry that the Indians had never seen before. She was intrigued by their curiosity and felt they were more like children than savages.

If the weather was good and they didn't have to fight off predators the Saints could make the trip to the Valley in about 80 days. On the 62nd day scouts showed up to tell them that the brethren were on their way and would be having dinner and a meeting with them and that they would stay the night and refresh before hurrying on to Zion.

She cheerfully continued, "We were circled up with one wagon just close enough to the other that only one person could squeeze between the tongue and the tail hitch when suddenly the dogs growled, and the horses nickered. In the east up the road coming in were Brother Heber C Kimball, and Orson Pratt, with Brother Fielding and John Taylor just a horse length behind them. My sister Annie was so excited when she knew it was them. At seventeen, she was old enough to be betrothed. She and Father had talked for hours about her responsibility to be discreet and wait for the Lord to reveal to Brother Heber her desires. As soon as she saw that it was them, she made herself busy around the campfire and helped prepare our wagon in case the brethren stopped by our camp for food or drink.

"Brother Kimball and Brother Fielding both came to check on us as of course, I knew they would. They knew us well from all the meetings in England. It was just getting dusk when a caller came and announced the meeting would start at 7:30 giving mothers and fathers time to put their young children to bed and the brethren time to make a circle around the campfire. Brother Fielding informed us that we might have visitors from a neighboring tribe that had asked to join tonight. In favor of Brother Josephs desire that all Lamanites be converted to the Gospel, Brother Fielding had agreed for them to come see what we did at our pow-wow's. He then smiled and asked someone to offer an opening prayer. About halfway through our meeting 8:30 or so some horses came in on the other side of our wagon circle and Brother Orson Pratt, who could speak with them without an interpreter, escorted them over. Brothers and sisters moved to make way for them to sit on the logs but they preferred to sit on the grass and watch us quietly. Then the fiddle played with some guitars, and we danced until 10: pm. The Indians laughed at us, and some even joined in. The next day the same band of brothers came in on their horses whooping and hollering, shouting at the top of their lungs, 'Wasitu, Wasitu, Mitakoyesin, Mitakoyesin'... Brother Clark, our wagon master, said that being interpreted it would mean, 'White man, oh, white man you are our relation, you are our relatives.'

"I felt so honored and blessed to have met a peaceful family of Natives. I felt that if Brother Joseph would have been with us, he would have done the same thing and invited them to hear the language we spoke in our testimonies and our prayers. During the whole meeting, I felt my heart and soul connecting again with Brother Fielding and I watched as he tried to involve the Natives in the spirit of our gathering. Some of the Natives spoke very good English and even asked questions about Our Great Father. One of them said that they had a Chief whose name was Prophet, 'like your Great Prophet.' He stated that Burnt Thigh, his chief had many wives and that he, Red Cloud was trying to make his one woman glad. He was very young but also very smart. He said that their Great Father is Tunkashila and that he watches over everyone even the little children as they sleep so that their dreams will be good ones. I felt the love Brother Fielding had for the Natives and I felt his way with them would be so inviting that they would not want to leave us. I watched my sister as she disciplined herself and cautioned herself not to betray her feelings as she had promised Father. She kept a distance from Brother Kimball, but I was watching him, and I could see that he favored her as well, and it would not be too long before the question would arise.

"On July 4th, we had a special day and camped early. We sang and danced for hours. Red Cloud came that night also. He said he was watching the horizon for us so we would have a safe journey and that if this place we went had plenty, he would come there also and live. He brought his pipe and Brother Clark and some of the other men smoked it with him. He told them that the bowl is like the woman, and the stem is like the man and that the smoke is the heart of your prayer going up to see Tunkashila. Annie and Aunt Millie were so pleased to know the roots of the people Brother Joseph had received the Golden Plates from and we all rejoiced that these friends were watching our backs across the plains. We sat a little distance from the savage brethren. They felt our deep sadness at being driven from our homes and the huge 'burdens' they called our wagons intrigued them and they worried that the carts made our trip so slow. But Brother Clark told them we would need the carts in our new home to feed our animals. Red Cloud said Creator fed his animals, and that he would say many, many prayers for us. Just before we reached the Great Salt Valley, Red Cloud had brought his wife with a little bundle of baby on her back, and he stood as we entered the Valley as if he was blessing us on our final day.

"It was the morning of the 24th of July. Word had come back to us that Brother Brigham would most likely live but that he had ordered a great triumphal entry for our First Day in The Great Salt Valley. "This is the Place" that is what they called Salt Lake for almost two years.

"Four days after the Saints arrived in the Valley Brother Brigham marked the spot for the temple. The Saints had already made several attempts at building temples in Kirkland Ohio and Nauvoo Illinois. Brother Orson Pratt was the original surveyor and placed a cornerstone marker in the southeast corner of Temple Block. Later in 1855, the official surveyor-general of Utah made it the base and meridian for all of the entire Great Basin.

"Sixteen days after the Saints arrival the first white child was born and she was given the name Young Elizabeth Steele. Young for President Brigham and Elizabeth for Queen Elizabeth. The first official building to be completed was a school house. The first teacher was Mary Jane Dilworth. President Young said chapels would have to wait they could have the services in the open on benches in the shade or tents; however, the education of the children was more important.

"The first year of the trek Brother Heber C Kimball had several children with the cholera, and he lost his first born 'David' from his second wife, Sarah. And though this impacted sister Sarah and Brother Heber's life significantly she was given a blessing that she would be a mother in Israel and have many beautiful children that would sing praises to the Lord.

"There were 82 deaths per 1000 among the Saints the first year. Most definitely due to the freezing temperatures and lack of preparedness. I believe the difference of being driven out by madmen and leaving by will and choice was the difference.

"Mrs. Dolly Madison and Mrs. Polk, both first ladies of the White House made contributions to the suffering Saints. President Buchanan gave 20$ and then ten years later sent an army against the Saints.

"One of my great involvements and passions was for the Railroad. It was Brother George A. Smith and Brother Brigham both who had in mind the great highway to the West Coast.

"In December of 1847 the Saints had some serious speculation as to who was the President of the Church. Hyrum Smith had died with the title. President Brigham conceded to and was voted in as the President of the Quorum of the Twelve on the 5th of December that year, and Brother Heber C Kimball was his first counselor. But still there was no Prophet to lead the people. In the beginning the president and prophet were separate callings.

"All these things and a Lion House for the President of the Church were crowding my mind as our Camp came into Millcreek at 5:45 on July 24th, 1850. I was ten years old, and the trip took 82 days 12 hours 45 minutes and 32 seconds thanks to Father's pocket watch.

"In front of the wooden skeleton of Zions Mercantile and Livery Stable we stopped and met the Relief Team. Each wagon was given its stewardship. Some of the wagons would rest for a day or two and head to other settlements along the Wasatch Mountain front.

"Brother Kimball led several wagon trains to the Salt Lake Valley. On one of his treks, his nephew was caught stealing, and Brother Heber gave him 15 lashes with a whip across his back. A very common way to punish was with the whip. Often Brother Kimball and Brother Brigham would accompany each other as they did on several moves with their families of the Prophet Joseph's across the wilderness.

"I couldn't help but wonder standing there in front of Brother Brigham with our papers from Father if he would be leaving soon with Brother Kimball to chase another team of wagons across the wilderness. My mind was stuck on what looked like serious poverty and the truth that Brother Brigham had 50$ the first year and 1700 Saints to care for and feed. That the dust was so thick that you could spit it out of your mouth after sleeping a night in the open. The truth that the snakes were as thick as the savage Indians.

"The very first hour of my arrival in Salt Lake Valley I met Libby. She fed me every necessary gossip and was a treasure of Pioneer strength. I loved her from the start. She told me right off, "At thirteen years of age I will be keeping my mind on caring for my baby brother and helping my mother round up items to send to the relief parties that leave the valley every morning at dawn. Sometimes going to California relief and some times to Nebraska Relief. Thank the Good Lord for the Relief we have coming in from the Mormon Battalion gold dust.

"I was so excited for the first time in weeks I felt a little hope. Libby asked Annie if she could be of any help. And Annie asked right away for some refreshments and a place for Millie to rest.

CHAPTER 13

Pioneer Day A Celebration of Independence

On July 4th, Great Grandmother and I went to Nephi and watched the fireworks and the rodeo. I was very attentive to her. She seemed unusually distracted and unsettled. As I watched her, it became apparent she was sad. My mind was trying to give me reasons to be upset too... my new baby Clinton was over 4 days old, and I hadn't seen him yet, I had almost forgotten what my boyfriend Don looked like. I felt so excited about all the new things I learned but separated and distant from what was going on at home.

I was standing at the cotton-candy stand when I started to giggle at my sullen silly self. I must look like the spoiled kid on the block.

Around the corner, Great-grandmother sat at the pic-nick table waiting for me to return. She had on a wide-brim straw hat with beautiful small flowers woven around the band, a summer dress, mid-calf length and it was white with ecru tatting and embroidery around the ends of the sleeves and the hem. It was tapered to fit her waist and spread a little to make a false impression of large hips. She had an elegant posture and from where I was standing she looked younger than I felt. An old woman came up beside her toting a girl about my age with a hat smaller but similar to Great-grandmothers. I figured from her sweet disposition that this must be Sister Kay. "That will be a penny, please," I heard the young attendant say. I slid a penny onto the counter and said, "Thank-you."

As I was walking to meet up with Great-grandmother, Wendy came skipping up to me with a bright, cheery face and a grin from ear-to-ear. "So, you are Vanessa's daughter, Nessie. I have heard thousands of things about you!"

"Really?" I started. Knowing full well she intended friendship, but not willing to engage in any kind to her 'Gossip.' I suddenly felt like the night was going to be too long. As I arrived at Great-grandmother's side, I asked her if she would like me to go find Uncle Samuel and ask him for a ride home. She smiled and willingly agreed. I was so relieved. On the way home, she was droopy. I said, "This trip back to the house is much too good for me. I really didn't want to see any more people or fireworks."

Great-grandmother calmly said, "All work and no play makes Jack a dull boy." I started laughing, and I could not stop. I had the giggles from hell. I was trying even to let myself get embarrassed so I would quit. But it didn't help any. Uncle Samuel started laughing and then Great-grandmother.

I tried several times to open my mouth to say, "but never a dull moment since 1840." I had tears running down my face because no matter how I stammered and stuttered, it kept coming out, "butter annulment sedate four tea." No matter how I tried it was stuck and I could not change the sentence so we all laughed.

When we arrived at the house, I was asked if I wanted to go back with Uncle Samuel, but I had absolutely no desire to go. So, I told Uncle we had a story brewing, and it was about to blow. So, he clicked his heels and saluted me, said, "yes, mama", and took off. I was so glad to be back at the quiet little farm house. It was about 7 pm, and I wanted to go to the cave, but I also wanted to tuck Great-grandmother into bed. As I untied her ribbons in the back and lifted her dress, I could see how unlikely it was to get a word out of her. She slid onto her prayer stool and thanked God for the day and for the privilege of my company and my happiness even though I felt so far away from my family. Then she had tears coming from her eyes, and she thanked God for her beloved Joseph and her children and her life as a wife and mother. 'I so miss him today,' she whispered. When she got up and sat on the bed, she asked me if I would be willing to comb out her hair. I combed it and braided it and then tucked her in.

My heart was so big I could feel it banging in my ribcage. I think she was like my first experience of loving purely for the sake of love. In my journal that night I wrote, 'Do you believe that we will know that the things we are doing are pleasing to God? All I need is to know that she loves me, and I am at peace with everything.' And I did know she loved me.

I got up to go bathroom one more time, and I saw the light on in Great-grandmothers room so I peeked around the corner.

"Tomorrow morning, I have a treat for you," she said. She was looking at a picture. I stepped over, and she showed me the picture. She had a beautiful hat on and the green ball gown from the chest upstairs. "This was our last evening together. There was an explosion at the fireworks display, and he was thrown from his seat. The fireworks event took place after the dance and the photography sessions. He was rushed home, here and the doctor was brought to the house. We had a nice comfortable buggy and the next morning we left the children with

Libby and drove to Millcreek. He never recovered from that blast and used a cane for 150 days before he passed.

"Tomorrow, you and I will go over that inventory you made of the things upstairs, and talk about the things in the denim box. Give me a squelch, and try to sleep now. I love you, Vanessa Alexandria Cooke," she said with love and compassion. But I felt like she was saying goodbye instead of goodnight. I think my mind was as determined to grow up as she was when she was in England; I wanted to manage all the things going on and still be in charge of the way I felt.

I met her at the corner of her bed just as she was opening her eyes; 5:55 am and I helped her dress and get a light breakfast. She was aware of how excited I was and started answering all my questions with, "In a bit, in a bit." As I attempted to give that inventory in little fragments she would retort with, "I know, I know." She was acutely aware of all the things up there and exactly where they were stationed. I was getting antsy when she barked, "Ok, let's go!" She was really going to go up the stairs with me!

"I will need to rest at the top. And you will need to come up behind, Ok?" She then pulled the first set of steps down and informed me, "These steps are more sound than the steps at the Ward house. I used to visit here once a week and do some cleaning but the last time I was up here I remained stuck until I had the energy to come down again. It's going down that is the tricky part. I think it is because I get so emotional when I come up here." She stopped talking and carefully fixed each footstep with accuracy, and continued, on like a pro. At the top of the steps, she took a little break on the small bench and rested for a few minutes looking around and making comments on the things she loved. "That is RoseMary my sister and I shared her all of our young life, and when my children wanted to play with her, I made it clear that she needed to be around to see all our ancestors. Most of my grandchildren didn't have much time with her, and you are the second great-grandchild to make her acquaintance. The rocking horse is a not the one from England but a very close replica. The books are gathered from the places I visited as I traveled with my husband. The telescope was a contribution from your grandfather John Willard Young, a very handsome and wealthy man."

She rose and went straight to the bedchamber door. Bowed her head and entered with such grace. She went to the bureau and opened the top drawer. She lifted out a stack of letters tied together with a tiny braid of hair, and a delicate little hair pin clip with a magical blue dragonfly on the tip.

"When your grandmother Delories went into hiding she sent me these letters and I kept everyone. She pulled another smaller stack out, and it had a similar braid with a green dragonfly on the tip. "I'm sure these letters have many answers you would ask about the heritage you feel you lack. You could spend days reading and rereading them and realize that so many, many undesirable things have happened to the Saints." She pulled out the last stack of letters; three to be exact and they were tied together with the same red ribbon the key from The Gran Hotel had. "These," she said, "are from my beloved husband, and this is from your grandfather, John Willard Young." She handed me the last one and said, "Let's start with this one." She sat on the edge of the bed and patted it for me to sit down.

"This room and the adjacent one were recreated in 1910. When the world changed because of the Manifesto Decree, everyone who had a testimony of the principle of plural marriage had to argue in their minds against what they had heard and what was speaking to their hearts. Sister Emma had fought for years with President Young about the legitimate heir to the Church and that the original revelation (section 132 of the Doctrine and Covenants) of plural marriage was in her possession.

"Your grandmother was married to one of many of our leaders who had their families taken from them. Because there was no provision for the children and wives who had been taken, and because the men had to disappear or go to jail, they could sign a document proclaiming their indulgence in the unlawful carnal sin, giving up the blessings which had been promised for eternity and given to them by the Prophet Joseph Smith. Then the wives and children could receive help from the bishop's storehouse."

"As a church, we don't believe in divorce we believe in eternal marriage. We marry someone we love enough to be with life-after-life. For the Church or President Woodruff, to insist that the unions be broken and the children considered bastards, was so unforgivable to most of us and causing a great upheaval and many were worse off than when they were driven out of Missouri."

"So many of us were ousted over the modern need for the Church to become money changers in a money changing world. There was a band of brothers who took their families to Mexico, over the border and started a colony there. There were others who kept their personal affairs completely private and when the Church found out, they excommunicated them. Originally there was a rumor that was sent out that only the polygamist who entered into marriage after the manifesto would be ex-communicated, but that was not the truth. Your grandmother Delories was cornered and told that her husband would be excommunicated if she didn't give the child she was carrying to another person to raise. Because it would be proof that either her husband had broken the law or that she was a whore. She had been separated from me and was living in Provo by the river, on a beautiful piece of property given to her by Brother John W. Young and only a very few people even knew she was married to him. She cared for herself and came here to deliver her last child who was born after the death of Brother John W. Young. Her bishop actually attempted to have her excommunicated because she refused to sign an agreement to give her last child to the bishopric to reassign even though her husband was deceased. They still insisted that she give up her child. I know now that the church was trying to be-rid of all evidence of John W. Young's children born after 1881."

"Late one night the lights of the raiders vehicle came up our lane, and they took her baby from her, leaving her crying and at the mercy of what we later called "raids." The rest of the attacks were very organized by Bishop Mark E. Peterson, who thought he was acting in the name of the Lord. He had circulated a war against polygamy. We had an inside infiltration group that let us know when and where the raid would occur. This room and the other room, were used by many people after that. Because there was such a huge need for the room it was like the underground railroad for a while and the music chime, let people upstairs know if someone was here. The room on the other side used to be unfinished with stair access from the hall downstairs, that exit was blocked off and covered in 1910. It was left for many year's rustic-looking so it would look like an attic room for the boys.

"Your Grandmother left here with the Allred and LeBaron brothers and went to Colonial Juarez where she lived until she came back five years ago. She tried for months to do any repairs, with your mother and find your uncle William before her cancer took her to heaven. Your precious mother really didn't know what to do. She had been raised by the new Church that what your Grandfather did and what her mother continued to practice after his death was evil. Your mother knew me but not well enough for me to tell her the truth and not well enough to trust with her abandonment and pain.

I raised my eye-brows and breathed deep, exhaling like I didn't want to ask the question in my mind. *'How do you know?"*

"You will have to ask that question and find the answer for yourself. In the Book of Mormon, 2nd Nephi The Lord promises us that if we ask with faith nothing wavering, we will have our answer; that promise is also in the book of John in the New Testament." I knew great-grandmother had read my mind. In these days who knows the 'truth'?

"Last night I was sad. I miss my beloved, and I remembered my first 24th of July in the Salt Lake Valley with my new best friend.

"We had arrived at President Young's home with our papers from Father. President Young read the papers and then said, "Well at least I know that you are familiar with Brothers' Fielding and Kimball and my Brother John. There are probably others you will meet whom you have known while in London and Manchester. He introduced us to the head housemistress Clarissa and said, "Please, I pray that you are studious and helpful. I am grateful you made it here without incident, many were not so blessed. I will do my best to help get your parents here as well," turning to Aunt Millie, "and your sister's family, here as soon as the Lord sees fit. You will be trained and informed what your chores are by gentle and loving hands. If you need me I will be easy enough to find, we all met for prayers at 4: AM in the summer and 6: AM in the winter time. Welcome to Zion." He turned like a good soldier and left us with our new guide.

"We were shown the gardens and the livery stables, where the women milked the cows and feed the chickens, and took turns working the soil in the gardens. There was a head gardener. He was lean and black. He was very courteous and pleased to make our acquaintances and said if we had questions he'd be the one to ask. He had such a brilliant and happy personality. I could tell he was no slave except to his passion for life and his love for his masters. I found it hard not to laugh when he called President Young, "Master President." I'm pretty sure he was funny on purpose. I personally heard President Young call him, "Master Young Jimmy," to which they both had a good laugh and all the young Young's as well. The respect the boys had for Jimmy was remarkable. I had never seen that kind of love and affection for a servant, which the Young family bestowed on all their 'help'."

"I felt like I was home the moment my clothes chest was brought to the basement dorms where all the girls lived and prepared for the day. The first level was nearly finished but even in its rough conditions, it was used for breakfast and classes for the 2nd and 3rd graders. There was a temporary building used for Brother Brigham's wives and their babies. While the building was being completed, the boys stayed in the hayloft in the barn. Brother Brigham had several children already married. He had married three of Brother Josephs wives as well, Sister Eliza R Snow was one of them, and they were helping the family as much as his own wives did. It was said that he married them for the love of Joseph and to bear witness that he was in support of the law of Celestial Marriage. But he wasn't affectionate with any of his wives that did not appreciate his affections."

"I had been in his employment from the 25th of July 1852 to 1856 before I had the first reason to have a real conversation with him about anything particular. We passed on the walk between the Lion House, (his beautiful families personal hotel) and his office. Later the office became the Hotel Utah and was the resident establishment for dignitaries who came to visit the Saints. I was passing him on his left side. I was bringing fresh morning milk for the morning breakfast. We had prayers at 4 am and then we prepared for the day's work and started breakfast at 6 am. It was early for Brother Brigham to be going to his office, but the usual time I came with the milk. He looked at me like he wasn't sure if I was welcome. I said, "Good morning President Young," and curtsied with a slight greeting. We had almost passed when he turned on his heel, (the way he so often did when confronted), and demanded, "where are you heading young lady unescorted this morning?"

The sun had just started rising. "I, Sir, am returning with the morning milking for your breakfast, and you might recognize me if I weren't dressed like a cow myself."

To which he smiled and stopped himself from scowling. "And I haven't seen a lady here since I got in from London." I answered him with a scowl.

He did not hold back. "Well, we shall have to remedy that, and as for the escort?" Meet me if you can Sister?...

"May Davis, Sir." I answered.

He stepped back and retorted, "I thought you married my friend Heber."

This time, I laughed outright, "My sister Annie, Sir. As for 3 pm, I think I can get Sister Clarissa to give me a pleasant break at 3 pm... if," I tilted my head, "I will tell her the President requested it. But be aware there is only one escort my father would approve of for now. He is still in England Sir."

He tipped his hat and said, "And we shall have to remedy that as well. Have a very pleasant day Sister May."

At 6 am Brother Brigham was served his breakfast at his table in the dining room, with a selection of wives who could attend at that time. He was served the same glass of cold milk he had received at Aunt Millie's hand a zillion time's before. This time, it slipped out of her hand, and she tried to fix the fall and leaned into him to catch it. His wives were amused, but he was not. "Excuse me...sister..." Aunt Millie was blushing and nearly ready to faint when he asked calmly, 'sister?'...

"M...Mill...Millie, Sir, I'm, I'm so, so, sorry, Sir..." She stuttered and choked trying to figure out how to fix this mess.

"I've had babies spit up on me, also the treasures of vomit. I think I can handle a little milk. His wife Zina stood and helped my broken Aunt Millie and the glass out of the room. "How long have you been serving me my morning milk, Sister Millie? And only one little mistake..." he shouted as she slowly turned her back to leave. He looked very confused standing up and about to take his leave. His wives were having too much pleasure in his mishap. "Nothing a little water won't correct. I'm going to sit with the children, where I seem to belong right now."

"I walked around the corner of the kitchen, where Aunt Millie had gone to wash her face and restore her composure. When to my almost terror, the headmistress had given Aunt Millie another glass of milk to deliver, of course to the table where the sons sat to have breakfast. Brother Brigham had just sat down and ordered a plate of steamed potatoes and a glass of milk. Aunt Millie had no idea whom she would be serving. And to her chagrin there he sat again."

"Brother, Brigham, are you sitting with the boys?" She asked.

He exclaimed, 'Well since this is my house, I think I should be able to sit where ever I like, unless you intend to baptize me with milk a second time, then I think I will pass on breakfast altogether.' The boys were having a great time. Brother Brigham leaned over to his son and asked him, 'How long has that young lady worked here?'

"Little Ernest Irving answered, 'Sir, I believe it was before I arrived'... holding up his little hand with 5 fingers. 'I am only 5 and one-half year's father'. Ernest was the third child of sister Lucy Ann Decker. He was very fond of John W Young. You could see them working or playing together. Ernest loved John and idolized him. They were seven years different.

"Brother Brigham ruffled his little head of hair and looked at one of the other older boys Brigham Heber, who sincerely shrugged his shoulders. 'Well, excuse me don't you think I should know who is serving food to you? What is her name...do you know that?' All the boys shouted at the same time...'Millie.' To which I nearly had to scrape my Aunt off the floor.

"I was larger than my Aunt Millie. She was very petite and had quite particular features. She looked like a painting of a duchess or an angel. But she was always dressed in these gingham or calico dresses with dark almost black, green aprons that came from mid-calf all the way up to our collar bones. The green made her look like a ghost at night.

"We slept in the same room. We had been together since we left England. Not one day had passed without us telling each other how grateful we were for each other. I knew her secret, and I was sure by the way the wives were behaving so kindly and attentively that she had shared her secret with one of them...probably Sister Eliza. She went to compose herself again and was dismissed by the headmistress. She ran downstairs where I found her complaining about her insecurities and failures. I tenderly reminded her what Father had said, "The Lord commanded that by Revelation all things will be done with two or more witnesses." I begged her to be kinder to the woman I call "Aunt" and I kissed her on the head, and gave her a sweet hug telling her it was from her sister, my mother, and that I was proud of her. We were interrupted, by Sister Eliza, she was always so very proper. I think she knew more about Brother Brigham's family than he ever did.

"Sister Eliza started with, 'I hear you have an interview with the President today at 3 pm?' She looked at me kindly."

"Yes," I said, "I'm not sure why, but I think it has to do with my comment that all our dresses are so lovely that it would be difficult to tell the difference between the cow and the milk barer. At which He laughed.

"She raised her eyebrows and asked if she could have a minute alone with my Aunt. On my way, out she said kindly over her shoulder, "I've made no mark on that man with what it takes to make a lady feel like a lady. If I believed in 'good luck' I'd wish it for you, today."

"I did a small curtsy and left them to talk."

"I was just sixteen, I had been well endowed with breasts that nursing mothers didn't have. I was discreet and unwilling to be boastful or proud of anything including my determination, which could easily have been mistaken for arrogance or false pride or even stubbornness. I had an active mind."

It seemed that great-grandmother had wondered from the bedchamber for a second; she left that world in the new Zion just long enough to touch me and she looked deep into my eyes.

"Like you, I loved the Lord more than the people and the things we had. My mind wanted to know what allows a Spirit to talk to us through the air without a voice? As a person, how does it tell us who we are to love, who we are to lean on, and what it wants us to do for others and ourselves? How does what we believe and what we have committed ourselves to start showing up for us as a human? You, my dear child, are not a child at all you are an old soul who has come to help set things back in order and pull some nasty skeletons out of some closets that people don't even know exist. So many of the Saints have thrown the baby out with the bathwater and have trusted the arm of flesh instead of the God of Abraham, Isaac, and Jacob.

"It is no accident that I have lived 106 years to see you find the same power that I found at 3 pm on that 3rd day of July 1856."

There was a strong presence in the room, and I could feel my grandfather. He said, "Listen with your heart not your head when your great-grandmother tells you how hard it was to keep a passion strong enough to die for, quiet."

She continued, reading my mind again. "Since the Saints had been ridiculed by Congress for not celebrating Independence Day in 1847 when they arrived here, President Young had gone to great lengths for an amazing show and plenty of entertainment since the ridicule.

"I arrived at precisely 3 pm at his office. Brother Heber was just stepping out with Brother Taylor. Their homes in Millcreek were coming along, and they were preparing the ground from the Granite Stone Quarry for slabs to build the Temple. Annie had told me that these men were Brother Brigham's right and left arms. Brother John Taylor had settled in Clearfield and the Bountiful area. And Brother Richards had attempted to stamp out the pain of losing Brother Joseph with study and teaching classes for the adults every hour of the day. He was writing the History of the Church and rounding up all the records of the martyrdoms of Brother Joseph and Brother Hyrum that had been written... He seemed always preoccupied at our meetings every Sunday in the Bowery. I curtsied and moved out of the way a bit. They both genuinely reached to shake my hand and say, at the same time, "Why! May, sister, May." They both laughed at their redundancy. And I smiled and answered jokingly, "Yes, Sir, yes, sirs'! Whatever have you done now?"

"I got a bit of a squelch from my brother-in-law and a tender smile from Brother Taylor, then I turned quickly to cover my blush and handed them the path to the door. Brother Brigham was standing. And said, "Good day Brethren. Could you see to it that my home is finished by 3:45. Is it too much to ask for a miracle?"

"No, not at all," they answered, grinning. To which they tipped their hats and shut the door behind them.

"You could not even believe how beautiful and tasteful, it was set up inside the office. His wives were still camping out, it seemed from being in there. I could smell the fresh paint and new wood. I almost felt lonely and the longing for comfort hit me for the first time as a slap in the face. I had taken a quick inventory before I said something that would put me in a situation that I could not recover from.

"Your office Sir, is very becoming of the President and Prophet of the Church. I believe the Prophet Joseph would be very glad, and I know my father would surely approve." I said every word very clearly and cautiously. Remembering I was still considered a child in England because I had not had a 'Coming Out Ball.' The position of a woman was tolerated because of her father or her husband. I had neither.

"Before I leave this life and with the will of Our Lord all of my wives and children will live in the luxury that they deserve and are working so hard to earn. I believe your experience here in Deseret has been limited, and the confinement has caused your candor on the walk this morning. Before I continue with my plans and how they involve you, I want you to know I have written to your Father beseeching him to consider how he wants me to proceed with you. He was forthwith concerning your sister Annie. With that said, are there any questions so far?"

"He had his hands folded in front of him. There was a picture of Brother Joseph on the wall to his right and a picture of the 'Last Supper' on the wall to the left. Behind him was a set of menorahs, each with seven candles and in the middle between them was a picture of the Savior kneeling in the Garden of Gethsemane and under it another of the Savior being betrayed by his brother Judas Iscariot. I felt again, lonely and at the same time curious."

"No," I answered abruptly.

"Very well then. I have decided that I agree with you. I am going to send you to the Relief Society President with this message. He handed me a sheet of paper, a copy of it on his desk in front of him. It was bulleted.

"I believe that I can count on you to fulfill one request, that is not bulleted on this development. I am aware that it is short notice for some of these conditions, but I have seen the Saints do anything, no matter how bold, once they put their minds to it. Do I need to go over each bullet?" He gave me precisely 30 seconds to read it. And cleared his throat.

"No, Sir. No need. I understand perfectly. About my responsibility to your unwritten request, what exactly is it?"

"He eyed me over wondering where I got my boldness from. And then he sighed."

"I believe that there is someone to whom you have affections, though I have entreated both, of the Brethren most familiar with your family, and neither has any idea, with whom you might have affections. It isn't a mystery that you have worked in my employment for 5 years, and I don't recall you growing up…it appears you arrived grown up…"

"Excuse me, Sir", I apologized, "have I missed the part where I must agree to divulge my affections? That seems contrary to etiquette. Does it bother you that I have considered my affections the Lords business only?"

"I felt his respect coming in like a wave of mercy. And I heard a dull voice say, 'By vision and by revelation only.' His face softened substantially. He cleared his throat again."

"I believe it is customary for a young woman to have a "Coming-Out-Ball" and I want to have a Ball-of-all-Ball's here in Deseret. I'd like to have your help doing that, however, it would be inappropriate if you are not betrothed or seeking betrothal. And as for the young men in Zion it would be a heartbreak to promenade you as your sister was in England: remember I was there. Where were you?"

"I stood up causing him to rise at the same moment."

"Brother Brigham Young, I will remain your faithful servant as long as I am in the service of my Lord, but there is no rush for such a proposal. I have just turned 16 years in May. The Lord knows to whom all of my affection has forever been. When the Lord feels it appropriated to reveal that to him, my heart's desire, He will and not one second sooner…is that understood. 'By vision and revelation only!' That is how I will fulfill your request."

"I was fighting every instinct to run. When I heard a still small voice say, 'In the mouth of two or more witnesses.'"

"Quickly then catching him off guard. I said, "Here is my word on your request. If my beloved should ask, I will not deny my Lord. Until then I will hold you to your word. That you keep me in your employment until my Father gets here, or my Beloved relieves you of my burden…Perhaps by July 24th, and I will behave more like a lady! Thank-you for your consideration, I am the perfect candidate for a Ball-of-all-Balls."

He could tell I was extremely vulnerable. "Have you considered running for Mayor?" He asked determinedly. "Please forgive me I have overstepped my bounds. Usually, I pass everything I do through Sister Eliza. I considered you officially permissible…" I interrupted him proving him right, "You mean, you thought me of age?"

He requested again, "Please, forgive me."

I interrupted him again, "And No, I haven't considered running for Mayor, I can hardly take care of my Aunt Millie, you stir her up nearly every day!!! And teaching the nursery the Deseret Alphabet, and my own studies, chores, etc.! No." Then the tension broke.

I breathed again, and he said, "You should. We could use someone who is as certain as you are that the Lord will fulfill His promises. The Lord is greatly pleased with you Sister May. You shall have all the blessings you desire, and if your beloved doesn't propose to you before the evening of the 24th consider that I have made it my personal quest as a surrogate father and guardian that he better be worthy and do so!!!." Passionately he raised his voice to be better heard and understood.

I smiled. "Thank-you. I suppose you frightened me. Using your station and omnipotence, (Brother Brigham had a look that chided me) to cause such a sudden engagement, of a minor, because I am so, headstrong."

He came from around the desk and went to shake my hand… withdrew it and brought me into a side hug. "Young lady, you are going to be an influential representative of the Lord. Continue to pray as will I. I hope it's not one of my son's. I'd have to die of embarrassment to have a son that has missed your diplomacy and graciousness."

I could tell he was reaching. "Very well then, I shall be a lady and not let you down, President Young. I see you will be responsible for announcing all appropriated suiting, and calling cards at your own residence. Very well, I shall make my first report to you on the effects of this proposal by say…tomorrow at 3 pm?" I paused for a good minute and said, "Please, forgive me for underestimating your ability to see the needs of a real lady, and if I have not been properly suited by midnight on the 24th of July I will go visit my Father and Mother and help them come to sudden terms about Zion. Thank-you for your confidence in me. Good day."

I walked out with the last word and didn't look back. Was I seriously that big of a problem? I speculated.

I said, "Great-grandmother if you had seen yourself yesterday at the fair, you would have been smitten too. I can't imagine any man not having his head turn in your presence. The Lord needed a woman to show the way, and he needs you to show me now."

She gave me a hug. "You do not need to ask me for permission to come up here. Neither do you need my approval to read these letters? You know where they are and how to care for them. Before I turn you loose, one more thing. This is the last letter from my husband, Joseph Fielding. He was 43 years older than I, and there wasn't a moment of my life with him that I didn't feel that he was the younger and more agile and more lovely. Perhaps I was just too old by the time I felt the Lord and saw Brother Joseph as my soul-mate. Either way, you will be shocked by some of these things and others will just enlighten you. Shall we go have lunch?"

"Great-grandmother will you please tell me what was on the bullets and how the Ball-of-all-Ball's went?" she seemed to ignore me.

There was a shawl on the banister that had been tatted, and the fringe was crocheted. It was blue and green with stands of gold and silver intermittent, the wisps caught the light and made the shawl look like it was alive. It shimmered. She handed it to me and said, "This is for you I bought the thread in Lebanon and made it while I was pregnant with Liberty one of my stillborn daughters. The thread is cashmere; very, very soft." I pulled it up to my face, and it smelled like the flowers in the vase in the bedchamber. I asked, "How do I thank-you, great-grandmother?" I asked innocently. Like there was really any way to thank her for any of this.

"Let me go first, down the steps." She answered, and we went for lunch.

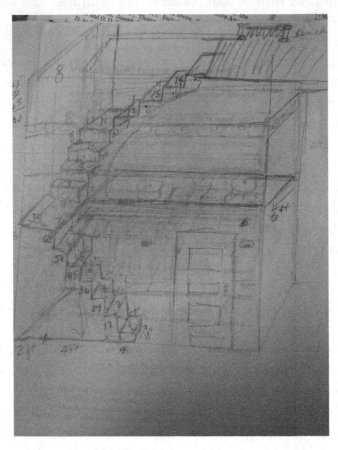

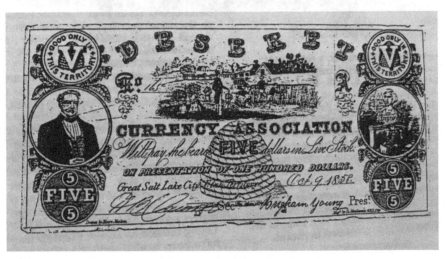

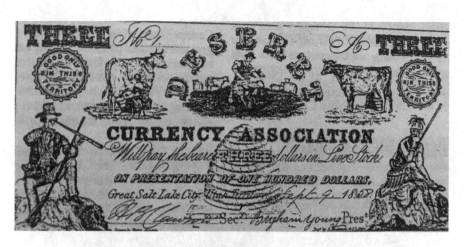

CHAPTER 14

Wendy KayDean Bunker

After lunch, it was sweltering outside and inside it was lovely. Great-grandmother asked if she could take a break, she wanted a nap. I was grateful.

"I need to have a conversation with 'grandfather' I'd like to visit the cave," I said softly.

"Take one of those nice sun-covers hanging on the rack. Don't stay until evening, please, I don't want to worry about your wellbeing, okay."

"I will be back by 3:30 and rest well". I cleaned up the table, rinsed off the two saucers and the two tea-cups, quickly tossed them in the little drain-rack, grabbed the hat from the hook, shouted, "I love you!", and I burst like a bullet across the road. I didn't bring a towel. I was not even concerned about that. I slowed down at the ridge where I heard the echo on the segment of stone that covered the lake underneath. I was so excited to have the magical place. I did a skip and a toss of my two braids in the air and shouted, "Okay, Grandfather, John Willard

Young, you bring it on," and I slipped down the entry-way into the amphitheater filled with water and now my misunderstandings and longings surfaced like the splash that echoed in the spacious opening.

I started my inquiry with Grandfather like a prayer, "I'm so happy to be a sister, and a daughter, a grand-daughter, I'm glad my father let me get baptized, I'm so, so glad to have this summer with May Alexandria Constance Davis-Fielding. I love her so much. Please take care of her. I know she is getting very close to you. I think I saw Great-grandfather passing in the hall with her last night. I know you were with us upstairs today.

Just exactly what do you want me to know that she married you after great-grandfather died? I already guessed that. That you were very in love with her as well? Who wouldn't be? You want me to forgive my mother for holding a grudge against her mother for 30 years? It seems petty to have a gripe over someone else's gripe. I guess my real beef with mom is that she stood in the way of me knowing…I think. Maybe she just wanted me to be old enough to decide for myself…no… she stood in my way.

"It must have been very hard to be raised by someone who hated your parents. I know that the Jews are hated just because they are Jews, and by the way weren't they hated long before they Crucified the Savior…Don't even try to pretend you're not keeping up with my extensive list of questions…you've been holding out for at least 4 days. We have to catch up. Did you finish the room upstairs…? Who knows about the hidden room? I suppose that really doesn't matter.

"I was swimming the length of the lake about 100 feet long when I heard the sound of footsteps on the terrace. I lowered myself to my chin and held very still.

"Hello, Hello!" Wendy called. "Your grandmamma called and said you would need this." She dangled a towel in the air and started stripping off her clothes as fast as a hornet. She was in the water before I could protest. An excellent ploy of hers I was beginning to gather.

"We didn't have time to chat at the fair, seein' that you-all had to leave right away with your gran-mamma. I wanted to get to know you better. Anyway, this gives us a chance to hang out a bit and talk…"

"I came to speak to my grandfather," I replied cautiously. "He and I haven't hung out for about a hundred years."

She ignored me…I was sort of glad. How would anyone reply to that? "When's your birthday?" She asked. "Mine is September 11th. I'm a Virgo. We are very picky with making friends, and lovers. I'm going to be 12." She was apparently trying to get me to respond.

I had doggy-paddled back and forth a couple times. She was an excellent swimmer as well. I was glad I didn't have to rescue her from the deep crater we were enjoying.

"My father has three wives." She bluntly stated. "I like them all; his youngest one is actually my second mother's oldest daughter…gotta keep it in the family, I suppose. I'm just joking.

Sorry. We are a part of the Allred group. My gran-mamma said I could tell you anything I wanted too. I want to tell you so many things. I have seventeen siblings. I love school. And I hate, hate, hate boys."

"Really?" I asked joking. "Whatever did a selfish boy do to you?"

"Oh, nothing. I just know that if I get close to one, my dad will kill him. My dad wants me all to his self. You know until I'm eighteen, old and useless…" She hummed a bit. "What do you think?"

"I believe you are a great liar. Now start over at the beginning and let's get this right. Your birthday I'm sure is the 11th of September. Your name is Wendy. Your grandmother said it was okay to tell me anything. Your father has three wives, and you like them all. The rest is horse-shit."

"You are good." She said. I hate school, I like boys, and my dad doesn't even know I exist. My Mother is a Kay. My father owns a large company called 'Dyna-flex Corp.' He invented a new cover plate for printing machines to decrease the cost of printing. He could be a millionaire soon. That only makes me less valuable. He comes over once a week looks in the door leaves a check on the table. Ruffles our hair a bit, sometime and then leaves like he never had a reason to come in the first place. Sometimes he will bring one of my other siblings to stay a day or two. You really should meet my brother Robert. He is so handsome and so smart. He is 16 now his birthday is the 27th of August, he's a Virgo too."

"Interesting," I interjected, "Don's birthday is the 27th of August as well."

"Who is Don?" She demanded. "He is your boyfriend." She wailed.

"Well if he is he doesn't know it!" I clamored.

"Well, when is he going to find out?" She demanded. "I'll tell him!"

"You are a hoot!" I said. He is my uncle.

"Oh, my heck, you are so boring." Wendy pouted. "What are you doing tonight?" There is a new movie playing at the theater on Main Street in Nephi at the little dump they have. I want to go. The theater in Draper is beautiful and has gold handrails and red-velvet-covered seats. The seats are terraced, and you never have to strain to see over big, bald heads."

I wanted to laugh at her crazy behavior, but I realized it was not an act. She was genuinely rude, but not ignorant. "What is the name of the movie?" I inquired.

"Seven Brides for Seven Brothers." Humming she started to climb out of the pool. "I'm turning into a prune." She wrapped the towel under her armpits and tucked it in. I was taller than her by about three inches, but we were the same age. I wondered what kind of home life she really had.

"You'll need to come visit me when you get to Salt Lake again. I'm leaving this weekend. My dad is going to Pinesdale, Montana for General Conference, up there. He will be assisting Brother Rulon with the sound system and the new building sites they are making." She sat on the terrace. Just looking at me. "You don't talk much, do you?"

"No, but I have lots of questions," I answered.

"Well ask me one. If I know the answer I will tell you if I don't...I do know how to find out!" I was sure of that. She probably had a gossip ring the size of Cincinnati.

I was thinking of my friends back home, there was Jonny, and Don... "Well," she challenged, "hit me."

"Are you a member of the Church...", her astonished look made me go on..." of Jesus Christ of Latter Day Saints...!" With a duh... already...attached but not vocal.

"Of course, not! Why would I be a member of the very organization that wants me taken from my parents and given to strangers to raise rather than my own...simply because they don't have the balls to live the law God gave Joseph Smith a C.O.M.M.A.N.D.M.E.N.T to live?" I went to put my hands up to shield her explosive response as she was spelling commandment forcefully, and she said sighed, "You really don't know anything, do you? Sorry, you poor thing.

"Okay," she continued, "Have you read the Book of Mormon?" I nodded, "Yes." And I was thanking God it was sufficient because I could see this was going to be lengthy.

"Have you read the Bible?" Again, I nodded.

"You are aware that Abraham was given his posterity and the bloodline of Christ because he took Hagar to wife?"

A 12-year-old, I'm thinking, is giving me a Biblical history lesson, oh my God, I asked for this…I shook my head slowly…no…and she continued.

"Have you read the Doctrine and Covenants?" I nodded again, yes.

"Have you read The Pearl of Great Price?"

I nodded and added, "Twice."

"Oh," she asked, "why?"

I answered, "I liked the way things were explained better than the other books you asked about. But I have read the Book of Mormon three times, and I'm working on the fourth."

She shook her head, "No! That doesn't count. You aren't reading them to understand something you have a question about? You are reading them because you have tooooo!" she stammered. I was shaking my head, no, and she said, "Well okay you don't have to. But are you actually looking in that book for the answers to your questions?"

I interrupted her with, "Are you always very headstrong and rude?"

She paused and offered, "Sorry." I've heard all these adults talking to convert people and explaining over and over again all the crazy, stupid excuses that demanded a Manifesto, and it all comes down to one thing. No, respect for the law."

"So," I retorted, "You don't live the law because you want to but because you are C.O.M.M.A.N.D.E.D too. What's up with the hypocrisy?"

She slipped back into the water. "Aren't you all shriveled up?"

I looked at her like she was a Martian, and raised my hand up to look…" big deal!"

"Okay, I don't want you mad at me." She said, "and I don't want to get all preachy either, but there has to be a starting place. You'll figure it out…I think. You're real smart, huh?" She waited for me to come back from the cavern. I was swimming under water, "And you are a damn good swimmer." She had something crucial to say and I was keeping her from saying it.

"You see the thing is, the opposition to the Law of Celestial Marriage wasn't from the world it was from inside the Authorities of the Church. The men who couldn't live the law and love their women were cruel and hated the law. The men who loved the Lord and received their wives because they were filled with kindness and mercy, were finding it in their soul that loving their wives was as easy for them as it was for their wives to love and respect each other. Homes started becoming a paradise. Jealousy was rooted in the ranks of the authoritiers and all manner of lies were being circulated."

"There is another book you should read, actually volumes, called the Journal of Discourses. It is because of that set of conference notes that the New and Everlasting Commandment became 'to do as the living prophet says'. What happened is this: The Doctrine and Covenants as a book was sealed…no more could be added or taken from it.

She paused for emphasis…So then how would the Saints know when Brother Brigham, or Brother John Taylor, or Joseph Fielding Smith have a revelation about the Saints? And how then would it be recorded and documented as a commandment? Was the Lord done when Joseph Smith died? Then just throw all his hard work into his grave with him! Including the Golden Plates and the Urim-thumum, no one knew how to use those things except David Whitmore and after the Prophet's death, he was very shy…He came back to the church you know? My mother is a stenographer and like Willard Richard's keeps the notes for the cottage meetings and the firesides that go on."

She leaned into me and said, "I know the man who is an infiltrator and works for the people from inside the church…you won't believe it. Brother McKay and Brother Benson informed on their own church. They have other wives in secret as well, and they know it is evil to raid the homes of the polygamist families." She sighed again, "I love, them for that. I would run away if they took me from my mother. Do you know they are still fighting the people and putting them in jails around the country? There was a massive raid on Short Creek not too long ago, and another one is staged because the authorities didn't catch the 'ones' they wanted to punish the first time around. There are colonies in Montana, Texas, Arizona, Canada, Mexico, Idaho, Wyoming, and a very isolated colony in Missouri, it isn't even legal for Mormons to live in Missouri. But polygamist are not 'REAL' Mormons anyway. Also in California, where the 'Saints' can hide, from Mark E Peterson, the new Paul of Tarsus. If he could, he would have the Saints burned at the stake."

I knew it was getting close to my time to leave. I felt somehow glad she had come, but I also felt incomplete with going to the cave and talking to my grandfather. I rose and dressed gradually, focusing on all the new little distinctions, Wendy had uncovered for me.

She said, "I will walk with you to your place Gran-mamma is coming to pick me up at 3:30."

After the company, had left, I asked, "Great-grandmother how would you know the difference between a lie and discretion?"

"That is an excellent question? What are your thoughts about it?"

"I was surprised when Wendy showed up at the cave." I was collecting my thoughts not knowing how to compare the imaginary with the real. Great-grandmother was patiently waiting on my response.

"Well, I can see how the stairs were chiseled into the slate. I can imagine my spirit being guided to the Young and Fielding families. But I cannot imagine a God that would recommend a condition like Celestial Marriage and then send armies of persecutors to challenge them for trying to do what he had commanded them to do… I guess, and the secrecy was to protect them but in the end, the worst of the torture came from being driven by the church itself…I don't know? Who to believe, and that's ok right now because right now I still don't care if there is a good reason for people to still be living 'that' law!" I took a deep breath. "My thoughts are these…" I shook my head…

Great-grandmother said very carefully,

"There is a very excellent library upstairs. Many times, the things that concern us are more about how to perform than whether it is the truth or not. I don't think you lack the complexity of the subject. That would be overwhelming to anyone, whether they are in judgment of it or not. Go spend some time upstairs. The shelf on the east wall is the one with the answers."

CHAPTER 15

John Willard Young

The eastern shelf did have some fascinating books. But what was on my mind was the letter and the Blue Denim box. It seemed to me that before the answers to one part of the story were answered for me a whole new set of considerations came about. I felt like I was on a jerky roller coaster ride with sudden and uncomfortable jerks instead of smooth swaying. For one second my mind delivered to me a possible future with an understanding of my parents and their past. Then suddenly I was offered another possible future where their past and future were joined with a raid, like Wendy had said was still going on: and I might be ripped out of their hands and put in a foster-care environment with an all new lifestyle and a new story that my parents were evil.

In 1846, the people weren't upset about 'the rights of children' or 'the law of the land' being broken. What were the reasons that drove the Church to persecute the Saints so acutely? The murder of innocent children and pregnant women, how could they consider it ok? Then I visualized the furnaces that were as big as the living room downstairs that cremated thousands of Jews. Was it all the same evil nightmare? Was there a place in the story of mankind, where the pursuit of happiness was not interrupted, by blood-curdling insanity?

There were a few new books on the shelf at hand level. There was a whole set of Journal of Discourses at eye level. There were some books by George Q Cannon, Cleon Skousen, Willard Richards, Talmage and host of other individual authors' books on the shelf above my head. But what caught my eye was the set of new books. An original copy printed in 1919 of the Koran. What? The Archko Volume, published in 1929, Mary Queen of Scotland and the Isles, The Lost Books of The Bible, and The Forgotten Books of Eden, and the one that had been purchased and read most recently, The Story of My Experiments With Truth: An Autobiography, by M. K. Gandhi. There were a couple *Time Life* magazines and a few *National Geographic* magazines. There was enough reading for several intense months.

I looked...I paused...and I went in the bed chamber for the letters.

I read until it was too dark to read anymore. I cried several times, I turned over and lay on my tummy and asked the room "Is there really a God, out there, who has an interest in my life, my lives, my family? Where does this end: this miracle and this madness?

I knelt down beside the bed, my hands palm-to-palm with little or no room for my face. There were marks in the rug where knees had made an imprint before. I suddenly had a good question:

"God, Grandfather John, Joseph, Father-in-heaven, Oh, daddy, whoever it is that has dominion over me, I am looking for a path that will lead me towards understanding and light, one that will help me find direction and clarity about THIS. Is it you I ask for guidance? How do I know when I am on the right path? It seems to me that of all the people I've known, not many I realize. My great-grandmother offers me a crash-course in out-of-the-ordinary with the most abundant acceptance and faith. My parents and the Church offer me a course-of-mush with the least amount of faith and a constant warning that the slightest variation is damnation and hell. You probably don't want to hear this, but I just want to go night-swimming in the cave. Sorry, I got off track."

I listened to the fading darkness and smelled the flowers from the vase. There was something magical about my experience, but I wasn't able to put my finger on it.

I hurried quietly down the ladders and closed them with the least amount of effort, slowly and with serious caution came upon the very blessing I had asked for.

Sitting on the edge of the bed was my father. I had never seen such warmth of love in my life. I ran to him and buried my face in his pressed baby-blue shirt and cried. In a minute, I knew he was alone and that I was wasting precious time. I looked in his eyes; his handsome hollow face with goatee and dark wavy hair. "I didn't know I love you so much," I said.

"I must hurry home to your mother. No worries I was on bank business in Spanish Fork and stopped by. Great-grandmother has filled me in with some of the details. There is a bunch that I cannot talk to you about now, but I wanted you to hear me say that I know 'everything' I don't need to know about your time with Wendy and with your precious great-grandmother. I want you to search things out for yourself and not to worry about your mother or my view." He smiled the loveliest smile and hugged me again. "I know Mr. Bunker and his family. Dr. Allred delivered your brother, who by-the-way is cute as a bug-in-the-rug. In the next few weeks take care not to wonder to far from the ranch, and I trust May with my life and with yours. Later in life you might be asked if this time with great-grandmother could be considered 'child abuse.' I want you to place a great value on the things that are most important to you and then remember that what you think about most is what you worship."

He tilted his head a little, and I caught the light from the lamp as my reflection showed up in his eye. I started to cry again. "Are you homesick?" He asked.

I chocked, "OH, my heck! No, well, yes I miss everyone, but no I don't want to come back to Millcreek...I wait, hold on, do we live in great-grandfather's home in Millcreek?"

I saw a twinkle in both of their eyes, and I knew I was about to have the dream-of-a-lifetime. "Your great-grandmother made sure it was purchased recently, and we moved in there to keep it in the family." He said with 'Peter-Pan' look on his face.

"I told your mother I would stop by to see her grandmother and you, sport. But if I stay much longer I won't get home until after midnight, and I have a big day tomorrow. Go call your mother."

He said goodnight to Great-grandmother and kissed me on the top of the head as he walked past me. "Your mother is looking for the same answers you are my love. She is so profoundly and totally my gift, be gentle please."

I nodded my head ok and dialed the phone, "Hi, Mom," I shushed him out the door, "I miss everyone so much! How are you? No, no, no, he will be home soon. Oh, he's nursing, always nursing." I laughed as I repeated her words to me. "Mom, what made you give in to me coming here to stay?" There was a moment of utter silence. "Mom, did we get dis..."

"No, I'm here. I didn't decide, and I didn't choose either. Your father overruled me by a landslide when he asked the question, 'Why not?' and all I could offer was, 'I don't know.' That was such a silly answer, but I still didn't want you spending time sorting things out on the wrong side of the fence, with the enemy. When I told him that he just laughed at me and said, 'The only enemy Nessie we will ever have is Time; and she will never have enough of that. So, give her the next best thing, the love of a matriarch.'

"Mom, I love you. Don't worry there's nothing here I can't handle. I love great-grandmother I don't want her to die but I know she is going soon, and I will be grateful forever that you let me spend this time with her. I will make up lost time with Clinton until he's two. I love you too, good night."

I hurried and hung up the receiver. It was exactly 8:00. I slipped in and knelt beside Great-grandmother and kissed her folded hands while she was saying the last of her evening prayers.

She asked me what I thought of John Willard. I answered, "He was a shark!"

She laughed right out-loud chuckling like she was twenty-three. "You are so absolutely right, my dear. How did you come to that term?"

I looked at my reflection in her mirror, tipped my head and said in my most theatrical male voice, "Why, hm, hm. Well, it must be true I have the most beautiful wives in the kingdom, the most famous iron rails, the deepest gold, copper and silver mines. And I have generations of both…it must be true!!! I am Blessed."

"You don't approve of him?" She said in a twenty-three-year-old voice again. To which I laughed.

"Great-grandmother, I'm so relieved that my father came by tonight. I feel so safe now knowing that I'm not hiding anything at all from him, and quite the contrary, he made it possible for me to look at this life because he knew and wanted me too. It is because of John Willard's letters: I realize how impossible it was to keep the faith and be in the Church.

"I can see how he must have suffered letting you be given by your choice to the man you loved even though he had loved you since he first met you. Before he married his first and second wives he was desiring to be your partner. Also, I'm not surprised that great-grandfather Joseph had the wisdom to request your marriage to John even though you had no idea that he had wanted you. Twenty-three years old, three children under 6, a pregnant widow, with an inheritance worth $600,000, at the time that was close to a million, wasn't it?" She nodded, yes. "I have so much respect for the way they looked at your family and your life as a single mother."

"I know from John's letters that he really loved you, as a lover, but did you love him?"

Great-grandmother was combing her hair, the evening ritual I had come to admire. My reflection in the mirror has been severely in need of a make-over, but I was curious about this polygamy thing.

"Ok," I interrupted her meditation, "Were you ever young and restless and eager to be in love?"

She turned with her honey-blue eyes and whispered, "I was always a passionate person: in everything. That is why Brother Brigham was worried about me going to the ball without an escort. That is why he knew I had a sweetheart, and why he pressed me to agree to be betrothed. Even thou he was talking to a sixteen-year-old girl, the woman in front of him was worthy of the kind of love that a man has for an endowed woman not a child. He was concerned that I might be making a game of it somehow. But I had sworn to my father that by revelation only would I allow myself to enter the principle of Celestial marriage."

She continued her story, "I had walked from the Lion House to the Tabernacle. It was young Brother John who met me at the Ball-of-all-Balls on the steps, as a matter of fact. I was waiting for Brother Fielding and my sister Annie. Annie was big with child and having pre-labor. The heat had put women at risk, but the midwife and Brother Heber agreed that the ball would do Annie well. When I saw Brother John W Young getting out of his coach I smiled my genuine smile and then pouted immediately when I saw he was alone. He said that the ladies he had gone to pick up were under heat exhaustion, and his father would not have it that he be elsewhere. He smiled so graciously, very young, four years younger than me and he offered me his arm and asked if I would like to go in with him. He was twelve and his father's right arm in family affairs. He stood a good seven inches taller than I and had a marvelous tuxedo on. I was wearing the gown that I had designed in the beehive room at the Lion House. It was a light, soft peach color with a train of bows off the length of ties that bound my waist. I hadn't worn a corset much. Except for meetings, there was little to dress up for and the dances had been sudden and uneventful because we were building Zion, not award winning performances.

"The benches had been set to the sides of the Tabernacle leaving a vast and open arena for dancing. Several men were tuning their fiddles, and some cellos were being tuned. There were a harp and some flutes on stands in the rear. And there was a group of folks standing around the curtained area at the back of the stage. I had graciously taken Brother John's arm but curtsied and said thank you as I walked in and began the descent to the floor below where the dancing would occur. Brother Brigham had dozens of wild roses adorning the pillars that held the ceiling and the upper galleries in place. I was elated. As I came down the set of stairs leading to the podium where the master of ceremonies would be standing, I was handed a brilliant rose and a Shasta-daisy. I did a deep curtsy to the young man who gave it to me, said, "thank-you sir." And continued to where I could see Brother Brigham looking at what appeared to be a copy of an agenda for the evening.

"He turned and, bowed, 'Mademoiselle, you look lovely tonight, be sure to tell your dress-maker that the president of the Church and your Prophet approves.'

"I curtsied again, and answered, "Yes, Sir I shall.""

"He then thanked me for my hours and hours of preparations and the refreshments and the ladies arriving who would be 'coming-out' tonight. He asked me if it was his son John who ushered me in. I told him yes of course. He said he was concerned about the heat, and several of his ladies would be coming later after it cooled off significantly. He said he would be making some announcements at the beginning of the event and then in the interim. He wanted me to prepare all the ladies for the interim announcements to stand by their escorts, or fathers as most were, some widows had brought and would be the chaperone for their daughters.

"Because my father had not arrived yet, Brother Brigham would be my proxy-father. He then said he was finished with me and asked if I had any questions. I told him no and that I had not forgotten my pledge.

"When I turned from Brother Brigham to go to the refreshment booth, there he stood the most adorable, handsome, youngster I had seen. He looked exactly like young John Young, except in my heart he was mine. I had a perfect reason to use my new fan. Quickly, I curtsied and fanned two times and said, "Good evening, gentlemen, you look like twins." To which Brother John and Brother Fielding said, at the exact same time, "Thank-you. You need to have your eyes checked." We were all laughing. Brother Brigham, however, was not laughing. He motioned the brethren over to him, and I departed. Slowly keeping my balance, fanning as I went and wondering if I did need to have my eyes checked.

"Brother Fielding did not look like he was 59 years old. He was thin, sound, agile, soft spoken, and cheerful as young John Young...but to me he was ten times more handsome, looking at him from where I was, took my breath away. I was smitten to the soul, and it was getting harder for me to control my insides, and make them match my cold, old, reserved, mess…as soon as I could find a young lady, nearby I engaged in unfamiliar talk and laughed it off. I thought.

"I was taken off guard again when young John came up to me bowed formally and said, "Father has requested that all dances with the young ladies' coming-out be numbered. The chaperones have been given a list of the callers who have asked for a dance and the ladies cannot deny them."

"Yes, I know Brother John." I said sweetly, "your Father is my chaperone."

"He said I could tell you that I have the second dance with you." He smiled his amazing, terribly handsome grin.

I tipped my fan and said, "Now, how dare I say No, to that?" I curtsied and said, "My pleasure Brother John, thank-you. Did he mention whom it is I should expect first?" I raised my eyebrows. And he replied, "Oh, not at all! He wouldn't dare. Perhaps your chaperone knows, but our," placing his hand on his heart, "requests are satisfied with a number as well."

"So then, young Brother John, whose breakfast table is my station, do you get to dance all night? If so how many dances are there?" I was feeling a little overwhelmed at my new command. Was I even dancing tonight? I hadn't even considered whether I would be dancing. I had been so busy with all the details.

"There are 12 dances, 6 in the first half, of which I requested one with you and, also 6 in the second half but Father said, No! to my second request. And the last dance of the night is your choice if you last that long." He smiled his sheepish grin bowed the full length of a gentleman as I did a mini curtsy and turned on his heel, just like his father, and walked away, turning once to see if I was still watching him leave.

"I had turned to Libby, who was just as excited as ever. She asked me if young John was my first dance. I informed her he was not. She said she wondered who would be my first dance, and she wondered when the actual dancing would begin. I asked her who would be her first caller, and she said it was her new father, Smoot. Of course, her mother had been a widow, and now her new husband would act in the place of Libby's father. She was 3 years older than me but in some ways, she felt so young to me. I was backward, old at heart but young. She was young at heart and almost an old-maid.

"I suddenly felt like a guest, and I wondered with reverence and reserve what the night would actually look like.

"My mind was now in a flurry. Brother Brigham had two daughters coming out tonight. I knew I would not be his first or second dance. So, who would or...As I was contemplating this new issue, Sister Eliza R Snow came in escorted by, Alphonso Young. She was so beautiful. There was a sudden and silent hush that fell over the crowd. We had wondered if she had made an oath to wear black for the rest of her life. We had never seen her in blue satin with white Victorian lace collar and a train of white lace. Her hat was simple, but it was made with peacock and dove plumes. Her fan was blue and had black hills with white caps and white birds painted on the blue background. She smelled like honeysuckle. I was so excited by now. I went to her and said, "I felt so uncertain until now that you have arrived, I know everything will be perfect."

"She then informed me that because the President had two daughters coming out tonight, his first dance would be with me...she left me no room to think or to consider, his second with Emily his oldest and the third dance with Rebecca, the younger. "This would be the way President Young would have liked your father to have done the honors if the places would have been reversed." She finished with a gentle and very kind nod and rushed to her next victim. After she had finished her rounds making sure all the dancers were lined up. The music became very soft in the background.

"Brother John Taylor then went to the stage and had the podium removed and stood where it had been. He cleared his throat and shouted, "Good evening, my family and friends, I am so happy to be here with you tonight and for the opportunity to pray and dance with our Lord the God of Israel. He bowed his head and very carefully and loudly blessed the congregation and the artisans providing food and music. He blessed the young ladies and all the suiters and callers and asked for guidance in all the affairs of the Saints. I remembered he blessed all the other gatherings occurring that night around the world where one or more of the Saints were gathered in the Lord's name. He finished in the name of the Savior'. And then he turned to Brother Brigham and said I would like to introduce the Master of Ceremonies tonight it will be our very own President and Prophet Brother Brigham Young.

"Brother Brigham took the spot where Brother John Taylor had been after giving him an embrace and a pat on the back, 'I'm so glad we made it!' He said clearly. Then Brother Brigham made a little speech about how fine and delicate things are often overlooked because the more rough and demanding things are rough and demanding...I think he was talking about himself, it was as if he had made a joke. The audience laughed with him. He then informed everyone the agenda for the night, there were sixteen couples to take the floor for the first dance. After the first dance with the callers and their ladies, the second dance was open, and others were welcome to join at any time. There would be an intermission in the middle at about 9:15. When we reconvened at 9:30 there would be the sixteen couples chosen for the first dance of the second half and then the last dance of the evening would be ladies choice with as many dancers as could still remain on foot to dance.

"Everyone watched him like he was a Roman God. He came up to me and offered me his arm. There was a circle formed of gents with their ladies, just exactly as I remember Annie's coming out in England. First

Brother Brigham and myself, then Bishop Partridge and Emily, then Brother Joseph Fielding and Rebecca, then Brother Smoot and Libby, and on until one large beautiful circle of Saints and magistrates had displayed with pride and precious style their soft and tender daughters. We walked the full length of the ballroom in one big circle and then the dance began. A moment for each father to praise his lovely child and let her into the world and promise to be her refuge if there was ever a storm.

"When the dancing began, graciously I thanked Brother Brigham and asked him to please forgive me for all the childish and headstrong things I had said and done, and I tried to say that I knew I would be myself again. He only asked me if I was curious who my callers were. I said no, I would know soon enough. He then informed me that I would tell him who would be my choice for the last dance because he would need to inform me if that person had already been taken. I looked up at him and grinned, aren't you tricky…I thought. He then leaned close and whispered, "I promise I already know and that I will not tell you unless you inform me first who it is, you would tell your father."

"I have already told my father many times, and if you already know then I trust you completely, and I will leave the results to you and the Lord."

"Very well then you will enjoy the final announcement tonight. How is your French coming along?"

"Se pre'senter au devoir papa, (I have just begun to wet my appetite, I thought), "Merci, beaucoup!"

"I am also thankful and have been blessed to have your immeasurable sacrifice and attentiveness with my wives and children." He smiled at me with a father's kindness. Then he continued, "I am going to be a very happy man when your father and mother are comfortable here in Zion. I will also be concerned that someone as devoted and particular as your father is to his calling, would even be replaceable when he does leave England. England hardly knows what they will be losing, and I am very aware of *our* gains.

"He was silent for a while and then he continued, "This dance will be over soon. I must allow you the insight of the letter I received from your father and the willingness he has offered me is superior to most of my trusted servants. As a proxy father, I am entrusting you with the most confidential enlightenment. Your mother is of rich and intact Spanish and French heritage. I am asking you to do a courtesy for the church and indulge if you will please in a mission to France with one of my beloved apostles. Your father has given his blessing and will be seeing to your every need upon arrival in London. The mission president and his companions will be leaving in 3 weeks exactly." He was guiding me to the edge of the ballroom floor, and I was experiencing a sense of complete abandon. I noticed a very slight flick of his wrist and elbow and wondered if perhaps he had injured his arm. But the music faded slowly to an end as he bowed very low in the gentleman's fashion and I curtsied.

"I wasn't even able to say thank-you when he put my hand in young John's hand and yelled, so loudly I jumped, "The second dance begins." Young John bowed very low, I was perplexed and bewildered. Where was I now? My father's pawn: Oh no, father wasn't like that, I told myself."

"Looking at young John, I nearly fainted; He pulled me close and began the polka with the grace of a prince. He was so damn charming. I couldn't help but smile at him and with him as he burst me through the dancers faster and more deliberately than I would have dreamed possible. We passed his Father, who, you know was dancing with Emily and, they were cheering us on and in pursuit, which caused a serious on-the-floor conquest. I could see young John being the crowned 'king-of-the-evening' at this rate. Then as we slowed and he twirled me round and round the only place I could end up is on the floor or in his arms, he stopped short! The music had died, and I was in shock again! I was not amused. I was carefully and in an unruffled way fixing my hair, my dress, and I felt like I needed to put my head back on straight. Young John then carefully bowed as low as was humanly possible and said, "That is the best dance I have ever had since I became a man and could dance with a real woman." I blushed, dreadfully and he was putting my hand into the next hand on his right and on my left, when Brother Brigham shouted again, so loud I nearly covered my ears, "Enjoy the third dance." It was a waltz. Oh, my gosh, I was so relieved. Then I joined my eyes to the hand and the gentleman with his left arm behind his back, bowing like he was the viceroy and I was the chosen one, all the way to the floor. I wanted to laugh, I crept a smile...now I was enchanted. "Yes," I said, "you may", and I lost my breath. I could see stars, and I could feel my head going down, and I could cry. I took a very slow staggering breath, which cost me, a good three stanzas of our waltz, and moved my left foot just a fraction of an inch to keep from crashing. But Brother Fielding had seen the stunt pulled by young John and wasn't about to be let down by a little girl..."

I looked at great-grandmother, and I saw the reason that young John could not graft his magical powers over to her heart. She had upstaged herself. To her making, Brother Fielding's love of her was impossible because he was a man and he only saw the child in the carriage. Every time she looked at him he was unavailable and unapproachable. She had to ask God for permission to like him and love him every time it crossed her mind because he was so far above her station. She was truly a slave to her feelings. I reached over and touched her soft wrinkled hand, "Do you want to sleep now? It is 9:30."

"Heavens no! You just got me started." She smiled and continued. "I was lifted off the planet dancing with him. If there was ever, need to feel the presence of dashing love I could always return to that moment. There was no one else in the room. I wanted him to draw me close enough that I could smell him and feel the heat from his body. He was such a proper man of course, and he had never seen *me.* "My dear," he hummed, "Yes," I replied. "The dance is over." "Oh, oh, but I don't want it to be!" I stammered. He smiled and said very graciously, "Perhaps another, for the lady of the night, with mysterious shoes." I lifted my skirt with my left hand and looked down confused, raised my eyes and he was bowing again as if it was the last time I would see him...My heart was coming out of my chest. He had very gently unclasped my grip from his hand and put it softly in Brother Heber's hand.

"Oh, Brother Heber I'm so grateful it's you." But the music had started, and it was a promenade, usually the first dance of the evening. I would then be shuffled back and forth. There was no need to worry, but he could see something was troubling me. He attempted to comfort me by saying, "Annie is coming for the second half of the evening. I hope to get her on the dance floor. You were spectacular with young Brother John."

"Thank-you," I said. Turning and trying so hard to not be distracted and getting to the lineup. Brother Brigham and his wife Amelia, Brother John Taylor and his wife Mary, Brother Richards with his wife Natalia, Brother Fielding with his wife Sarah. It was as if the evening had started over with each of the men and their appropriated wives and then we girls. "Did you request a dance with me?" I asked, Brother Heber. "Of course, I did. Do you think I would let Annie down? She wants you on the floor the entire evening. She has been plotting for days who will dance with you next. She's quite the woman that sister of yours." He smacked his lips and smiled at me. I was sure that half of the advances and circumstances on the floor would have been highly disrespectable in the cathedral in Manchester, but here it appeared as a big luxurious family outing.

"The tabernacle was large enough to have four sets of promenades going on at the same time. Each with the standard eight couples. When the end of our promenade and the beginning of the one on my left were close enough that young John placed his sister's hand in Brother

Heber's and took mine so quickly it was hardly noticed. He whispered so no one could hear, "I told you I'd get another one in tonight." And he winked at Brother Heber.

"Brother John Young, are you flirting?" I had just asked a question but it sounded like an old lady in the back asking the question, and I had to laugh at my own question. He replied, tapping his foot and exaggerating the hands-on hips, "I believe... I...am!" Everyone in this new line-up was congratulating him and egging him on. I shook my head like this was my brother Henry in front of me. And to everyone's surprise, I said, "And may the best girl win." He carefully passed me back to Brother Heber and tipped his imaginary hat, while doing so. Rebecca said as she passed, "Don't mind him he's smitten."

"When I got back to Brother Heber's arms, I was confronted, again by my heart and the strange events of the evening. I was to be an example of the Gospel and of Zion. I would have been given a choice with the callers in England. Here in Zion, I was given the opportunity to trust my surrogate father and being a remarkable lady in doing so or else complaining. It was perfect so far. But it was so incomplete. How was I to get Brother Fielding to recognize my intentions without flaunting them to the crowd? He was a married man, and I was just a child. Brother Heber gathered me in for the last turn of the promenade, and the group did what I had never seen done before and yet they did it like it is done every time. The outside passing promenades kept right on dancing around the other three groups and put themselves into the next line while the other three couples did the same. If we continued this way for the next few minutes, all the groups would be with all new members. Oh, how fun it was. It was a very long slow and happy dance with so much going on in the dance and people cheering from the audience. I was beginning to sweat when, the music came to a halt, this time, I caught the same inconspicuous movement of Brother Brigham's, and I knew then he was controlling the minstrels.

"I next danced with Brother Richards, and it was a two-step. Quite short, I was glad; he relieved me to Brother Brigham's son Alphonso, a married, happy man and handsome, much like his brother young John. I knew he had moved. I asked where too, and he informed me that his family had purchased most of the land south of Benjamin and north of Nephi. They were looking at orchards and farming as well as ice-blocking in the winter from the fresh water lake in the valley. He said he was very excited about the new home he was building for his wives and that there would be two sides complete with all the same needs, but each of his lovely wives could build her space the way she liked it. He said he had been doing some traveling for his father in Europe and that he was very excited to hear the announcements at the interim."

Great-grandmother was getting drained, and I had understood something clearly at last, that love had kept her living so many years. It was burning in her beautiful blue eyes. I knew it was time to go to bed, but I needed one more question answered. How did she handle the respect of Brother Fielding's wives and have a marriage that masked all others?

As she had so many times, she read my mind and said. I will tell you the rest right after breakfast. Tomorrow the Relief Society will be meeting here at lunch time for their annual inventory.

CHAPTER 16

A Honeymoon in France

As I washed my face and brushed my teeth the next morning, I could feel the pull of the cord on the light in the closet ceiling, and I wanted to go turn the little music box on, so I could warn all the people hiding upstairs that strangers were coming. My serious concerns about my family were being erased, and I was collecting imaginary memorabilia to take home to Millcreek to hide in the attic I had never even tried to go into.

The sun brought me a beautiful and welcome day. My room was on the back of the house facing the eastern mountain range. It had large French windows and a door that opened onto the porch. The door was always locked so great-grandmother never needed to be concerned about someone coming in from that entrance of the house.

On the west side of the room was a dressing room that had a wardrobe with an eighth-inch gold inlaid around the cornice, the feet and the handles which were inset. When I opened the door the first time, I had to step out of the way because the shelving and the hangers came out at you when it opened. On the north wall was a beautiful dressing table. The vanity had mirrors that floated in or out to meet the center one. They were very old.

I went from my room down a short hall to the kitchen turned right and on the right, was the house bathroom. Straight to the west was the hall that leads to grandmother's room and the stairwell; I hadn't gone to the room upstairs yet, that was the perfect copy of the sacred bed chamber. On the first left was a doorway that would get you around the corner to the living room and the parlor or turn left again into the pantry and straight across from the pantry door was the entrance into the kitchen. Between the house bathroom and great-grandmothers, room was another door usually locked, which would open into her private bathroom. Both bathrooms had large claw bathtubs and beautiful tile inlaid porcelain, finished floors and walls that went three feet up. The water basins and marble vanities had gold inlaid drawers. I had not been in great-grandmothers bathroom to study it or see her things yet but when I went into her room at 5:55 she asked me to go in her 'water-closet' and get the stockings hung on the rack around the tub.

I helped pull up the stockings great-grandmother asked to wear, and I asked her if she would like me to plait her hair again? She said, "Not today it needed to be fancy for her tea-party." She sprinkled a little water on the brush and handed it to me, requesting that I comb it all into one narrow stream running down her back. She then twisted in tight and pulled it into a lovely French knot and placed a hair-comb with cobalt sapphires, rubies and diamonds inlaid beautifully like a flag.

"Great-grandmother I fancy a scar right here on this side of your neck with stitching marks on it."

"Yes, yes." She answered, "That happened in my travel from New York to Texas in the suffrage era. I was 47 years old and had been the instrument in so many powerful men's lives. All, were not Saints. But all the causes they championed for were great opportunities, for the Saints.

"It started for me at the ball-of-all-balls. When Brother Brigham announced that he was reopening the mission fields and wanted every young and married man with a desire to do the will of God to go into the world and be 'fishers of men.' He read a list of about twenty brethren he intended to meet with him Monday morning, and on it was young John, Brother Heber, Brother Alphonso, who smiled at me, and it went on and on. He said he was offering every man, woman, and child an opportunity to clean their lives from any hate or distraction that had gotten in the way of their salvation. At the Sacrament meeting tomorrow, upon taking the sacrament they would be cleansed of the aversion and resentments we had felt toward anyone, anywhere, anytime and be made perfect in the eyes of God, with a new life spreading out before us all. He was on fire, and the people saw him as if he was transfixed. Then he shouted, at the top of his lungs, "Dance on be joyful for the Lord God is a merciful God. He then danced the first dance of the second half of the ball with Eliza the Prophet Joseph's wife. They looked like a fairytale and we the first dancers of the second half could hardly begin for watching them. They waltzed as if they were on ice-skates crossing the floor.

"To my astonishment, my sister had not arrived. I was very concerned and was about to look up Brother Heber, whom I could not find at a glance when my first dance began with Brother Smoot, who was very sweet and talked about his widow and her family: Libby and her brother Jimmy. He spoke of friendship and the towering responsibility it is to grow up. I felt compelled to thank him at least 60 times. The dance was so extra-long. He placed my hand in Brother John Taylor's hand, and it was another waltz. Brother Taylor read what he thought was a great concern on my face and told me that Monday morning the list of brethren would be meeting at the office and be set apart for their callings. I hadn't heard his name on the list. He read my mind again and stated that I should stay awake because more announcements were coming. I then asked him if he knew where Brother Heber had gone. He said there was a little rumor that he had been called out to meet with the midwife. I shouted, "Annie!" Drawing attention to myself right or wrong was paralyzing to me so I shook it off and danced on, but I wanted to know if my sister was in labor this time. Young John then whispered something in Brother Taylor's ear and left abruptly. This was the skaters waltz, my favorite waltz, and the band played it through from beginning to end 4 times. When it finally came to a close, young John was back, and Brother Taylor put my hand in young John's, He bowed like a knight and very genuinely backed away with a beautiful smile. "Stay alert."

"Was I getting tired I asked myself. Young John asked very sweetly, "May I have Brother Heber's dance? He let us know that if he was called out for his second dance, I could take his place. Your beloved sister is in early labor, and as your brother-in-law, Brother Heber requested a second dance with the lady of the night…however I'm a surrogate brother, sort 'a and offered to take his place should he need to leave, hence my casual awareness that I might actually get a second chance."

"You are having way too much fun with this entire caller's secrecy, don't you think, *brother*?" I chided him. But he was undaunted and kept the polka going steady and was a constant refreshment and distraction. He placed my hand in Brother William Cooke's and said he would go check if I was needed. I thanked him and I was ever so grateful that there was a long pause before the dance began. It was a double-shodish, a two-step created by Brother Allred for dancing with two of his wives, Brother Cooke was betrothed to Joy, a beautiful and smart teacher, whom he was sharing this dance with me for her. I felt complimented by her genuine compassion. We made a jubilant set on the floor, and it was the first time for me I had never done the dance so we had some kind laughing amongst ourselves.

"Brother Cooke then generously, placed my hand in Brother Brigham's again. Brother Brigham bowed, I curtsied and, he said, 'My dear, your sister is attending to family matters and sends her approval and love. She is very aware that your last dance tonight will be with your choice of husband. There isn't a man here that would not consider it a privilege and an honor to be your choice, including me, he touched his heart. In the last few weeks, your manors and example have been that of a royal born lady. I support you in your choice and so does your father, but the rest of the world is still dreaming. When you request this final dance, if he says, "no", I'll get a shotgun! Not so!' He expected me to be shocked, and I wasn't.

'But you have been utterly discreet. Becoming of a loyal servant. You know he loves you, but you also don't know if he will allow you to be his wife. I guess as the surrogate father of the soon coming bride I'm a little worried about you being let down.'

"Thank-you," I said politely, "the Lord delivered the children of Israel from the Red Sea. I believe your revelation of my *choice* is sufficient to prove He can and will deliver me."

"One last thing', he lowered as he whispered into my ear, 'I positively request that you tell Brother Fielding that I asked you to ask him to walk you home tonight.' He then gently kissed the top of my head and left me with Sister Eliza.

"Stepping up to the stage Brother Brigham announced the last dance. Requested help from the deacons and priests to help rearrange the benches for tomorrow's services. Called the evening the most successful experience of his *Young* life, to which brought a good laugh, he acknowledged all the beautiful ladies still there and having left early, then bowed to take the hand of his most recent wife, my Aunt Millie. Standing and facing Eliza I felt empowered and yet perfectly humbled, almost humiliated, and she said, 'I have a message to give to you, please come to my room after the dance is over, I have called Libby to take your place in the clean-up.'

"The last waltz was just starting when someone requested to replace a string on the main violin. Sister Eliza then looked me in the eye and said, 'You have been a vibrant and active influence tonight, I would be honored and blessed to be called your mother.' She then lifted my hand a turned me slightly to see if all the young men had been chosen. Standing beside Aunt Millie who was still praising her husband was my mark. I felt so small and so young, and almost stupid. I smiled back at Mother Eliza and almost skipped to Brother Fielding's side. Brother Brigham said, 'I think you have a caller, Brother Fielding!'

"I curtsied and asked, May I have this dance?" He placed his hand on his heart and turned to see if I was talking to someone behind him, (RASCAL) I wanted to say.

"Oh, oh,' he turned and handed his glass to his second wife, Sarah and skipped up, bowed low and said, 'Seriously of all the glory available tonight you choose this rubble: me!'

"I felt my tears and a story of rejection compelling me to desist, but instead, I stood taller and braver. I wasn't sure what to say so I was silent. I wanted to make the experience memorable but not problematic, and I was getting stronger by the second. We waltzed passed young John, who rolled his eyes at me. Then we sailed by Brother Brigham, and my Aunt Millie, who both acknowledged us."

"Then I heard my own voice ask, "Why are you so surprised that I will choose you. I will always choose you. Are you going to the Monday morning meeting at the President's office? Your name was not on the list."

"Neither was yours.' He answered me. 'But you will be there as well.' He took my shock as a real reason to continue, 'I can inform you because we will be working on a similar assignment.'

"I think I was going into rebellion; I wanted to run…when had I decided how this last dance would go? By the way, it was sorta' just dumped on me that I would have a choice and then here I am with all the things that have happened tonight to create a whole bunch of meaning...I stopped...Brother Brigham requests that you walk me home this evening. Is that favorable, with Sarah?"

"He looked into my eyes and reached for a handkerchief in his pocket, and carefully wiped a tear that was hung-up on my eyelash. 'I think we should ask her, and I wish I could read your mind. I'm not... very good at...this...whatever is bothering you? I have never seen you cry, even when you left your parents, I was there...come...come? Have I let you down completely? I'm sorry.'

"My sister is in labor, Brother Brigham has decided that my talents for communicating in Spanish and French will serve the Church. He decided that we girls would ask the last dance, you don't know anything, anything I have no idea what to do next, I will not leave for Europe, as a piece of luggage, it would be a scandal, I need to meet with Mother Eliza...Sister Eliza tonight after the dance."

"Have we ever talked before, in this life,' he asked me? 'You are truly a picture of elegance and dignity. I would consider it an honor to walk you home, you are lovely.'

"The music stopped. 'This time, you didn't object to the music stopping,' he smiled.

"I ceased to believe in the dance before we started...But I made a promise to Brother Brigham, and I will keep it."

"I could see myself packing my bags in the Lion House and putting my goodbyes together. I sighed, "I believed Brother Brigham and myself when I committed to leaving back to London if I was not promised by midnight. I thought it would be more acceptable to his family if my headstrong ideas and anticipations were out of the way," I said, out-loud to him.

"Oh, my dear, you are quite right, having you around could easily be considered torment.' He said.

"I should slap your face! I wanted to shout but I stopped dead in my tracks. I felt a good 10 inches taller and ready to defend my own honor. "And quite rightly," I was about to say, and I can walk my own self home, when his beautiful Sarah said,

"Brother Fielding, I believe you are the sense of torture here. We shall call a trial, and you shall not be acquitted. My love,' she took my arm and began the circle that formed the last prayer of the evening, 'Let's take a look at those tears.'

"I wiped them hastily away and bowed my head, not caring who was holding my hand on the other side. After we had said Amen, I turned to Sarah and said, "I feel so embarrassed, please forgive me, I can walk myself back now, please, it's only a block and a half."

"She linked her arm in mine. Folks were leaving in all directions, Libby, faithful Libby was showing her mother's husband how to disassemble the punch bowl and fountain. I hurried out least someone should stop me, and I begin to breakdown again. Sarah lived about three blocks east and one north of the Lion House. I had walked the distance many times with one or more of the children to keep them from getting smashed by all the traffic carrying building supplies from the canyons and the quarries.

"It was a bright night. I asked if she knew what time it was Sarah said, 'It's time to examine the way your feel. I understand how you feel, but do you? I can feel your pain and your excitement and all night long you were bounced from pillar to post if some men are pillars, and some are posts.' We both laughed at her joke.

"I guess I thought too highly of myself...at least to myself. I assumed that my feelings were virtuous because I had not flaunted them or been given to them. And then when my moment-of-truth showed up I realized it was all a myth. No one even knew I was in love and always had been..."

"I started to hold back my pain again, and she pressed me to let it out, 'Do you think that because you feel strong enough to cry that it makes you weak? Let's go see how Annie is doing. She could probably use your passion and strength now.'

"We hurried along moving first north 3 blocks and then east by 2. It was quiet inside. We carefully pushed the door open and saw that the light was on. Brother Heber was standing sentinel. The light was just good enough for me to see fathers watch. It was 11:15 we heard the shriek of a newborn babies cry and I started to bounce on my toes Brother Heber split and then bounded back again with his new baby. The attending midwife was giving orders, and her attending nurse was moving as fast as she could. The baby was quiet in his father's arms.

"Brother Heber was crying, 'I am never sure how this miracle occurs for me, but I always feel like I am In the presence of God when I hold a newborn.' He let me kiss the baby's head and asked me to go check on Annie.

"She was lively. She wanted to get up and be with her husband and the new baby. I went and dragged Brother Heber back in the room and made him sit in the rocking chair near my sister, beside the bed. I reached for her hand and his and put them together. "I'm so proud, so blessed," I said. "I will be back to check on you tomorrow, I made a promise to Brother Brigham and I must keep it."

"Annie gave me a kiss and a squelch and said goodnight to Sarah, and we took off.

"Sarah your house is on the way let me drop you off, please. And can I tell you why the tears earlier tonight?" I begged.

"Oh, I wish you would,' as she pulled her shawl over her shoulders, 'I know why. Maybe you would rather I should tell you?'

"She paused and then went on, 'my sister and I are married to the same man. But he is not the same for me as he is for her. He is my cloud of sunshine; he is her thunderstorm and salvation. She can't live with him she can't live without him. He can't tease her or be friendly with her he must always wear a uniform it seems. With her it seems Mayor, advocate! She lives for the world, I live for the day. She is 10 years older than I, but it feels like she is my grandmother. She loves order, he loves order as well, but she calls his chaos.'

"How long have you known that you love Brother Fielding as a lover and a man?'

"I sat right down on the grass! The only person I ever told was my father. He had asked me before I left England if I wanted a Patriarchal Blessing and he gave me one; promising me that if I was faithful to my heart that the Lord would provide my husband with the truth of my wedding-right. He said that I had made a covenant before I came to earth and that it was the cause of such a growing and hopeless attraction. But in the blessing, I was told that the man I loved had also chosen me and in time he would remember the covenants he had made, and that we would be sealed for time and all eternity. Sarah, I am only sixteen, but I have known only one love in my life, and it was him...I was five. I remember how, I was angry because I was too young to be baptized. He was married to your sister then, but to me, he was the same age as my brother Henry. Brother Fielding sees me as a little girl, in perspective, he would be committing a crime. You are his wife, and I have confided in you. Tonight, at midnight I will be leaving Zion, I promised Brother Brigham that I would torture his home no more and that if by midnight I was not betrothed I would return to England. Brother Brigham thought I was twenty-three and then when he found out I was fifteen and soon turning sixteen, he pledged the ball tonight as in keeping with the tradition of my homeland and my absent father's love. But as the time drew nearer and as he became more familiar with me and my Aunt Millie he realized that I showed no favor to anyone including his sons. He got angry with me, it seemed, and accused me of playing a game of sorts. I told him that the Lord had delivered the children of Israel from the Red Sea and he could and would deliver me. But in fact, if my beloved had not proposed by midnight tonight I would return to my father's house, and rid his house and sons of my so-called torture. And then my own beloved accused me of the same thing: at the very moment I was sure I would be delivered, he agreed that living with me would be torture.!" She started laughing hysterically.

"Oh, my love! You are torture. Don't you understand? That the masks men wear are to keep them safe? Brother Fielding may be 50 years old, but he is still a boy at heart. If he doesn't marry you, I will! That is what every caller was saying to you tonight. Why didn't you ask him to marry you tonight before the clock struck 12 and your coach turned into a pumpkin? Because you don't know if he loves you in that way, and you assume because he was shocked that you would pick him, instead of some fiery, gangly tom cat, that he sees you as a child. But quite the contrary. He sees you as the wife of a nobleman. You must be the one to make him worthy.'

"Oh, Sarah, my time is up!"

"Now, listen here, are you a silly girl or the woman of your dreams? Come; get me home. You have to meet with Sister Eliza tonight.'

"We had stepped onto her sidewalk. She bade me stay just inside the door to wait for her to grab me a shawl. She came back, quickly and gave me a kiss goodnight.

"I went as far as the edge of First South to the gas lamp and looked at my father's watch. The stars were magnificent. I said, softly, "I'm so sorry I didn't do my part." I heard footsteps running toward me, 'Sister May. Please wait, please.'

"It was that voice I feared the most…no not the voice of God…

She smiled at me and continued, "The voice of Brother Fielding...I could handle no more rejection tonight. Maybe I could handle a goodbye after I had packed my bags and had my trip east secured. But not this evening. I kept my head down and walked slowly on. He ran up beside me...What was I to do now? Say, "go away?"

"He was panting slightly from running down the hill and huffed, 'Sarah said if I didn't purpose to you right now that Brother Brigham would. Is that why you were invited to the meeting on Monday as well? Ok, please, stop...will you marry me? Please.' He was then breathing heavily as a pouting Tom cat.

"Neither of you needs to pity me! I'm not an old maid! Stubborn maybe, I said under my breath.

"Maybe I behave too old but only because I have waited forever to hear you ask me. You did a terrible job. Pity and all that." He tried to touch my elbow to slow me down. I knew as soon as he was near I had sped up my step.

"I just asked, you to marry me. Would your father approve of a hug and a little kiss," but he had already taken advantage of my bewilderment, and I was engaged in an embrace before I could pull on the reins. He had kissed my forehead and said under his breath, 'I would not allow someone as noble as you to marry an older codger like me.'

It felt like time stopped and went on endlessly.

"Is the dance over? I don't want it to be." I whimpered as he picked me up and twirled me under the lamp light.

He set me on my feet and said, "Details you always want details. The very first question you asked was, 'Would all that power go to our heads'? From that moment, you have never left my head. But Sister May, he was struggling with words that matched his gratitude and concerns, 'why me?'

"Only God knows." I said with as much dignity as I could muster. We both laughed, and I pulled up my father's watch again. "My father's promise to me was that in time You would know! Brother Fielding, you have made the mark. It is exactly 24:00 hours and now Brother Brigham won't have to charge me with criminal behavior."

"We slowed down as we cornered the Lion House block and paused a moment, being very quiet and present to what had just happened. My love was so pressurized, and I felt like I would explode but I knew there was a great future ahead of us now.

"He held my hand the rest of the walk, opened the door for me and touched my cheek as I said goodnight.

"I could hear him whistling the Skaters Waltz as he returned to his home and his beloved Sarah."

It was July 17th baby Clinton was two weeks old, and I had only 53 days left with my Great-grandmother. She and I had finished our breakfast, and I was wondering what would happen if I asked to run to the cave.

She turned to me and asked, "Do you believe it? That the very second that my covenanted mate arrived was the very moment that I had promised to give up.

"On Monday Brother Brigham set Brother Fielding aside for the French Mission and made Brother Willard Richards his first counselor and Brother Orson Pratt his second counselor, he set apart several elders to be missionaries in the French mission. He sent several to the islands, and he announced that we would leave as soon as we could get our affairs in order. He told the Brethren there would be a very special dinner served at the Lion House Wednesday evening at 6:00 sharp he expected all of them to be there.

"Wednesday night Brother Fielding's wives gave me to their husband as a wife and helpmate. Brother Brigham married us for time and eternity and told us as soon as the endowment house was complete we could receive our endowments there. The dinner was in our behalf. We left that night by coach to St. George; we stopped in Benjamin at Brother MacDonald's house, more like a mansion. It was very much like an English Bed and Breakfast.

"Sister Eliza was the one to nurture me and helped prepare my mind for the wedding and the assignment to be Brother Fielding's French guardian. She was the most cherished woman I ever knew. Her love for Brigham was so dutiful and perfect, but her love for Joseph was abiding and deliberate. She admired and treated Brother Brigham like a brother.

"I was not allowed any chores. I had a wardrobe to prepare, and all my goodbyes to the children were short and simple.

"I had gone to see Annie on Sunday, and she had already heard that I was betrothed. She was so excited and a little interested that I had done such a good job of keeping my heart private for so long. Aunt Millie and Sister Eliza orchestrated every extra pair of hands. By Wednesday evening I had a wedding dress that I had designed. Very simple, very elegant with many, many hours of lacework and embroidery I had been working on since we crossed the Atlantic Ocean. I created a new dancing gown, for public outings, made new underwear, purchased new shoes from the mercantile, new socks three new hats and a new shawl that matched a new coat! All very breathtaking and lovely. My father had been notified that we were coming there first, for a week, and then on to Paris and then to Spain."

"Great-grandmother," I said, as I cleared and washed the table intensely, "Would a trip to the cave today be alright while you are meeting with the ladies this afternoon?"

She looked me over as if she was measuring me and said, "I would like you to meet some of them, but all of them you shall because we can't leave anyone out. After that, you can go and gather some Brigham tea from the west lakeside, and we will make some sun tea tomorrow from what you gather. We have exactly 40 minutes before Mary and her first counselor arrive. In the drawer over there are some small pruners and in the pantry, is a nice canvas bag for the tea. We have enough time to complete this story.

"When the Prophet Joseph had been assassinated in Carthage, some of the Saints didn't wait for Brother Brigham or Brother Heber. Some of the Saints knew there would be a significant move to the Rocky Mountains because they had met at the School of the Prophets with the Prophet so many times and had heard first hand that if the persecution did not stop then, there would be a refuge in the Rockies.

"I think the Prophet was waiting for a revelation about leaving. In section 58 of the Doctrine and Covenants, the Prophet reveals that it is pleasing to the Lord that a man not be commanded in everything. Brother Fielding believed that the efforts of the Saints would have been futile if everyone waited for the Prophet to secure their way for them. Some had been prepared to leave for a long time. Most of the Saints believed that with the Prophet gone the Church would fall apart, and the Restored Gospel would be just an old memory. But many knew that the Gospel would spread to all the inhabitants of the Earth. The moment the Prophet was martyred some folks got up and left to catch a ship to California, some had wagons and headed out on the Oregon trail, some went south and did the Santa Fe route. There had been fur traders and Trappers that used the watersheds to make their living. One of the beauties of being a member of the Church and being married when I was young was the respect given to me as I traveled with my new husband and his companions.

"I was married on Monday the 28th of July, and had our wedding dinner at the Lion House; nearly as complete as it would ever be, on Wednesday, the 30th of July.

"We were met in Saint George with Brothers, John Taylor, Heber C Kimball, George A Smith, and Joseph and John Young, who then traveled on with us into England.

"I had taken some few things with me in my chest that had traveled the ocean already. Of the things, I had taken were an excellent French dictionary, some sewing, and stationery with pen set.

"On our way to St. George there were many small towns and single dwellings along the way. When we finally arrived in California we were met by a host of Saints and as the Saints had taken the practice of Dancing at every occasion they could, I had the chance to try my new ball gown.

"I believe there are two times in my life when I felt like I had achieved the rank of royalty. The first was my walk down the stairs into the ballroom at the Hotel owned by one of our members in San Francisco, and the other was when I had my first child, who was born while on our first mission together. Both times the feeling was present with the look that accompanied my beloved husband. He cherished me beyond words and I could feel his pulse and his longing for me from the bottom of the stairs and from the edge of the delivery bed, it registered in his eyes like music does in a lullaby. When I reached the lower step, he bowed as he did the first time he danced with me, in the Bowery, and then he swooped me off my feet and twirled me around the room like I was a child. He whispered in my ear, his mustache tickling me, 'My love I have waited a thousand years to have you as my own, and I shall stay preserved to love you for a thousand more! I promise to never grow old on you, my heart and head are far too much in love to have you feel left behind. Will you marry me?'

Great grandmother had become entranced in her thoughts and I broke the silence with,

"Great-grandmother, in one of your letters I read that he died more of a broken heart than from the explosion. Did he know how badly it had affected you?" I watched as her eyes as they teared up and she straightened her face ever so carefully.

"While we were in London with my Mother and Father it occurred to me for the first time that I might outlive him. I had morning sickness, not badly, but enough to slow him down a bit. He treated me as if I had always been a princess and had always been in his heart. Later as I watched him with Sarah, I knew why she was so dreamy with him. He truly was a splendid man and loved as deeply as I ever did.

"I got side-tracked; yes, in England, I told him that if I lost him for some reason that I didn't know if I could go on without him. I would choose cyanide over a life without him. He called an extraordinary meeting with my parents and his mission companions and requested a blessing for me. In the denim box is that blessing, I was promised that my love for the Lord and the Gospel would grow. That I would be a living example to women all around the world, and the Church would call on me to teach the art of transformational love: to love the Lord and to love your husband as yourself. It was Brother John Taylor who sealed the blessing. We didn't have telephones back then, and there had not been one minute before My Beloved had requested of Brother John Tylor to seal and assist in the blessing. My Father had anointed and when the blessing was over Brother Joseph turned to me and said, 'If I were the Lord that is what I would have said. Know that you are loved by your Heavenly Father and all of us here for choosing to be a Mother in Israel. You will be strong, and you will never be alone.

"But at that moment, he was sealing his own love of me with a looming doom. So, when the explosion happened he was already aware that his time was up. I had grown and learned from 10 years of love and marriage to be away from him, but I have never left his soul.

"Our first child was born in Spain in a little hostel on the side of the sea. We had just served a thousand new converts with the message, and we were signing ordinance papers when my labor began, unexpectedly and very hard. The lady of the Inn noticed my face and my situation. In her broken English said, "Que, be time, com, com." She made up the bed and sent the waiter off for a midwife. When Brother Joseph figured out what was up, he ran to the Mistress of the house and told her he was the doctor to deliver the baby. But she insisted that it was a woman's work he could stand and hold the water and then if he was very careful he could hold the baby.

"When he informed, her he was the father of 10 children and that he had delivered 2 of them himself, she said he would be very happy then to have the woman's help. I could hardly keep from laughing at them, and I was making little jokes all along to keep them both happy with each other. My labor was very, very hard and I felt my body going somewhere. I wasn't afraid for the baby or myself. I felt like I would not be able to raise him, and a lonely feeling came over me. Brother Joseph then anointed my head and gave me a blessing calling on the angels to help with my first trial as a mother. The baby was finally crowning, but I couldn't feel anymore, so Brother Joseph lifted me up to give me a rest more from the pain I often had in my lower back, and as he let me slide back into the bed, I finally had a bearing down pain. The first one, the midwife was so excited she announced that the baby would be here very soon, and someone go get the wine. In one complete push, the little man was born in his bag of waters.

"As soon as the midwife broke the bag, he took his first little piss all over the room and his father. There were a bunch of hoot's and holler's that ran from one end of the street to the other, and half the countryside came to serenade me at the window with violins and guitars and mandolins. In 30 minutes, everything was cleaned up, and I felt like dancing. There was a party going on downstairs it reminded me of Angelina's birth in England.

"When Brother Joseph brought me our very own child. Hyrum Joseph Fielding, and Joseph looked in my eyes I could see eternity. I was the mother of his child, the love of his life. I immediately wrote letters to, Sarah, Father, Annie, Aunt Millie, and Mother Eliza. I was the happiest woman alive. I believed I had arrived.

"July 4ᵗʰ at 6 am, my honeymoon was over. Now I would be tending to two; my precious husband and his little heir. The use of my Spanish and my French for interpretation was constant. Hyrum wasn't eight hours old when I was called to interpret for the brethren the agenda for the next two days. The ladies were to gather white clothing, fitting of everyone for baptisms and the meals for three days of celebration along the (river).

We both heard the gravel as it moved under the weight of a slow-moving vehicle. Great-grandmother promised me we would continue at the soonest possible time. I stayed and met the lovely ladies and then rushed out the back door.

One of the most beautiful things about 1946 and the summer time was that I had it all to my self. I figured out that I didn't like being alone, I liked company, but I really didn't like to talk much. Just like Wendy pointed out. So, while I was on my hike looking for Brigham tea and gathering it: I looked at what might be in the way or if I had a valid reason for not talking.

Did I speak at home? No, not much. I might actually, be to blame for not knowing more about my family. I was quite talkative in school.

I asked all the questions, much to my classmate's demise. I was very curious about how things work and why they work the way they do, and what would you want those things for anyway. But mostly I just like to go! Run! To the park or the hills up Millcreek or even to school.

I had soon gathered an entire bag of Brigham tea and was about to head for the cave when I heard someone talking. I stood quietly waiting for the direction of the sound travel, and I saw the people and their purpose for discussion. Behind me to the west and over the ridge was an old beat-up wagon and mule with a funny haircut. It appeared to me that these were not local people. I soon figured out what they were up to and didn't go to investigate. They had made a very simple fence, and they had a long narrow flat table-like board coming off the back of the wagon. They were shearing sheep. I watched for a little while, and I wondered how long they had practiced shearing in these parts and if they spoke any English. One of them had nicked the other with his shears and before he could continue he had to bandage it so the blood wouldn't get on the wool. I considered that they probably knew about the cave, and I hurried to get my own enjoyment in before they needed it.

I was in the cave, and I felt safe to talk out-loud. So, I listen to my voice as I asked great-grandfather if their lives would have been complete without polygamy and if he only had great-grandmother as his love would he have been satisfied. As I listened to my voice and the small vibrations it created in the hollow of the cave it occurred to me that I didn't like the sound of my voice. I didn't like it amplified. So, then I decided to sing, muffled as it was so far under earth I wasn't concerned about being a disturbance. And then it hit me; I was more concerned about being in the way. Jonny and I always left the house and sought our own company than the company of our parents. As I sang the skaters-waltz underground, I felt like a muse. And when I asked great-grandfather if he liked it when I sang or when I talked, or laughed I answered myself, "of course, you do," I said.

My eyes had so adjusted to the light that I could see the walls of the cave. At the back towards the north were sections of slate that had slid with time into natural shelves. I stepped out of the pool and walked about seven steps toward the wall when I saw a stone box about the size of a cracker jacks box. It was completely dry on this side of the cave. I picked it up very slowly and on top of it was inscribed "Vanessa for you". I put it back and considered that there must be another set of words it could have said. I dressed quickly and looked again at the box. How long had it been there? And then I wondered how it had been protected from being scavenged by someone, like me? When I reached the opening, my eyes were blinded even though the sun was at about 7 pm and I turned and sat on the slate-slab until my eyes were adjusted again. From there it just looked like another piece of slate against the backdrop of the cave.

I was at the last step when the guys from the sheep-shearing expo saw me leaving. I smiled casually and waved for them to enter. I could tell that they wanted to know if anyone else was inside. I suggested no with sign-language and headed down the hill. They repeatedly said, "Thank-you, thank-you" until I was gone.

When I arrived back at the 'little mansion' everyone had left. Great-grandmother was just finishing with her bath time and brushing her beautiful long hair. "I see you met Juan and Pedro. They have been employed to shear the sheep since we began homesteading in 1862. They came up from Salt Creek in Arizona as was requested back then with their fathers. They are probably nearly sixty by now. They start in northern Utah, going from farm to farm along the west side of the Salt Lake, and the Utah Lake and complete in St. George around the first week of September. They will go into Uncle Samuel's office tomorrow and turn in the wool for shipment and collect about a hundred dollars for their work for us here.

As she was explaining to me with sentiment the extensive accounting of sheep husbandry over the years, I noticed a light switch by her bed near the dresser. I was looking at it realizing it had probably been put there to be covered by the chest. It was on. It occurred to me that at about 8:30 she would reach over and turn it off after prayers and before she went to sleep. I got up and ran to the pantry and on the switch panel for the light was a knob that had "off, low, medium, high and frost". It would seem to anyone else that this would be a control for the pantry, but I knew it was not. I came back into great-grandmother's room and said, "He was a veritable, genius!"

To which she replied, "If only I could tell you. There is not enough time for everything. But we will try to give you what matters most. Okay?"

"How was your meeting?" I ventured.

"The ladies were very happy to see another member of my family. The old crowd is long gone except Sister Kay. I suppose I have reason to be tired. They always ask if we need to move the meeting some other place; like the ward house. And I always say if they still want me to be at the meeting it would be more likely that I would come if it were here."

I plaited her hair neatly and asked how we take care of the Brigham tea. She told me it will be okay, just like it is for days to come if we don't get to it. I told her I had been reading at night and that I had finished my "Wizard of Oz" book. She asked me about it; if it held my curiosity? I told her there wasn't nearly as much magic in the book as in this place, and she smiled at me, a mysterious smile that made me feel like I had no idea.

She told me that when she was teaching school one of the ways to get children's curiosity peaked was to have them find a mystery in their project. She loved a good mystery.

"How long did you serve in France? Do we have time for that tonight?" I asked?

She said, "Yes."

And then right away started again, "I stayed another year and four months. Then I left with Brother Kimball and Annie. Anne had brought one of her children with her and had left the other with Mary, Brother Heber's seventh wife. Annie had been his thirteenth. Sarah had just arrived to take my place. I was so excited to see her as of course so was Joseph. We went shopping together and bought her a new hat and a new pair of shoes. We wore about the same size so I gave her two of my dresses; I certainly wouldn't need them where I was going. We laughed, and I love her so much… (There were tears in her eyes,) I'm just a little sensitive," she said changing the subject. Could you please bring me the denim box?"

"Of course," I said. Jumping up and going to the shelf to retrieve it.

All the things in the box were ordered; that was evident, and from the way she went from the key to the third item, it was evident that the key was always first in her mind, but not in the order of the events. She handed me three tickets to the Opera in the Odeon-de l'Europe, Opera House in Paris.

"The three of us went to that together. It was like a dream come true. I tripped on a patch of slippery sidewalk and spread my legs like the splits, I was seven months pregnant. Sarah stayed with me every minute of every hour until the baby was born, sleeping by my side. I ran a fever, and I had moments when I would vomit until I would black out. Joseph was busy keeping the Church affairs straight and spending time with Hyrum. Brother John Young spent hours with all of us. After a week of labor and hard, impossible headaches, we got a letter from Brother Brigham. Back then there was no telegraph or phone, of course, the fastest ship in the fleet could make it 14 days 22 hrs. The letter said that Brother Heber had served long enough, and it was time for him and Brother John Taylor to come home. He then said it was the Lords will that the valiant and the strong in spirit be called to greater things in heaven. Some have gone to the other side old and well-seasoned, some will leave us before they even arrive. He blessed Brother Fielding and his family and hoped that my experiences with my father and mother would give me the kind of support and love that I well deserved for being on a mission and having children born in the covenant while so far from the comforts of Zion.

"Alphonso delivered the letter, two hours and 45 minutes later our baby was born. He was blue and not breathing, he probably weighed 3lbs, but he came before the doctor could arrive. Sarah would not believe the baby was dead. She massaged his little body and worked his little legs and arms and cried and cried and begged God to have mercy. After 15 minutes of praying and crying and massaging him, he squeaked. Brother Joseph and Brother John gave him a blessing and said that his name shall be Alphonso for bringing hope, to a very dark hour. He was so small for almost three days we kept him by dripping my milk into his little mouth. When the doctor finally came to check on Alphonso, he reported that there was no manner of a miracle that could have made Alphonso stay alive through the delivery or the next day of his life, because he was too young to have kidney function yet. I was so weak and so sore and bruised in my legs and crotch region that I could not walk yet, but I was more worried that if I let my body slow down, it would stay slowed down."

"When no one was watching, I would get up and walk Alphonso up and down the hall with my breast leaking milk into his little mouth. On just such a walk I heard him say to me, somehow, I don't know how, "Mother, I love who you are, I am going to go with my brothers now. They are taking me to see Father." He was seven days old and died in my arms. I felt his spirit as it lifted into the heavens and released his body. I sat down and cried. Sarah found me in the hall and brought Joseph to me. He sat with me and begged me to forgive him for bringing this to us. I turned to him and cradled both of them tight and said, "Brother Joseph this is God's doing not yours and Alphonso will be the one to come and take you to the Lord, like his brothers, your sons came to get him and take him to see Our Father in Heaven." Brother Joseph looked at me and asked, 'How do you know this,' and I replied, "Just before his spirit left his tabernacle I heard him say his brothers had come to get him, and he was so happy and excited. He said he would see me again and that he loved me just the way I am." I stood up and walked away with never a pain in my legs or crotch again. We had the body exhumed, and I took it back to Zion in the casket the next day. Brother John Young accompanied me back we went by ship to Philadelphia, and then by rail to Council Bluffs, and then on the Oregon Trail, we started with the Clark company on October 5th. But because of my weakness I then took a coach from North Platt to Salt Lake.

"Baby Alphonso was born on the 12th of August and died on the 19th. We left England on the 30th of August. I took my little Hyrum to show off to my parents, and I wore black until I arrived in Millcreek with my new family.

"The ships were faster the rails were faster, even the wagons were much faster. We arrived on the 30th of October and on the night of the 31st we buried the baby Alphonso in the City Cemetery on Capitol Hill.

"Things had changed since I had left. Two years and three months. Enough time for a whole new look. The town was busting at the seams. Brother Brigham Young had informed the young men that they could either marry so they could put their income to use building a better Zion or be sent out on a mission to gather those who were eager to know the ways of the Lord.

One magical thought was that the iron rails could pass through our state and give relief to the traveling Saints.

CHAPTER 17

Married Again and Homesteading

Many hours I spent reading great-grandmothers lovely letters over and over again. I spent the time while Great-grandmother was napping. In the attic watching, the time fly by in a world of fashion and delight. In this very narrative experience, I could hardly ever catch my grandmother out of the *archetype* of Matriarch. Often, she spoke regarding "we": a collective group of people who I thought might still be around.

Coming down the ladders; which by now were, like she said, "easier than the ward house steps," I found her with the denim box. It was just before lunch on the 24th of July. I knew there was so much she still needed to tell me. She needed to clear the air for a very important future for us.

"Great-grandmother," I asked, "You are getting ready to go out already?"

She looked at me and said, "I'm really just undecided about what to wear. All things come to an end, and I can see that this is my last 24th. I would like to have it beautiful and as memorable as when I spent it with Brother John, and not threatening to my heart as the last one was with Brother Joseph. But that is not what you were going to ask me now was it?" She turned and looked me straight in the eye. A chill went down my spine and I looked at the intention in her lovely blue eyes.

Beside the closet, next to the swinging doors was a chair for her to sit on while looking at her wardrobe. The chair was made of handcrafted wood, and the cushion was hand stitched tapestry with a mother cougar and her cubs playing together. I had so much reverence for her things, and as I almost fell into the chair, my first consideration was for its soundness. I was falling as careful as I could, considering I was about to faint.

"I guess my head just caught up with my body." I apologized. I waited to see if I could in any way avoid my question, but then it occurred to me she already knew what it was.

"I have been so preoccupied, since my visit with Wendy in the cave with an idea that now I feel is more important…well actually it's probably two questions: what will happen to all of THIS, I waved my hand around the room as if it was the world, "and how important is it"?

Oh, my. I wanted to say that everything you've been and done must be inherited.

My emotions were reading on my face, a face that I would carry with me for a very long time into my future. My face must have looked like I was about to crumble.

"And that everything is only as important as it would seem to someone who knows…but that makes me cry…" I wept.

She had her hand on the old gown she was going to wear tonight. It looked like the gown Betsy Ross would have been wearing to make the flag. A pinafore type apron with ties that would fall over a bustle in the back. I knew she would inspire children at the event to look at the past, and probably some gawking adults as well. She lifted her hand and held the gown in her lap gently, like silk with her soft, long fingers, of course, she played the piano, her hands were so precious. I started to tear up again and proceeded to use my hand to wipe my tears when she offered me a white hankie. The edges were tatted, and the inside had a white on white heart with doves tying a bow at the top of the heart. Inside the heart was an *M & J*, around the entire tatting on the inside, was an inscription, May, *and Joseph forever and ever, where one circle ends May the next begin. Love Libby, yours also forever, and ever.* I took a second to read it and then almost started crying again. "Why is this so hard?" I demanded! "I don't understand."

"When you don't understand something Vanessa, you get angry. Maybe you get angry because you are afraid you will be left out? I think that somewhere in your experience you have felt or dealt with some of the abandonments of your ancestors, or maybe, you're just a kid?" She smiled at me, and I was encouraged to see the souls we had become as we had spent time together over the summer vacation. "Be specific for me so I can look at it with you." She requested.

"I want to know if someone will come and take all your stuff to the Salvation Army when you leave? "go *home*" And I want to know if the Gospel is true? I believe it is, then how did the Gospel have the right to take my mother away from her mother and father?"

"And if the Prophet had it revealed from God Almighty that the Law of Celestial Marriage would be lived until the coming of Christ, with not ONE YEAR, going by without a child being born into the covenant as a witness to its truth, then why did the Gospel give up? And why is it so hard to keep that covenant now if the Gospel is true?"

I sighed and felt like a whole bag of beans had been taken off my shoulders.

She asked, "What are you wearing tonight? Let's get dressed and go get some Country Fried chicken before the show, okay?" "I just have jeans and my Sunday dress," I answered.

"Here let's see what I have for you." She went to the far side of her closet where some articles of clothing were hanging in plastic wrap and proceeded to pull a couple dresses out, laying them on the bed.

"Well now don't just sit there! There's a whole wardrobe of clothes that would be delighted to be worn, pick anything at all. In the Blue, Denim box is a playwright that my mother wrote when she came to Zion. We did a significant performance in the Capital Theater and John was an actor, and I was a 'drama queen' so just take your time. We have thirty minutes to lunch, and four hours before the show begins. If you choose and get dressed, I won't stop the story. But I must confess I refuse to go out tonight the only one in proper style." She was animated.

I looked for the next 20 minutes and apparently, she had already made the arrangements for our ride. I looked and looked and finally picked the only thing that could possibly reflect what I might want to be…it was the 'Gone with the Wind' dress that Scarlet O'Hara wore when she broke for Red. "Very Romantic," I said and began to dress. She twisted and braided my hair and in the end in front of her beautiful full-length mirror was Scarlet…for sure. I was adorable, beautiful and not twelve at all. "We must ask Uncle Samuel if he could be your chaperone tonight, not proper for such a fine lady to be out without an escort."

She began with; "Libby made the kerchief for me when we went to Joseph, Utah to homestead. After I got back from France with my Hyrum and my little Alphonso I could not be consoled. I think I had a condition they later called *postpartum depression*. I tried to keep myself busy with the important things of the Gospel. While Sarah was with

Joseph in France, I stayed with Hannah his first wife. I tried so hard not to irritate her, but there was not enough perfection in her world and no mark for acceptable. I would have rather been her maid than her sister-wife.

"At one time during Sunday services, Brother Brigham came up to me and with the kindest reproach and said, 'France was not what you would have had it be, but the Lord is sure to call your blessings to you.' He then gently pinched little Hyrum's check and said, 'He looks just like his father, and he has his mother's inquisitive eyes.' To which Hyrum said, 'tane-to.'

'And his father's charm, I see.' Brother Brigham then asked me if I could stop by and see Mother Eliza.

"Mother Eliza gave me my first real makeup, a cake of color that was made from the softest clay. And a little brush that was made of skunk hair. She said it had been shipped to the Zion City Mercantile by request of the drama class for Sister Mary who had been the first instructor for the Salt Lake Theater in1850.

"When I arrived in July of 1852, I immediately sought out the fine nature of the Saints, dancing and acting. That has never changed throughout the years. The Church has always been able to make money in entertainment. I was greatly in love with the arts, and I wanted to speak seven languages and have a pallet of paint and all the musical instruments I could learn to play. So, needless to say, Sister Mary and I got along very well until she passed of pneumonia in the fall of 1852. As a student, I could hardly believe that her efforts were not more appreciated. Then when her things were gone through by the family some of the educational items were sent back to the school and redistributed to the some of the actors. Mother Eliza was very involved and had gathered a cake of make-up for me but never felt it was appropriate until she had mentioned to Brother Brigham that, 'May needs some encouragement.' She showed me how it covered the black rings under my eyes, and she asked me if I would consider taking on the new role of support for the Salt Lake Theater Company that would be opening soon? I told her I would consider it an honor and that Brother Joseph would be greatly appreciative.

"We started acting classes the next Monday. I was given a two-hour block of time, and we began with the Taming of the Shrew, by William Shakespeare.

"To my great and wonderful surprise when I got the mail the following week I found out that Mother and Father were coming to America and would be bringing my Uncle Seymour as soon as they could make proper financial arrangements to come to Zion. Uncle had not remarried, and his lovely daughter was now nearly seven years old. I was ecstatic.

"Hyrum and I were living in the upstairs of Hannah's house, and we were very grateful, but having Mother and Father in Zion would change everything for me. My color changed I became alive and happy, health began to triumph, and I heard myself singing on the way to class on Tuesday morning. Libby had been anxious about me and probably was the initial reason for Mother Eliza's involvement. She and I had become such friends. We spent hours together.

"I had left France August 30th, 1858 and by January of 1859, I was not looking good. But on the 15th of January, I had a job, news that my parents were finally making their way to Zion and I had news that Brother Joseph was being replaced by Brother Alphonso Young, brother Brigham's brother.

"I ran from school ecstatically and took Libby in my hands and twirled her round and round. I was so excited I asked her if she would marry me. I stopped still. I looked at her and asked; why you haven't married Libby you are nearly twenty-five years old now. When Joseph is gone, we could can and garden and tend the family together...oh, well of course if you too would like to have each other. He will be coming home soon, please think about it. She stopped me and reminded me how hard it was for me to stop Brother Joseph in his tracks and to imagine her impossibility. So, I embraced her with a genuine scrunch and told her if she didn't have a suiter by midnight the first week he came back. I would ask her again.

"I told her Joseph would be home in March, and they would be here to be sustained at April conference. My whole "self" changed. I wrote to Mother and begged her to send me the copy of her play script she had made for the school in Honeybrooke.

"I received it in six weeks' time and on the 1ˢᵗ of March, we started as a class to practice from her manuscript: <u>Fathers Five Wives</u>. It was a funny play that went over very well in Honeybrooke before the Gospel was taken there and converts began to find out that Mormons practiced polygamy. It was about the virtue of a man and his political station. He had to keep his wives from finding out about each other, but his children were the ones who pulled the plug when they ended up in school together. It was so hilarious and still used in the school after they found out that Mother and Father had adopted Mormonism.

"The Bowery had been used since 1853 for social entertainment, and the Saints were well known for their entertainment. I gave the manuscript to Brother Brigham, and he gave it to Mother Eliza. She made a few suggestions and requested the title be changed to <u>Fathers Seven Wives</u> and said it would increase the comedy plus the frustration. She promised that it would be a_great success and that the Jew and Gentile would love it. She was right of course. One of the key points to the play was the Fathers desire to get them <u>all</u> into one big Commune. He would often talk to his best friend, who kept his secret and was fond of several of his wives. The Father thought that if he could get them all under one roof, he would be better able to manage the children's needs. Within seconds, the audience and the cast would be in hysteria. It took well trained and seasoned actors to play several of the parts. In

Honeybrooke, Mother had a team of students between 15 and 18 years of age playing the roles and she did very well at teaching them to cast. I was so excited. Libby was right there every step of the way encouraging and helping me.

"To my complete astonishment, Brother Joseph was home three weeks early. I turned the corner on State and First on March 15th and there he stood. His big grin from eye-to-eye and ear-to-ear. I could hear my enchantment screaming out of my flesh when I was less than twenty feet from him I couldn't hold back, and I ran to him with no thought of the public or anyone. I did not care that the world witnessed my love for that man. And with my love for him I was not discreet I was open. 'I love you, my May-using wife. I missed your little outbursts more than I realized. And there's my little man.'

"Fah-do," little Hyrum said.

"He picked up Hyrum and through him into the air. 'How did you know it was Father?' He asked.

"Hyrum answered, 'Pi-toe.' We laughed at his attempt to say picture and then walked back toward the third north and third East home. I was so in love.

"Brother Joseph moved us to the Millcreek home by November 30th, and I delivered our Rachel Angelina on December 15th. She was ten days early. Brother Brigham had asked Brother Joseph to go from settlement to settlement giving encouragement and passing on the word of the tithing settlements being paid in land and other properties.

"I had traveled with him while on the school breaks one from June to August and then again at Harvest time, around the 1st of October. We went to St. George. We had traveled to Bear Lake and Garden City and then to the gold, silver, and copper mines in the state. Brother Brigham had sent a team to study the existing minerals and gems available for the 'Deseret' resume. The railroad had been the first request the Saints had made after arriving in the Great Basin.

"The domination of area for statehood was massive; a mini country! One of Brother Joseph's consent companions since returning from France was Brother young John Young. His interest in the welfare of the state and the political challenges amazed me. As we traveled, I grew to understand young John through the eyes of the surrounding land. He viewed everything as if it was alive. His relation to the Natives was so keen, and he could be with and converse with anyone. I often felt like there was not one thing he did not know something about or had some curiosity for. He was genuinely intelligent and interested in being enlightened. On the 20th of December Brother Joseph was informed that he could choose his home in Millcreek for the future, but that Brother Brigham wanted him to go to the middle of the state and homestead. Brother Brigham said to choose any parcel of land that appealed to him and set up a township and city ordinances and elect a mayor within the first six months of establishment.

"He asked us to go along the State road that went to Kanab. Highway 89. The same road that runs to the east of this house. Brother Brigham said he could choose his companion travelers. But he could not have Brother Heber C Kimball or John Taylor or Wilford Woodruff they were already heavily engaged in commitments to bring talent and economy to Deseret.

Brother John Taylor gave the October conference a great delight when he informed the congregation that a Mr. Fourier, a French man and a communist would be very proud of the communal efforts of the Saints except that there would be no significant profits in his pocket. He said that some of the towns would be set up in 'Orders' that would establish peace by the design of universal ownership and kindness; love unfeigned. Orderville was created for that reason and would have been a standing example of the Law of Consecration if it had not burned to the point of disrepair and families with children had moved away so there were no inheritable rights.

"The town and the museum still exist but not for the same purpose. Brother Taylor was a very gentle and soft-spoken man except under the wind of what he was passionate about. The most of which was the Prophet Joseph and what he taught. He said the war of the Deseret had just begun and that we needed to watch because the fire would start inside the very Church itself that the damage caused by Army's sent against us would not amount to the dissidence among the Saints themselves.

"Brother Heber spoke as well and to my knowledge he had the largest harem of wives; 34, I think, and he had 67 children. His ability to organize and unite families and cities was astonishing. He should have been called the Church "marriage advisor." He was not as soft spoken as Brother John Taylor, but he was a happy man. I heard him called "The Lion of the Lord."

"On April 30th Libby married Brother Joseph and on May 1st we took off with our little family to find a new home. Brother Joseph's first wife petitioned Brother Brigham for a health release and begged to stay in Millcreek. Sarah stayed for about two months with her sister and helped her let the rooms out and then came down with Brother Joseph on one of the freighting trips. It was not acceptable for a man to have more property than he could provide for or maintain but the resourceful Hannah made it work very well. When Brother Joseph or someone else needed a room, it was always prepared courtesy of Hannah and her lovely daughters Rachel and Ellen.

"There is a beautiful and heavenly place over the hill and south of Salina where Libby and I and sometimes Sarah, began to build a dream world. Against the crooked and worn sky in the east are hot springs. We did all our laundry there and bathed. It was there I met two important people. I was bathing my little Rachel Angelina she was smiling so sweet, and I was cooing at her. Libby and I were so happy together. The clay was so rich and so many different colors, yellow and green and bright red, there was a dark black and a very uncommon blue. We made different pots and cups and plates. We were harvesting that day, and I had been carrying my little Annie in a bundle on the front. I had just taken her out of the wrap and cleared a little stop in the warm water to lay her down in when she stared at something over my shoulder, and her eyes were focusing on it and me. I was very aware that shock would not work in *any* case. I continued cooing at her. I realized that if someone had wanted me dead the item of surprise was over. So, I cooed, 'You, beautiful little angel do we have a guest? Do we have angels watching us? You are my little angel, should we say hello? Hello. How are you, I asked? My name is May, and this is my beautiful daughter Rachel Angelina Fielding.

"The woman behind me had the face of a goddess. She smiled and said, 'I know this Brother Fielding, he makes a good friend. For much food. Trade good.' I wrapped my baby in tight against me. I wasn't about to have her asking to trade the baby. She was the daughter of Chief Walkara. She spoke little English but more than the Navajo I didn't speak.

"She was very careful, and her body language suggested that she really wanted to touch the baby. I let her feel Little Annie. She was very gentle and so sweet I think she was about ten or maybe twelve. 'Papoose,' She said. Baby…I said. She said, 'baabee.' Baby, I repeated. She carefully caused the 'a' to be a long 'a' sound. And I cheered her on. We said baby after each other several times, and she spread her arms a little and was asking to hold her. Annie's little precious body; was I going to trust the maiden with my little life? I carefully handed Annie over, sitting closer to the maiden and trying really to understand her. 'Baby, papoose, hoka…gone, hoka…gone.'

"She had a look of such sadness in her eyes. I was young and not very bright about all the dangers of life but this I could see was a common expression of a mother. I had lost Alphonso. I knew the hurt I saw in her eyes. I pointed at my chest and said, "My baby," I pointed to Annie, "Annie,' I said. She repeated "Annie." I shook my head, yes. She shook her head, yes. I pointed to my belly, "My baby Alphonso, baby...hoka, gone." She smiled and tipped her head.

"Then she pointed again at her belly and said, "Hoka...gone".

"I had seen something moving in the willows, but I knew I was already cooked if I didn't stay very still. Where was Libby? Libby was in the mud cave at the bottom of the hill. She was taking what we called a 'mud bath' then she would come up on the hill and soak in the warm pool of water and dry off in the sun. The movement had me a little more than concerned. The young girl smiled and stood up. She motioned someone over. He was tall and very naked, except his loin-cloth and his feather and his long hair and a smile.

"Apparently, all men of every nationality know when you are checking them out.

"He was quite proud of himself. He sauntered over all naked like and said, 'This is my Mary', she tapped him on the ribs and said something in return.

"To which he replied, 'You have this baby, and now you have another that is gone, baby boy, he died? Yes.'

"I was shaking my head, yes.

"Mary wanted you to meet her father, Chief Walkara. She wants you to talk to him about you can have another baby. Mary had a baby boy he was little,' He held up his fingers and put out his palm and drew across it with his pointer finger, like the baby could fit in his hand.

"Then Mary had another baby boy, little,' he held up his hands and cradled a very small but bigger child. Mary had another baby girl, girl breathed and sang only one song, and she died too. Mary wants you to teach her to keep the baby alive. Come to her Father's house.' He went to reach for me.

"I was shaking my head no, no, no, no. But he said, 'Please', and she copied him, 'pwees.' I told him I had a sister here, and a little boy that needed me and I had to talk to my husband who was down at the house.

"He said, 'FINE' and stomped his foot and took Mary's hand and stomping off he stuck his nose up in the air: another very common human trait. I was restrained, but I could not help but laugh inside at his total body build and strength yet childish behavior. I was afraid I had made a big mistake. I will tell you the rest of the story after we get back, tonight."

We then went to Nephi and at 1: pm. We had Country Fried chicken and mashed potatoes at her favorite restaurant. At 4:30 we rode a Ferris wheel, and we listen to country western music at the bandstand. We sat in saucy chairs that had been carried in by Uncle 'mysterious' Samuel, and at 7:00 the stage was cleared, and we watched Father's Seven Wives. The volume of laughter and excitement that was generated by that red-neck crowd superstitiously caused me to see if I was dreaming. I pinched myself.

Great-grandmother shifted herself in her chair and said, "It's real. Mother published her play under a pseudo name Margarethe Ballantyne. It was suggested by the Relief Society, ten years ago, to find a play that would be fun and actually enlightening for the High school in Nephi. We were all sent out for two weeks to look for something. Ten plays were brought back and looked at this one was chosen. Each of the plays was presented in a plain manila envelope tossed and turned. If it was mentioned who had offered it or where it had originated, it was discarded. I read each play meticulously as did everyone else. We then had a vote. This one won 10 years ago, and it won again this year. The play takes about six months' time to practice."

"I think they did a lovely job. I was laughing and crying at the same time."

I told her it was marvelous. Clapping and hooting at all the right times and in all the right places. I felt alive. We then watched fireworks at 10: pm.

There was a rodeo that had been going on all day. After the fireworks, you could hear all the frightened animals crying and the natural anxiety of the people as they fitted themselves into their cars. A couple of the nearby farmers had ridden their buggies into town and had parked their buggies in a particular place, assigned to the 'buggies brigade'. Uncle Samuel was one of them. Great-grandmother and I looked as if we were from the 18ᵗʰ century stepping onto the buggy platform for the ride home. We both heard 'Sister May' and turned to see who called. A great amazing flash took place. The new reporter from Salt Lake City had just taken a picture of us in our regalia. Later it was published, _The Eldest and Most Fashionable Lady, with Her Prodigy_.

CHAPTER 18

An Endowment of Love

I took such pleasure taking her home and helping her get into her evening gown. My little mission in Kaysville had become my most important thought. I was consumed. She agreed to tell me more in the morning, and I kissed her hand as I was leaving the room.

After prayers in the morning, she started right off with the answer to yesterday's question.

"All these things," She waved her hand around in a big circle, as she spoke, "and all these lives get passed to the next generation. By using the changes made in the social environment and our faith we get to see the plan of God unfold.

"My mother's play has always been a success, and a young man even turned it into a book. My Love for Brother Joseph was manifest in each of our brilliant children. What is most important is not who you are or where you come from...oh, yes, that matters, but what _is_ really important are the choices that you make because you get to live with the outcome of your choice.

"I'm so grateful I came to America and to Zion. I am more thankful that I married Brother Joseph and that he helped make the selection of Brother John. I don't think I would have chosen Brother John, but I did choose to consider it for the sake of Joseph and for my children.

"When I found out how long Brother John had loved me, I was unbelieving astonished. He was a strapping twelve years old when he fell, head-over-heels for me. He was twelve years old when I watched him flirt with me in public, and he thought I would choose him as my betrothed. I thought of it when I read Brother Joseph's last will and testament to me and when Brother John asked me to consider him as a 'second dance.' I cried, and I was so lost and confused and afraid with my three children and one on the way. I was twenty-three, Hyrum was seven, Annie was four, Sarah was eighteen months old, and I was six months pregnant. I had loved Joseph for eighteen years of my life, and I could not imagine my life without him.

"When he died, I was given a special blessing by Mother Eliza and my mother in the endowment house. A mother's blessing. They washed my whole body bit by bit and then anointed my entire body joint by joint, organ by organ, including my head and brain and blessed each part with holy oil. And then a blessing and a promise that I would be surrounded by the warm light of my guardians and the children I had lost who were waiting to see me on the other side. They promised that Joseph was giving me everything that he ever gave me from the Grace of Heavenly Father's throne and that he would continue to throughout my life. I knew I was loved beyond words, and I felt him touch my cheek during the blessing, and I leaned into his touch, and I felt his warmth.

"The first person to come and see me after William Patrick was born was Brother John Young. William was born on the 6th of April 1864. Brother John stayed his distance as he had promised and allowed me one full year of mourning and one full year of soft reminders that he was Brother Joseph's choice for a second dance. I was so seasoned with heartache and worry, and I was so concerned about the Kaysville home. Brother John would not allow me to worry when he was able he took care of everything. He was twenty when we married. He had married his first wife when he was eighteen, and he married his second wife when he was nineteen, and he would marry me at twenty. Few men ever lived that could have given me my space and love at the same time the way he did"

Great-grandmother paused and clicked her tongue. Sharing her surprise at her own memories.

"We can come back to this story. For, now we have to go back to the story about when we were homesteading in Joseph.

"I had come down the little hill to where Libby was mud bathing to find her staring off into space, a towel wrapped around her body. She looked at me, stood up and started walking up to the hot springs. I could tell she was perplexed.

"I just encountered some Indians. I'm worried Libby they might come back. They wanted something from me."

"I was following her up the hill again, tucking and turning Annie into her little gown.

"Uh-huh," she mumbled.

"Libby," I stammered, "did you hear me?"

"She looked at me with a faraway look that was haunting. It still haunts me.

"Did you ever consider that your husband is down at the house making mad passionate love to another woman?"

"My mouth dropped open I had to shut it with my hand and give Annie a breast to nurse as fast as I could. I was leaking all over the place. I plopped down on the log we had fashioned near the pool as a bench. "Libby, are you okay? We might be in trouble."

"I'm pregnant." She said with no mood at all.

"Oh, oh, oh I'm so, so excited for you, for us!" I was dancing with little Annie up and down.

"Did you not hear me, May!" She shouted, "He is having sex with another woman in your house."

"Libby," I murmured, "Libby...look at me, look at me...I'm okay with that. It's our house. He loves me when I'm with him, and he is the father of our little miracle. Libby are you jealous, of something?" I coached her and looked at her soaking in the pool. "Libby, it's getting too hot for Annie I want to go back now. Can you please come with me? I think we are going to be paid a visit this evening by Chief Walkara, come on now okay."

"She stood up to put out her hand to me and stepped onto the little reed mat we had made so our fresh, clean feet would stay clean while dressing.

"On the walk, back I could tell she was still not communicating so I waited until we could see the house. "Libby," I asked, "did Brother Joseph hurt you?" She spun at me.

"What on earth would give you that idea?" she asked me. "He is the kindest person, man...I have ever known. He loves you so much. He looks at you with such awe and respect. Sarah is so much, he is so much older than both of us. I'm not handsome like you. I guess I never considered that marrying him would be the same as Sarah being with him. I...I'm really, not jealous for me, sorry, I'm jealous for you. I have loved you May since I saw you walk down the road from Emigration

Canyon, what a great name, and you asked me if I would marry into your family. I feel strangely put-out by Joseph being affectionate with Sarah. I guess I always have been it's just now that I'm pregnant…and well I missed my cycle by 30 days…"

"30 days I screamed. Oh, Libby, I'm so happy for us. We are so blessed."

"I don't ever want to lose you," she cried and managed to walk faster and get closer to my side.

"Libby, have you been afraid to tell me because you thought I would be upset at you for getting pregnant? Do you realize how happy this makes me? I can hardly wait for you to tell Brother Joseph."

"I was almost skipping. Hyrum had seen us coming and had jumped off the lumber wagon and started running toward me, his little legs were not keeping up with his head; he almost took a face planting. Libby grabbed my arm harder than she had intended and spun me, taking me off guard and I twisted my ankle. We had a little wagon we were pulling behind us with our fresh washed laundry and some mint and willows we had gathered. Libby let go of the wagon and pushed herself between me and the ground blocking the fall so that Annie would land upright. I'm sure it looked very confusing from where Brother Joseph and the boys stood. Like the game 'we-all-fall-down' only we looked like we were dancing.

"I wasn't badly hurt but I was terribly worried about Libby and by then Hyrum had caught up to us. Brother Joseph had hopped off the wagon and flashed to help when he got to us he reached for Libby first helping her up with such tenderness, and then he looked at me like… 'Well, wasn't that interesting.' And then when he said it. We all started laughing. Libby stuck her finger up to her lips, to silence me. I shook my head, and she shook hers back at me. Brother Joseph was baffled.

"Okay," I interrupted him. "I encountered some Indians today. The girl looked like she was twelve or thirteen. But she was married, and her husband was there with her. She wanted to hold Annie, so I let her. She then tried to tell me she had lost a baby that it had died. I somehow communicated to her that Annie wasn't my only child and that I had a little boy that had died too. Her husband then came out of nowhere and said I needed to go with them back to their camp to see the girl's father, Chief Walkara. He wants me to show them how to heal her. Apparently, she's had three babies die already. She looks too young."

"Libby seemed relieved that I had changed the tune of our possible conversation, after all, it was her right to inform Brother Joseph he would be a father again. But Brother Joseph was concerned about our encounter with the natives. He immediately sent our fastest boy, Sarah's youngest, Edward, to Marysville for some backup. Brother Joseph told us that the couple had probably watched us to see which home we were from and then would go back and to their camp for Chief Walkara. He asked me if I had seen a horse. I told him I hadn't even seen them "it was Annie" who let me know they were there.

"When we got inside and had settled a little I looked at my ankle which was bruised and had started swelling. Sarah had made chicken dumpling soup for dinner, and the boys were going up in the wagon to bathe and bring back water.

"In three days time we would have running water. The pipes for the water had been laid, and we would have the hot water coming from the hot springs and cold the water coming into the house from the creek box, by Monday evening.

"I turned to Libby and whispered, "If you call putting a barn roof on, 'mad passionate love' we're in trouble." We both laughed. I could tell there was still something troubling her.

"We went upstairs. It was unfinished, and our clothing chests looked like toys against the largeness of the room, with the sunshine coming in between the rafter-slats. There were tarpaulins; large, rolled up canvas drapes, hanging from the rafters. They would be lowered for sleeping and dressing arrangements until walls could be put in. We were pretty sure the roof would get finished before it rained too hard. It had sprinkled a little but never rained yet.

"The next day there was going to be a large work project, and several of the town folk were coming over to help put on the roof.

"Kathryn Harrison the girl I got close to on the trek across the prairies was helping with the new settlement in Marysville, not far from Joseph our little township. We came all the ways from Winters Quarters together. I was so excited to see her again and share our love for the Gospel and our families.

"When I got back downstairs Sarah took Annie from me and handed her to Brother Joseph. She proceeded to set me in a chair and lift my skirt. It is so comical, even now, that we all trusted each other so much and let people administer to our needs in such a personal and abrupt fashion. Brother Joseph turned his head. She ordered Libby to bring the pot of water from the stove. Then she stood and went to the shelf and pulled vinegar and salt from it.

"We had put in a garden, but it wasn't ready to harvest yet so there was no cayenne. So, she yelled at Rhea her youngest daughter, who was standing in the yard, to bring her a swatch of Brigham tea off the plant next to the barn. The Brigham plant was about six feet tall. We had been very careful not to hurt it while putting up the barn or the fence. Rhea brought in about thirty stems ten or twelve inches long. Sarah dropped a hand full of salt in the water and a cup of vinegar.

"Brother Joseph said to Hyrum, "Oudh, looks like were having mommy for dinner tonight," as Sarah twisted the tea all together inside the pot of nearly boiling water.

"Then Sarah said, 'Now we have a roof to raise tomorrow, and you won't have a broken ankle to keep you from doing your share of the work,' frowning from ear to ear.

"I said to Hyrum, "That is Aunt Sarah's way of saying, 'I love you and I'm sorry to be so bossy.'

"Hyrum said, "I think we should eat you anyway."

"To which his father so proudly agreed, 'I think so too! Don't worry Sarah', he said, 'if your remedy doesn't work I have a whip.'

"I believe that we are all having way too much fun over my failing, I mean falling." I looked at Libby. 'But Libby's the one who got plastered.'

"Come on now, Libby we'll just have to put your whole body in the pot," was Sarah's reply. Sarah then looked at Libby and caught her as she was passing out.

"Brother Joseph jumped from his station throwing Annie gently to the floor and caught Libby in his arms. He lifted her like a rag doll and took her up the stairs two steps at a time.

"I knew it!' He shouted, 'We're pregnant.' I started clapping my hands and singing, 'Here we go 'round the mull-berry-bush the mull-berry-bush the mull-berry-bush.' Hyrum joined in, and soon we were making a mess with the pot and were chided by Sarah.

"Brother Joseph stayed up there for quite a long time and when he returned we were ready for dinner. The boys had come back, and the water had been rationed to the animals, and the tins with fresh water were lined along the unfinished porch. 'Libby is going to be a mother now so I want a little kindness shown to her while she is in the family-way.' Brother Joseph announced, 'She's still a little shy this being her first-time with-child.' He said very happily. Then he said a sweet prayer over the food as we were all holding hands, then he stood and took a plate of soup and some rolls upstairs. 'I wouldn't argue with the man-of-the-house if I were you, it could upset a few termites.'

"Papa what's a termite?" asked Hyrum.

"Why, son you are the very termite, I was talking about." Brother Joseph responded with a magical grin.

"Oh, Brother Joseph,' I rebuked. "Hyrum, dear, termites are little bugs that eat the wood." I countered.

"And I saw him eating a stick of red-willow today. I think that qualifies him for a termite." The boys outside had heard the bantering and had joined in with their own interpretation of termite.

"The boys were strung-out on the porch and the steps going along the wall on the outside of the building; a natural exit. It was still too hot for an inside formal dinner. Brother Joseph, Sarah, Edward, Libby, Rhea, Hyrum, and myself sitting at the table, with Annie in her cradle.

"At about half way through dinner we heard a war cry. Brother Joseph said to the boys on the porch, very sternly, 'Don't move a muscle. Keep eating like they aren't there at all. Just don't look at them or return any hostility. Brother Joseph then stood and went to the porch, and watched as the Indians did their hoop-ta-la. When they were finished, and had kicked up enough dust. Brother Joseph asked, 'Are you boys hungry? I have food and flour.'

"Brother Joseph good man, kind to family and to Natives. We want to make a trade."

"Well, that makes me happy." Said Brother Joseph. "Where is your father? I think he is the one I will trade with."

"He comes," said the loudest one.

"This is good, this is good." Brother Joseph was stalling the band until their father arrived.

"He comes." The loud one shouted again, in one of the boy's ears. George kept his cool and didn't even blink. Then they started their hoop-ta-la again, and we could see Chief Arapeen and his daughter and son-in-law and another rider coming along beside them. They came up to the yard, and Chief Arapeen asked Brother Joseph if they could visit.

"Brother Joseph asked if he and his family wanted to come inside or meet outside. Their Chief then lifted his hand above his head and swung it around and shouted "Hoka-hey!" Which basically meant 'get lost all of you'? He then came inside and introduced his daughter and his son and the man with him was their medicine man. He spoke very good English and was very soft spoken.

"Chief Walkara's wife had died giving birth to his daughter Mary. The chief had many other wives, but none of them wanted to raise a sick baby so her mother's sister raised her. Later when her mother's sister's husband died, "a good death", the chief married Mary's aunt and she became his daughter again. Mary was always very small. She married when she was fourteen and the first year she did not get pregnant, so the medicine man was asked to check her and the man. The man was good, but she was too small inside to have a baby. Her man was going to give her away but when he took her to the place to give her away she was in labor and had a baby. It was a little girl that breathed one song and then she died. It made Mary very sad, her husband asked her to forgive him maybe he was too hard on her. They went back to the medicine man, he said she could try again. The next year she had another baby. It died, very small, and only movement, no song. The next year she had another baby it was bigger but had no song and no movement. The medicine man said she was broken. But now the man loves her for trying so hard. Makes the man and Mary very sad. Then the Chief proceeded to tell us that his daughter met one of Brother Joseph's wives who is very strong and can have a live baby and a dead baby too. The Chief wanted to trade, he wanted me to go and study their medicine, and I would teach them ours. It was a good trade he said.

"Brother Joseph looked at me and said, 'Well you are now officially a medicine woman. What do you want to do?'

"I thought of all the things I wanted to say, like: Are you kidding, seriously, I know this isn't a joke and help me here, please? I looked at my little Hyrum and my sleeping Annie and then back to my beloved husband, and my mind was swimming in possibilities, but they all ended in not happening very well.

"Chief Arapeen spoke and said he would give me my own tee-pee for my family. I could come there for a week, and study and then the medicine man would come here. I could tell by the way the medicine man was talking that something wasn't right. The Chief then said that I would take me years to learn their ways and that the medicine man could learn our ways much more quickly. I think we all agreed. I knew that a trade it had to be fair. I asked if the medicine man would teach me for two weeks. I would stay and learn everything I could and then he could come and stay until he was satisfied. But I would need an interpreter for a while. It was agreed, and Brother Joseph shook on it.

"I know you are wondering what in the world was I thinking. I knew I didn't have the kind of medicine for Mary that was conventional, but while I was in France, I had studied with the pharmacist Jules Remy, who had given me the rich understanding of Herbs and mixing them. I spent two years as often as I could with the teachers in France and before I came home they gave me a certificate for completing Botany and the Herbal sciences. In the US, there wasn't even a school like it. So, when I was in the business of teaching Drama at the Theater in Salt Lake in the morning, I was also teaching classes for the Relief Society and leading Dr. Charles F. Winslow and Dr. Jeter Clinton in their studies as well. Dr. Winslow was the first cremated soul in Utah. We don't have time for all my lessons while you are here this summer, but you may go take another look in the pantry if you like. She patted my hand as if saying thank-you for being here with me and stacked the plates together for me.

We had just finished our breakfast, and as I walked past the kitchen window, I saw the young man who came to work in the yard; William. His arm was in a sling, and I could tell his devotion to a particular, weed was getting the best of him. I sped out the screen door, sighing as I went, "be right back," and came right under the hoe, grabbing the weed at the root and gave it a good yank. Great-grandmother was standing at the back porch door and shouted loudly, "Good morning, William, bring me that arm."

As he came over, he limped as well. He strung together quite a few passionate long sentences and then leaned into Great-grandmother and whispered something.

"I can't understand you there is no need to whisper," I said.

Great-grandmother and William both smiled, "You are quite right, William, it is not a break, it is worse than a break, and I'm glad you had the wisdom to sling it." Great-grandmother went to the pantry and pulled a jar off the shelf at hand level, she brought it over and handed it to me. I opened it, because of course, it was too difficult for her to keep the grip and because she didn't want William to try to open it. It smelled very strong. As I was shaking my head with disgust and utter amazement, shivers running down my spine and welling up in my gut.

She said, "Asafoetida; a fetid nasty tasting herb but it's an incredible medicine; used mostly on animals." William smiled. "It is used for many ailments in animals internally and externally but mostly for humans, we use it on top. William is a bona fide Chief Walkara great-grandson, and he is quite the animal lover. He can speak English well enough but prefers his Native tongue. He was one of the spry young bucks out there last night wrestling with bulls and broncos. He does it *every year*, and it makes him a bit of money.

"William smiled again and said something else. She smiled and continued, "And it gives the girls great cause to see how handsome he is." Great-grandmother laughed. They had both been sitting at the kitchen table. William said thank-you, leaned over and kissed Great-grandmother on the top of the head and tipped his imaginary hat to me and said "Good-day." Then he left.

"Where were we?" great-grandmother asked. "Oh, yes, the pantry. I think we should take our tea and some for William and sit in the shade, now."

I helped get her comfortable, took William his tea and took a bit of milk to Mademoiselle. When I got back to Great-grandmother, she was snoozing soundly under her beautiful straw bonnet. I went to where William was working and asked him how his arm was feeling? He said, "The old woman is very good. I have no pain now. I like it here. Do you like it here?" He had a beautiful deep accent, he was very handsome.

"Yes, I love it here. I am very fond of the 'old woman'.

She is my great-grandmother. I will be very sad to leave in 33 days." He looked over his shoulder at me.

"Are you Mary's grandson?" I asked.

"Yes. Mary is my grandmother, and your Great-grandmother was the person who took care of me. My father went to the talking wars in

Japan, and he did not come home. I am 50 years old now, and I have a small family in the meadows of Ephraim. But I stop here to see my good friend and medicine woman. She helped my Father get born and two of my aunties. My Grandmother passed the way of the falling leaves last year. She was 104 winters old. The old woman helped me say goodbye in a good way. She is a beautiful woman.

"My family will be glad when she is gone to see Brother Joseph and Brother John Young. He was a very handsome man. They were good for each other. She was his other skin, and he didn't want to leave her.

"Stupid church. I have many stories from my people that make us sad. The old woman is wise in a medicine way. Thank-you, for the tea. It is a pleasure to know you and to know you love the old woman. Don't be sad for her to go home she misses her other skin, and she is very cold, (he touched his heart) without it."

He finished his work and left in his quiet way. I walked to the small orchard in the back and picked some apricots and a couple of sprigs of asparagus. I reflect now on the silent presence of peace and tranquility that surrounded me on her property and the curious way that as I walked and looked about I was fed as if the air and the earth were feeding me through my awareness and my senses. I remember looking at my hands and wondering if the skin was aging as I looked at it. I wondered what responses were going on in the trees and grass. And if when I visit later would the plant life remember me? I felt the crisp asparagus as I chewed and considered its cells and thanked it for its life, and I felt connected and happy like I was being fed some super awareness. When I came back, great-grandmother was ready to finish the story of the city called Joseph and her family there.

CHAPTER 19

Midwifery and Pots of Gold

"It was so warm and beautiful in the mornings. When I woke from my little quadrant of the floor upstairs, I could hear the soft snoring of my family in their different places. The boys always slept in the barn. Rhea was thirteen and stayed with her mother. Sarah had Rhea when she was 48 years old and Edward when she was 50. She was getting ragged around the edges, and Brother Joseph made sure she didn't do anything she didn't need to do. The struggles of the new life the Zion and the struggles in Nauvoo had caused a sad and powerful aging condition in almost everyone. Brother Joseph was timeless and endless. Sometimes he reminded me of what it might be like to be 'God', going from village to village giving love and encouragement to others.

"Brother Joseph took Sarah, Rhea, and the boys back to Salt Lake the next Friday, and it was the last time Libby, and I saw Sarah alive. Her leaving was difficult for me, and I missed her as I was waving goodbye on the hill. We had a family tradition to walk and watch as the wagons were leaving, waving as they drove out of sight. Having the Home set up and the water running was a real luxury. I had such a warm love and compassion for her help and felt the love and sacrifice she had given for our family. She passed in the Fall. Libby and I inherited Edward and Rhea. Their help in raising the family was vital as things progressed.

"I wondered when I would be called to go with the Medicine man. But he didn't come back until Brother Joseph arrived two weeks later.

"One of the gifts of a medicine man is his ability to remember how things occur for his people. He is like a record maker. In the beginning, they lived by word of mouth and only some things were recorded. The markings on the cliffs in the 9-mile canyon and in Fremont are probably an artist's graffiti left by someone who had the passion for painting and leaving their mark on the settlement."

"The night that Brother Joseph returned with the wagons Chief Arapeen's son was waiting for him in the yard. I think he had been waiting for his return and watching so when he got close to the farm he could race ahead of brother Joseph and deliver his message. He said he would be back in three days to get me."

I interrupted her with, "Great-grandmother, weren't you terrified?"

"Oh, for sure there were things I didn't understand, and I surely didn't trust the dark-skinned creatures, but over time I had become familiar with their calm un-displayed emotions and the talent they had for reading ours. They have an uncanny way of reading the bodies language and measuring the way we behave. I was relieved that Brother Joseph was back with us.

"Brother Joseph brought young John Young and two excavators to pitch a line over the mountain for a road into Kanab for better travel south which later became Arizona. After the Monroe Highway, which became Highway 89, they were to chase another line over the summit at Daniels pass and into the Uintah Basin calling it the East Highway, which later became Highway 40. That road would join the trading post in Whiterocks with Denver, Colorado.

"So, I had three days to get my things in order and then I would be learning another medicine for my family. The fear I had was more about how I would be able to learn everything quickly so I could get back to my home and gardens and family.

"Brother Joseph arrived from Millcreek Friday evening about dusk. He was so happy to be home. On Saturday morning, I packed a picnic and loaded myself onto the excavation wagon with the men, leaving Rachel and Hyrum with Libby. We headed up the mountain. The men where to stake out the first trail over the mountain and I to find the last of the herbs I wanted to take with me for my new training. Mountain echinacea, juniper, rosemary, mountain raspberry and lemon mint were important for my first attempt at getting Mary to stay pregnant. I was also gathering fresh red willow and thistle for blood cleansing, primrose, for nerves and composure. I knew I was in for an exciting time.

"I was fishing in the water for some roots of the snake-grass when I saw something very shiny in the bottom of the pooling water. I reached in and brought it up to my eyes. The nugget of gold was astonishing to me. It is the same one on the dresser in the attic. That was the first piece of gold I had found in nature, and it was smooth and glittery, soft, and hard all at once. I was calling out loudly for Brother Joseph and realized they had moved up the mountain further than I had expected. I put the nugget in my small pocket that was inside the larger pocket, where I put my ring when I was making bread or pulling weeds, and though I was curious about how much more was in the pool I wanted to get Joseph's attention on it first.

"I was coming up the incline with a large bundle of red willow when I was struck with sharp piercing fangs of a Rocky Mountain Rattler."

She reached down and lifted the hem of her summer dress so I could see the marks in her skin that I had seen before, and I saw above them the cut she had made with the stone from the stream, and she continued right on,

"I kicked it off and dropped the bundle of red-willow on it screaming at the top of my lungs to get the brethren's attention and then immediately reached into the water for a sharp rock slicing the area below my mid-calf deep enough to cause a good flow of blood. The rattler had started moving away up the incline not attempting to attack again but as young John was the fastest down the hill he approached seeing the snake and hitting it in the head and knocking it out, he felt it safe to wring its neck. As it was dying, I asked him to preserve it for me. I planned to use the venom to help heal myself. And I had to forfeit my picnic idea.

"We quickly gathered my herbs and headed down the hill in the wagon. After arriving at the house, I was fevered, and I knew I was losing time so I milked the venom left from the rattler's fangs and put a few drops in some cow's milk and drank it down. After about an hour I was sick as-a-dog, but I could tell that the magic of the venom I had ingested would soon be enough, and I would shortly be sweating out the vicious toxins.

"I can see by the way you are looking at me that you are shocked. I wasn't sure it would work either, but I knew from my studies in France that the process had been used before and that the antidote for most disease or illness is exposing the immune system to its properties. So, I had my first real-personal shot at trusting what I had learned, and it was on myself. That really gave me the courage to go out and deliver my remedies to the world.

"The whole experience with the medicine man was far more alive than we have time for tonight. Let us go eat dinner and maybe we can cool off in the house.

I interrupted her vibrant delivery as I helped her rise from the lawn chair with, "Great-grandmother, how did you bring yourself, after making your home in Joseph so perfect and inviting, to leave and come here? It seems like the area where you had made your home in Joseph was much friendlier than here, and it had natural abilities that aren't here; like hot springs and streams with fish and gold.

We had fresh cooked asparagus, mashed potatoes, with creamy white gravy and fresh apricot pudding with cream on top for dinner. I can hardly write about it without tasting it and tearing up. The things we smell and the things we taste bring far more presence to our experiences. I still miss my beautiful grandmother to this day, so very much.

I had cleaned up the dinner and washed the table off. As I was walking back to write my thoughts down in my journal. Great-grandmother called me back to her room.

"Sometimes in our life, we have things that stand out like they are so different from everything else. There was a dessert I had in Spain that was like nothing I had ever had and never will have again, but it is so choice that my mind cannot forget it. I will never encounter it again, but that dessert shaped me in a way that I continue to be. It was so delicious and so tart that I could not stop tasting it. I have no idea how it was made or what it was made from, and its color was so fascinating at the same time. So, my way of being was shaped by curiosity and intensity. I want you to consider that the roads and the cities have been shaped by your grandfathers and that some of the choices for development create the desire or, you could say the desserts, that have been forgotten or displaced. It took hundreds and thousands of years for the rolling hills of France to become what they are today. It has taken lifetimes of study for us to know and trust some of the medicines we have derived from mother nature's resources. Your perfect brain is not confronted or tortured by the experiences you have. It is comfortable because that's it's design. What makes us uncomfortable is simply the way we choose to interpret our experiences. You have the strength to shape your resources and your experiences, and it is a matter of your conditioning as you move into adulthood and your choice whether you do or do not."

I embraced her passionately and went to my room. Sometimes because I was young and eager to be out-and-about I would read late or write in my journal all the things we talked about during the day but that night I was so tired. I slept like I was on a buckboard being throw from one side of the wagon to the other.

I started my period that night and when I woke I was covered in blood. Great-grandmothers profound message was lingering in my mind and body. It wasn't the first time I had my period since I had come to stay but it was the first time I had looked at it as if it was part of my own creation. She comforted me about the blood stains and sent me to the pantry for some hydrogen-peroxide and helped me clean the bedding up. She made a tea of desert-rose blossoms and put the tea in my bath water. As I walked from my room to the bath in the soft flannel robe she gave me to ware I felt like I belonged exactly as I was; short and soft and feminine. She said we would give the day a rest and stay close and comfortable all day and even nap if we got restless or tired. And I did.

In the evening after lunch and before dinner we were resting in the porch area on the east side of the house. It was screened in and a breeze was trying to get thru the small spaces in the screening. It was cool we had our tea and she had some ginger snaps we were sharing. My condition was the perfect segue into her subject.

She began with, "It would seem out of place in life for a young woman to walk into a tribe of savages and attempt to cultivate from it some kind of use or likeness. The world did not offer that kind of relationship opportunity for me but my beliefs about God and medicine did. An agreement to study with the savages was my way of accepting my future as well as acknowledging my indifference to the standards placed on society.

"In nature if your fear is bigger than your predator you will begin to lose before the attack occurs. Your mind is designed to care for everything even the unseen things. Like parasite's that live on certain life forms or organisms that are smaller than the eye can see. It happens though, that almost all antidotes for any abnormality is within arm's reach.

"Now, there are diseases being created by science that have powerful destructive properties but the nature of life itself is to live, so then the cure is somewhere in the science of the thing. I don't like that method of discovery and I feel it leaves a door wide open for evil pursuits, but my curious mind has always seen another possibility. What if the diseases I have are not yet present to you because you haven't yet been exposed, and if by exposure to these new diseases causes your immune system to fight and be even stronger than mine?

"I only concede to that thought when there is sufficient time to heal from the exposure. However, to be ignorant of the exposure is deadly. Like the snake bite. I became a message to others that everyone doesn't die from a bite and that it's possible to recover quickly by using the appropriate antidote. And having too much snake venom in your stomach will kill you as well.

"I learned so many things from the medicine man and I didn't record much of it but what I did scribble down was burned in the fire that took out our home in Joseph.

"The most important thing I learned though and most useful of all was the nature of nature and how when nature is respected she takes care of herself and she provides for those who gift her back for their taking. I left the village giving thanks for everything, everything has a life and a message to offer. If I listen I will hear its medicine, I will see its likeness in the patterns around me.

"Babies are a woman's parasite. The woman is infected by the nature of love-making and the growth can only exist inside as-long-as the space is safe. When the space is no longer safe the parasite removes itself the same way it got in. What is most curious is that the antidote for the baby is its father. He has been known throughout history to fear and kill his offspring not knowing what it is or how it came. Wars are interesting ways to kill offspring. This unruly nature inside nature occurs in several animal kingdoms where the mother protects her young from the father.

"What happened to the Natives here is explained by a certain kind of love for their creator which turned a woman's gift into a power.

"Women are feared and respected because they have a power men do not possess. Their people have created songs and dances and ceremonies to honor the life-giving power of the woman. Yet as time went by they also experienced a sense of super-power at how vulnerable women can be, how meek and soft. They have threatened their women that if they did not have the power they would be rid of them; like Mary Walkara with her husband.

"I helped Mary reverse her cycle so that she was fertile and then strengthened her uterus so it could hold onto the child longer. It took me months to satisfy my interests in their medicine. It wasn't just herbs. They use sound and vibration and darkness and color for their healing. I didn't want to go and I didn't want to leave when I left.

"While I was there I taught many of the things I learned to their medicine man. But he learned very little from me. What he got was more of an awareness of what we don't know and that as time goes on for the white man and his undying curiosity leads him to destructive paths, and that what he didn't know was just waiting for him to learn.

"The one thing that I gave their people that they did not consider is the need for comfort during delivery. The need for cleanliness, oh, not that they were dirty, but that the babies' needs were proportional to the strength of the delivery mother. And that the women of the tribe be given respect for looking out for each other, instead of creating distance and discomfort for an expecting mother.

"I gave the medicine man a-heads up on the smallpox and the chicken pox and rheumatic fever and started his people on the antidote for them. The antibiotic that they use to keep their system strong and healthy was around them but they did not know how to use it. Wild garlic is powerful antioxidant and it grows everywhere and red-willow is a blood purifier and the tea we call Brigham tea gives energy to their aging and children and hydrates them when they have had heat stroke or sunstroke.

"While I was gone, almost six weeks, my family came and went. Libby came to visit me, and Brother Joseph even brought young John Young. He was amazing and spoke enough of their language to arouse conversations with the braves. My Hyrum and Rachel were staying with me all the time but when Brother Joseph left Hyrum wanted to go back home with Libby so I let him. Libby was getting big and I knew I would be getting home in time to help her with her confinement.

"While I was training, we went to several camps and administered many remedies. I helped train one of their older women to deliver babies that were turned wrong in the birth canal and upside-down and we even delivered a foal for a mother horse that was being born with its back first; with a C-section. It was the chief's prize mare, and she was beautiful. She healed perfectly. He was grateful and rewarded me with my own horse and a beautiful blanket.

"The relationship we created was a very good thing. The Black Hawk War was about to break out and the conditions and terms of our stay in Joseph would be greatly questioned.

"I was needed for deliveries among the Saints and gentiles as well and the snake bites and remedies for infectious diseases was a constant demand. These things were on my mind but the lump of gold in my pocket was of considerable more weight. As soon as Brother Joseph came back with the next freight shipment, I gathered my courage and asked him to take me back up to the place where I was bitten. He said we would leave in the morning.

"I put together my picnic and climbed aboard the excavation wagon, again, and headed back to my water hole. When we arrived Brother Joseph asked the other men to go on and he stayed with me. I had pulled my basket off the wagon and he lifted me down like a ballerina, setting me on my feet and kissing my cheek for all the world to see. I blushed he said it looked really good on me. The driver clicked his cheek and the horses took off. The wheels grinding the gravel stones as they turned.

"I took his hand as he took my basket and I stopped him as he pulled me up close to his lean chest. I was so torn by my need to let him know about the gold and my insane desire to devour him. But he was more torn. He was so conflicted by my resistance, I saw a look of worry and caution in his eye.

"What's the matter," he muttered, as I pulled the nugget from my pocket and handed it to him. I started walking and talking excitedly at the same time. He was studying it and had put his teeth marks on it as well.

"I want you to see exactly where I found it and I haven't had a minute since I was here last to tell you." We climbed down the embankment and steadied ourselves in the water that had receded over the last two months' time. There in the bottom of the pool were several hundred little pieces of gold just waiting for us to gather them. I pulled from our picnic basket three clothes I had disguised as napkins. I put one in his hand and took the other two stuffing one in my belt and beginning to drop little pieces in the other. He was just looking at me with a questionable grin.

He said, "You are so constantly inspiring. You realize that there is no such thing as free gold anymore?

"Yes," I said but this isn't free it nearly cost me my life. If it hadn't been for the snake bite I would not have reached into the pool for a sharp stone and come up with this…" pointing to the gold in his hand. I also know that the Rhoads and Arapeen are protecting the gold from their mine for Brother Brigham's use in the church.

"Ok,' he said. "I get it. You really did learn a lot from that medicine man." Then he pulled me from the water and treated me like I was some kind of siren, intriguing him and beguiling him. He kept looking at me like it was the first time he had seen me and I was a mystery to him. He loved every second we were together and when we had filled the basket with our treasures he put some small pieces of mica on top of some red willow leaves to hide the gold beneath. Then he carried a few larger pieces of mica in his hands up the road to where we were picked up by the brethren as they came down the mountain returning for the night. Mica was often used to finish counter tops and thresholds of doorways.

"We went back again and again scouring the area for every evidence of gold. I went up alone and gathered pots of gold and stashed it and he cashed it in privately. He hid some of the gold and turned most of it into materials for our houses and for his neighbors. He was very careful not to draw attention or to create concerns for how he was achieving abundance. He was very, very generous. 70% of our findings went to the church. 10% of all we made was turned into tithing 10% we used to improve our circumstances and those around us and 10% we hid in safe and remote places.

CHAPTER 20

Roads and Railroads

"In 1861 when Brother Joseph and Brother young John went with the missionaries to carve the road to Denver he intentionally reported that the land was a wasteland. He talked to President Young and the way the world looked at the Uintah Basin was all the same, "valueless". Keeping the public's eye off the Basin kept the resources in the Natives and Church's hand. But we knew what was hidden in the valley and in the mountains and it was the cream of everything."

Great-grandmother rose from her chair very carefully and cautiously leaving me there in my reverie, to bask or to be bewildered.

Sitting in the cool of the porch and listening to her tell me the history of the world pulled me to the edge of my seat and I knew she was never going to give it all to me. I wondered how I could find out all the stuffing's that were getting dropped as we went along in her story.

She read my mind and said loudly and determinedly, "There's no way to get through it all, but there are some things that must be told.

I have no idea how you would ever tell these things to others so that they would benefit. I just know that you need to be the one to hear it.

"Would you like me to start dinner," I asked her?

"No," she replied, "Your Uncle William, your mothers' brother, is bringing us fried chicken and strawberry-rhubarb pie. He will be here in thirty minutes. He is bringing his wife and children.

"Oh, what can I do to help get ready?" I inquired.

"I suppose you can set out eight glasses for tea, bring in the sun tea from the table out back and put out eight plates and service for each." As I set the table I was very present to the value of family. I didn't know my uncle. I had met him at the family reunion five years before. His children, my cousins were completely foreign to me. I did not feel related at the moment to anyone.

Great-grandmother came from her room. She had refreshed and put on a new sun-dress and re-pinned her lovely hair. As she came towards me I could tell she was excited.

"William Gilbert is my grandson because his mother is your very own grandmother Delories, but he is also my son because his father is John Willard Young. I love him twice, once for being born to such a treasured life and twice for returning when he found his true-identity.

"I would like to take a trip to the cavern with you and William Walkara on Tuesday around 5: pm. When he gets here I will inform him and by then you should be done with your "moon" cycle."

I looked at her, raising my eyebrows and pulling back my chin. She smiled and said, "Doesn't your period come one time in a month?" I nodded my head, yes. As she continued, "Then it is a cycle governed by the moon, hence a "moon" cycle. I nodded my head again and said, "I like that better than 'period'."

My Uncle was a sharp-dressed man, his wife an elegant woman Miranda Smoot. She was a quiet woman and disciplined her children with a modest amount of guilt, very similar to my mother's way. Her children were quiet as well, at least the ones she brought with her. They had a married daughter and a married son; both living in Allredville or as some called it Spring City.

"My Uncle and his wife lived in Richfield about fifteen miles from where Great-grandmother had lived from 1859 to 1862. The four children my uncle brought with him were familiar with the little mansion. The older boys Clark, 16 and Calvary, 14 went to the cave to swim but the younger two were girls and wanted to go into the attic. Sally was 10 and Evangella was 8. Great-grandmother said we could go to the attic where it was cooler and get acquainted with each other, while she and the adults talked.

I let Evangella pull the handles for the stairwell and the switch for the light. We all giggled and had fun with the mystery of it all. They had already been instructed about the delicate care of RoseMary and treated her with the utmost respect. They talked about her aging marks in the porcelain paint on her fired face, and the smell and texture of her old clothes and shoes. We all sat on the floor in front of the library and looked at the children's books, with RoseMary the teacher from Honeybrooke, England and the books which were so old and quaint that I was mesmerized by them.

"The girls and I very quickly became good friends. Sitting on the floor and looking at us from a crows-eye view I felt so very much older and removed from their child-like expressions and chatter.

In the bed chamber, they showed no interest or signs of interest in what might be in the drawers. Evangella was curious about the stained-glass window. I lifted her up so she could touch the little blue birds. I was excited for the first time about being a big sister and wanted to meet

Clinton. I told the girls about him and that I wished I could see him now but I was so glad to be with Great-grandmother.

It was nearly 10:00 when they left. Great-grandmother and I went to the end of the walk in the front yard waving good-bye, and I stepped out into the road and walked a-ways waving to them and saying, "See you later! Thanks for coming!"

Great-grandmother was smiling and I'm sure missing her grandson already. It still wasn't dark out yet but I was very tired again and eager to climb into my soft feather bed.

On the way into the house I asked Great-grandmother if Mom or Dad called while I was in the attic. She said they had called and that mom was coming down on Friday night and staying over on Saturday. I was so excited about taking Jonny to the cave, and about seeing mom not pregnant but I was so excited about seeing my new little brother and my dad. I could hardly wait. I was curiously concerned about what Mom would really think about me now.

It was Sunday the 28th of July, we would go to church and have a long day of being tucked into boring things to keep me quiet. But Great-grandmother took advantage of every second with me now and I could tell she was getting worried if we would complete all the stories and lessons before my time was spent with her. Brother Kimball picked us up for Sunday school and dropped us off after. He picked us up again for Sacrament meeting at 3: pm. Sister Kay dropped off a meat loaf and some apple-crisp for our dinner and before I could clear off the table Great-grandmother had started with the story of the roads and railroads. She moved so fast thru the times that I was feeling left in the dust a couple times.

We talked until 9:30 and then she went straight from prayers to sleeping. She was out so sweetly by the time I came back with my pajamas on. I kissed her softly on her beautiful head and walked quietly to my room. Where I wrote until midnight trying to catch all the little things she had said.

"The day I showed Brother Joseph the gold we found, I conceived Jonathan my third son. He was born May 30th 1861. Between my conception of him and his birth a hundred things happened. His pregnancy was so fast I wasn't even ready for him when he came. Years later looking back on my life I could see a pattern…I would get pregnant and a billion little experiences would light up our world…maybe I was just more alert when I was pregnant…it went like this:

"We harvested all our crops and a calf was born. I was attending a birth every other week. Sarah passed away the last week in November of pneumonia. We left for her funeral and came back right away for fear of being caught in a winter storm. The weather was wonderful but Libby was days away from delivering her first child. I felt she would deliver between the 19th and the 28th. Brother Joseph came back with us. He spent hours fixing things up for the winter, teaching the boys everything there is to know about farm life. He found out while we were in Millcreek that I was pregnant again. He wondered if I was glad and if I could handle all of my responsibilities.

"Sarah's youngest children, Rhea and Edward came to Joseph with us to live. There was a lovely school house about a half mile from our home and Edward could drive the buggy back and forth for them to go to school. Libby had become very close with the school teacher. She was the daughter of Oliver Cowdery. Libby asked Joseph and I if Emily could marry into our family.

"Emily was considered a spinster because she was not married and 25 years old. We discussed the feasibility of her coming into our family. We all prayed about it and on Sunday the 30th of December Libby asked her if she would marry into our family and if she would consider

Brother Joseph an honorable husband. Emily was already prepared she said she had been given a message when Rhea and Edward had started coming to school that she would be loved by them as a mother, and that she needed to give them time and space to accept her as a teacher and a friend."

"Brother Joseph said he would go see President Young about it after Libby had delivered. At that moment, Libby started hard labor right there in church and we all started laughing about it. As we were shuffling everyone around and getting Libby into the buggy to return to the house, Edward came up and asked,

"What's so funny?" We all started laughing again much to Libby's chagrin, and she grabbed her belly and started breathing slowly and heavily, while Brother Joseph answered, 'Looks like you will be having a new mother.' To which Edward replied, 'Looks like a new baby to me.'

"Brother Joseph returned his comment with, 'And that…Gather the children please and see if you can get a ride home…'

"He was interrupted by Emily who said, 'I would be happy to bring them home. I will take them to my place and feed them all… and then bring them home about 5:00,' she said, with a question mark after it, and Libby nearly screaming.

"Yes, very well thank you,' Brother Joseph said as he hopped into the buggy and we took off. It only took fifteen minutes to get home but Libby was having one continuous contraction it seemed.

"I walked in the door set a pan of water on the stove and cranked it up while Brother Joseph got Libby out of her clothes and into her nightware for delivery. I had no more than said, "Ok, let's check to see how far along you are," when she began to involuntarily push. Brother Joseph jumped up and grabbed a pan as she hurled into it and I was fishing for a cord around the baby's head. She was fully engaged and the head was coming down the birth canal without any assistance. As Libby rested for half a second the head was continuing to slowly come down and in ten seconds another baring down pain came and she pushed so hard that the baby girl almost sped past me onto the floor. Libby's labor was all of one hour and five minutes.

"We missed Sacrament meeting but had our baby safe-and-sound.

"We had cleaned the delivery room (living room) up and Brother Joseph had already buried the placenta in the garden. We were all upstairs, where Brother Joseph had carried Libby. In her room with a happy sleeping baby, Libby was in heaven.

"The children arrived at 5:30, afraid of making any noise and went quietly as a mouse walking through the kitchen. Libby was already calling her little girl Virginia. The second the door opened and the children walked in Virginia started to cry. Libby said, 'She wants so see her family.'

"One by one each of the children came in to inspect their new baby sister. One by one Virginia checked them out and seemed to agree that it was true she was here and they were her siblings. But when Emily walked through the door to check her out she started to wail, and wiggle. Libby handed Virginia to me as she sat up to nurse her but the baby kept screeching and crying out. Emily began to leave and little Virginia cried even harder. I walked close to Emily and she started quieting down and when I handed Virginia to Emily, she was quiet as a mouse and Emily had tears running down her cheeks.

"Oh, baby girl,' she said, 'I have waited a lifetime to see you and hear you cry. You are so sweet. I love you, too.' Emily looked around the room and we were all very touched by the precious reunion that just occurred in our home. Brother Joseph asked if he could drive her home and Edward followed him in our buggy. At about 6:PM it was pitch black out so Joseph and Edward would be coming home in the dark.

They had a gasoline lantern that hung from a staff on the harness of Tad the lead horse. I saw them coming and opened the door for them as they returned. It was going to be very, very cold.

"We now had five children two of which were very capable of being adults.

"Wednesday Brother Joseph left for the city to speak with President Young and another pass at getting some of our gold exchanged. As it had been made illegal for anyone to possess gold he needed to find a silent partner that would be brilliant at keeping our secret safe.

"I trusted him completely and I had no idea who he had chosen for over four years. I later found out and was very grateful and surprised by his wisdom.

"The stretch of roads that were built were funded by volunteer labor and a few tithing and tax dollars. The roads were created mostly of surrounding materials and by removing debris.

"Upon arrival in the Salt Lake City. Brother Joseph was called to go about the settlements and collect tithing and any surplus dollars. The Brethren had determined that they could get the railroad to come through Utah even if they couldn't buy statehood. The longest road in the state would be State Street: Highway 89. Running 501 miles from Page in the south to Garden City in the North it was carefully designed to go through the most occupied cities but missing St. George and side-by-side the railroad. And so, would Highway 189, being its alternate around the inner cities joining outer cities. They had also discovered that they could have their own inner state railroads and that they could use the rails to transport anything. Even though the iron horse was a new thing it was becoming a huge thing.

"At sixteen years, old Brother John Young became a powerful tool for his father, he was sent to every sight to inspect and to gather information for his father. He became Brother Joseph's right hand man as Brother Kimball had been taken from him for other engaging church matters.

"Brother Joseph Fielding Smith was kept in the mission field and directed the establishment of church offerings and organizing the church around the world. Joseph Fielding Smith's biggest effort was in Hawaii where he lived most of his life and caused great attraction to the church.

"Becoming a territory of the United States because of the efforts of the Mormon influence. He became the face of the church longer than any other living man. He was very unfamiliar with the politics of the nation or the church. He became a pawn for Heber J Grant and Wilford Woodruff and Franklin Richards son of Willard Richards.

"In the beginning, Utah was called the "State of Deseret" and became a territory in 1850 before I had even arrived. It didn't become a state until 1896. Though I know you have taken History in school, there are things about our states history that you won't learn in school because it would disturb the fragile nature of Politics. There were five other states granted statehood before us which had applied for statehood long after us, they did not qualify for Statehood and took significant acreage from our territory. We were the 45th State but we had applied for Statehood in 1851. There were 31 states when we applied and 14 were granted before us and of them 5 did not meet the qualifications for statehood, and to beat that we qualified upon our first request. But California, Colorado, Idaho, Montana, Nevada, Oregon, and Wyoming took portions of our territory to shrink us and to force us to refile our request for statehood again and again. You might ask the question; how could these other states obtain land we had already qualified for and secured title for?

"Brother John knew that if he turned the wealth of Utah into a substantial profit for the nation, the nation would be compelled to secede. The "Wedding of the rails" at Promontory Utah in 1869 which began in 1861 and that ended the "Pioneer Period" in 1869, was one of the biggest effects of President Lincolns term of congress. The Union Pacific and the Central Pacific covered over 1,776 miles of rail, but inside Utah alone were over 2000 miles of rails.

"By the time, John W. Young was twenty he had two wives and was well known in N.Y. as well as on Capitol Hill in D.C. By the time, he was twenty-four he had become a lobbyist and knew James W. Barclay, Andrew Carnegie, President Lincoln, J.P. Morgan, John D. Rockefeller, and several other tycoons who had money and sway. He was bold and dashing and a great thinker. He knew exactly what his father wanted and he went about to make it happen. If it had not been for the Black Hawk wars and the Anti-bigamy law the entire history of our state would have been so different. If it had not been for the debt the church was confronted with, in which they had to sell the very land the temple sat on and most all other church grounds, the church would have been an empire not a statehood.

"We received a letter on January 6th of 1861, that Hannah had also taken ill and that Brother Joseph and her sons would be looking after her for a while. The letter came at the hand of young John Young, with an accompanying letter to Emily. In which Brother Joseph explained that it was not his desire to cause discomfort to any member of his family, and definitely not to her. If she was still desirous of the arrangements we had all talked about, he wished for her to take comfort in his family while he was away and that he would be returning as soon as he felt that Hannah was properly cared for. He informed us that we would be moving Hannah to Ogden and that my parents would be taking over the management of the Millcreek home. Until further notice he was a humble undeserving man, in the service of God and his fellow brethren. He signed it sincerely Brother Joseph F.

"Few of the Saints knew that there was a weasel in the hen house (the church) and that modifications for statehood would come from major compromise, something Joseph Smith did not believe in or condone. The idea of giving up principles for standards was unthinkable and considered a violation of integrity and honor; a violation of priesthood law.

"One of the creations of wealth was through the genius of Brother Joseph Fielding and his design to keep the funds from gold separate from the government. It was apparent to him that all developments would be confiscated and distributed by the agents hired by political anarchists. So, keeping the gold findings and the silver and some copper privately controlled was his way of assisting the church and his family.

"John W. Young was a rich man he didn't need the church's money for his housing in N.Y. while he was a lobbyist, but he wasn't going to let them use him up as a lobbyist and keep him from his properties in Utah for free. There volumes of trouble in the attempts to "buy" congress. But paying the wage for his services and the attempts to "buy" congress, would not be coming out of his own pocket while the church was forfeiting their inheritance.

"As early as 1878 he no longer called the church "the church" anymore he called it the "committee". He had lost all hope in having a sovereign state after being excommunicated for not giving up his wives. The "committee" so rejected him, but because he was the son of Brigham Young they would not publicly deface him. But they hated him for trying to keep his wives and the right to religious practice. President Cleveland knew him as "the respectable polygamous, the only man I have met who would hold his head high and be proud and honored to be married so." The church didn't want any more embarrassment or association to their name with polygamy anymore. It was exhausting to Brother John and he felt betrayed like the Prophet Joseph Smith.

"You will find a Railroad Pass in the denim box for Brother J.T. Skinner, Signed by your Great-grandfather John. W. Young. The passes were one of the benefits of providing services to the Railroad and to John's other business opportunities, or to his family. He was a very kind and a generous man. He had been involved in tithing collection since he was ten years old, according to Amasa Lyman in his presence, John W. Young was ordained an apostle when he was ten years old, with his brother Alphonzo and then again in front of the "council of twelve" when he was twenty-four. He had been the official record keeper when he was called to be President of the Salt Lake Stake in 1868 for six years. In 1866 on July 1st Joseph Fielding Smith was given Amasa M. Lyman's place in the council of the twelve. Never had anyone been removed from office because of location in the history of the church. Amasa had gone looking for the relation of the Natives and the Prophesy made by Brother Joseph Smith that the Lamanite would construct and lay the cornerstone of the New City Zion.

None of the priesthood records for John W. Young were acknowledged after he was excommunicated and the church was left to believe that he was an apostate and had given up his priesthood.

"I was set up here, in Kaysville by then and it was easier because of him for me to get around and be of service to my people.

"I had my own ways of making an income for our family. When we were in Kanab I had accumulated respect from the community and taught four-hour days at school, while Libby watched the little ones. We had a lovely home and marvelous gardens. Rhea and Edward would share the load every day. When the road was completed from Page to Garden city Brother Joseph had moved us to Kaysville. The house here was just a stick frame.

"We had moved our things two weeks after Duke, our fourth child drown in the Sevier River. He was playing near the edge of the creek while we were visiting the cite ordained for Orderville. He was fourteen months old. I had moved him three time away from where he kept trying to get in with the older children. Then Brother Joseph got in the water with him and splashed and played. I had never been as happy a mother as I was to see them playing so.

"Before we went to sleep in our tents, he took my face in his little hands and said, "Mommy, wub, woo. Wub, Hym, wub, Achee, wub Pa." I scrunched him and squeezed him and tickled him. Then he continued, "Wub Ed, wub, Weea, wub, Wibby, wub Vit, wub Pa. He had not talked much before that. I tickled him again and I said, "Did you find your little voice today." I tucked him into his place near me and turned over to check on Rachel and your grandmother Sarah Delories who had been asleep for about twenty minutes. She was four months old. Then I went to Edward's and Hyrum's tent to tuck them in. Rhea was staying in Libby's tent and Brother Joseph was still at the campsite with Brother John Taylor and Willard Richards. When I came back in my tent Duke was gone. I dashed about frantically calling his name and grabbed a lantern from the yard and ran to the river. His diaper was on the bank. I screamed at the top of my lungs I could see him floating in the water about a hundred feet down the River. The water was only three feet deep in most places, but he was floating faster than I could swim. I tried anyway but it was Brother Joseph who ran along the bank and fished him out. We took him to Salt Lake and buried him next to Alfonso."

Great-grandmother paused and took a silent moment, breathing slow and softly as if to wash again a memory of life and suffering from her mind. Then very slowly she started again with a refreshed voice and clarity.

"My mother and Father were established in nice little cottage that had been where Hannah and Sarah lived before the house in Millcreek was built. Brother Joseph's older son lived with his wife in the Millcreek home. My parents were such comfort and support for us. Hyrum, Rachel and I stayed with my parents. Libby and Emily stayed in Millcreek. I hadn't seen Mother Eliza since Sarah had passed away and it seemed the only time we spent any time together it was over a death in the family.

"On the way to Salt Lake we passed this farmland which Brother Joseph had bought. I felt such a strange responsibility for Dukes passing.

It was like he was saying good-bye to everyone while he was holding my face.

"The lake on the west side of the valley made me cry. For so long I could just feel his little cold hands on my cheeks and touching my eyes. I finally told myself that Alphonso needed him more than I and that he had come to take Duke to play in the waves of heaven.

"It was my little Duke running in the willows that caught my eye and drove me to the lake and the cavern. I had been so busy I hadn't paid any attention to myself. When I slid into the opening I was so excited. I knew it wasn't actually Duke running but I really believe he loved the water and wanted me to love it again. I could tell that others had used the space. I could hardly wait for Brother Joseph to bring in a freight load, so I could bring him up there. I waited for him. I didn't want to take the children near the water again without him. I seriously needed to give up my pain.

"I want you to know that now I actually think it was Duke running and showing me the way.

"I want you also to know that I had become so appreciative of Libby and Emily. They had become the resources of health and happiness. They both treated me very sweetly and gave me respect and always requested agreement on their projects. Emily got pregnant about the time we arrived in Kaysville. She had taken to teaching again in the small school house in Kanab and then in Mona about two miles from us. While I taught the upper education in Nephi. I took fifteen-year old Rhea and little Sarah with me for four hours and Emily took her new baby James, he was born in April, Edward was thirteen and Hyrum was seven. Libby kept Rachel to play with Virginia. Libby was tending the house and the gardens and the laundry and planting trees with Brother Joseph.

"We had from the end of June until school began the first week in September to get everything ready for winter. Emily found an old friend at church from her youth at church and they became good friends. Rebecca Whitehorse's husband had left for the gold in California and never came home. She had waited for five years with her parents, heart-broken, when she got official divorce papers from him. She decided to give herself to work and became a maid at the Nephi Livery and Stables. She worked for a good man there and went to church every week. She lived in an eight by ten-foot room and paid for it by washing laundry for the manager and his wife. Her earnings she was putting away for her future. When Rebecca met the family, she fit right in.

"Soon Emily asked the question. I, of course, had seen it coming. It was the first time I heard Brother Joseph complain, 'I want to know why an old man like me would put up with a brood of girls like you?'

"I hit him on the shoulder and said, "We will keep you young as long as you want. I'm the crankiest and most boring of us all."

"To which Libby, Emily and he agreed, and I hit him on the shoulder again. He raised his eye brows and said, 'Don't expect me to give in all the time, you have been very old lately.'

'To which I said, "You're right and I want to make it up. Lets' invite Rebecca to come over Saturday after work and we can all go to the cave." They were all very agreeable.

"Brother Joseph then told us he would be going to Salt Lake on Tuesday and check on Hannah and then be back by Friday with another freight load.

CHAPTER 21

Trip to the Cave with Great-Grandmother

Monday morning Great-grandmother and I watched as a dust-storm built itself into a massive looming being, getting lower and lower and causing no visual access outside and inside. There was a sense of waiting and wonder. Soon the window sills were covered with dust thick enough to write in. At about 3 pm we were cleaning up the dust with rags and polishing different items with soft steal-wool. Inside the glass cages, there was a film of soft dust as well.

In the bottom of the biggest bureau was a delicate wooden box. It was obvious that it required a key to open it and that it was very precious. It was graciously ingrained with opal and ebony; the pattern was of ivy and dogwood blossoms. There was a very beautiful flying "V" that had streams of turquoise and amethyst running through it.

Inside the pantry where the doors had been shut there was very little dust, and it only took about half an hour to clean it up. We took a little hike up to the attic and as I expected the dust was almost nil in the bed chamber, but the hardwood floors needed dusting. I loved Great-grandmothers respect for the dust and the tenacity to keep working until it was completely cleaned up.

When we were coming down the stairs, I said, "I hope that doesn't happen often." I carefully watched her finish dusting the last few steps of the ladders and slowly go to her chair by the window.

She looked at me and said, "Occasionally the Earth needs new particles from distant places, and they are moved from their places by wind and rain from the clouds. We will soon have a rainstorm that will help energize the dust particles and create definition in color and depth and some new plant life."

We had an early dinner and then sat and watched as the sun became very red and beautiful while she told me the story of her confession to Brother Joseph as she sat in her favorite overstuffed chair in the living room facing the big picture window.

Then she started back at the beginning it seemed;

"A two-year mission was an idea that came after the Mormon Battalion came home, well most of them came home, many stayed in California and created possible incomes of gold for their families. But the mission fields were actively used as a resource for growth. Many of the converts were seen as assets because of their education and abilities: carpenters, printers, masons, iron engineers, architects, artists, sculptors and every manner of the craftsman was sought after.

"Even a steamboat captain was recruited for the 'City of Corinne' a steamboat that floated a restaurant and an entertainment club out on the Great Salt Lake and then they built one on the Utah Lake. The materials for the 'City of Corinne' came by way of St. Louis in January of 1871. The great 2-ton ship was 150 feet long. In the fall of

1871 a large hotel was constructed at Lake Point to accommodate and attract people from around the world. Corinne was bought in 1873 by a gentleman who used it for field trips and research on the lake. Then in 1875 your grandfather John W. Young bought it with the idea of entertaining diplomats and congressmen. In September of 1875 myself and your grandfather and the future president of the United States, James A. Garfield were aboard the entertainment ship having a splendid time when I suggested it be renamed 'General Garfield.' We broke a bottle of wine on the bow of the boat, and the future president gave a marvelous speech. We had the time of our lives. We knew it would be humiliating to the people of Corinne because the entertainment was suggestive and the parties wild with liquor. Then in 1904 someone set fire to it and burned it to ash. They have never reconstructed a boat like that.

"Let us go back to 1854 when I was newly arrived in Salt Lake.

"I was very preoccupied with my work and very present to Brother Joseph's wives' abilities. They were part of our immediate Relief Society Quorum and Hannah had trained and developed so many of us with talents over the years. One evening we were making quick tied blankets for relief packages, and we heard that a two-year mission was being called in England to wrap-up the printing business there and to create a church printing establishment in Zion. Hannah forthwith said, "I know Joseph will be going because he is so reliable and knows the people and country so very well, but sister Eliza I really need to be here assisting with the Relief Society. I pray I am not called to go with him, perhaps Sarah would like to go?"

"Sister Eliza nodded her head as if understanding her request but not having a knowledge of who would be chosen. I walked out with Sarah and asked her what her thought in the matter was? She sighed and said it would be hard for her to leave Rhea and Edward because they were only six and four. But what the Lord wanted her to do she would have the courage to do. As I walked her home, I felt so apart of their family. I was only fourteen, but I was always so certain of myself.

"We heard footsteps and turned to see Brother Joseph and Brother Heber walking towards us. As they approached, I said, "We heard that the Council is calling a mission to England to acquire a good Print Master, and most likely you have been chosen, Brother Joseph, for that mission. I hope you stop in to see my father and tell him we are doing well and that I miss them?"

"He said, 'Why sister May I would be delighted to do just that I think we will be there to capture your father and bring him safely to Zion.'

"I didn't know whether to sing or cry…my heart was racing right out of my chest. He was just so intoxicating to me.

"Oh, please. Please bring him back. I want him here so desperately." The conversation had shifted a bit, and Brother Heber and Sarah were talking about the possibility of no wives going on this particular mission. I reached for Brother Joseph's hand and realized too late what I had done…so covering my mistake, I said. "I love my family so much, and I miss them dreadfully, but I love you also. I want to be with you eternally,' and I pray you be very careful while away for so long…' and as I said it I looked into his lamp-lit eyes and saw what I thought was true kindness but also attraction…I believed he understood me, and I made it mean that he loved me the way I loved him. But I didn't see him for two years, three months and twelve days. It was awful having him away, and I would constantly ask Sarah how she could stand it. By the time, he returned I was sixteen, and I had waited longer than anyone I knew to be with the man who was my soul-mate and eternal companion. After-all for me, I had been waiting since I was five. So, for me it was nine whole years.

"Sarah had pretty much figured it out, but I wasn't answering any of her questions about it. I wasn't withholding from her to keep her in the dark, but to keep myself in check and I think somehow there was a fear that if I shared my ultimate desires, some other power would stand in the way of me achieving those desires."

That could have been Great-grandmothers segue into the Ball-of-all-balls, but instead it was her segue into what seemed to be her love of entertainment and the arts and her transition from Brother Joseph to John W.

At 5 pm William showed up in his pearly buffed truck. He looked like he came prepared for the day as if he already knew what we had planned. He picked up the basket and Great-grandmothers wicker chair in one hand and her parasol in the other. Then he looped his arm into the crook of her arm as if they would be taking a stroll. I had two towels and a sun bonnet on.

As we crossed the dirt road in front of great-grandmothers little mansion, I turned back to look at the stained-glass windows and wonder about the architect who built the house. I wondered too how so many people lived in that five-bedroom house.

I knew it had been less than a week since I had been to the cavern, but I was amazed at how tall the cattails and bulrushes had grown. As we cleared the south-end of the lake, the grasses were about a foot taller than me, and William could barely see over them when he stood on his toes. The path had been mostly preserved by the years and years of constant wear, and it was so fun to be hidden from the world's view and to be so close to perfectly content and passionately connected to my surroundings. The dragonflies and the damselflies were having a blast darting in and out between us. They were like friendly dervishes chasing us up and down and around.

Great-grandmother was like a magical muse bringing music and love to everything. She walked ever so carefully and not so fast as to wear herself out. When we reached the dry incline, where I first detected the echo of the cavern, she stopped and turned back to look over the valley from the north to the south. She let her eyes rest on the house and then said thank you to William for helping her make her final trip to her sanctuary. He smiled at her and said, "For you, my lady I could move the moon." His accent made him sound so loving and romantic. He was so gentle and respectful.

I had created the sport of shooting bottle rockets, that's what I called them, from the heads of the echinacea coneflower that grew among the bulrushes. Sometimes I would hit the side of my shoe so perfectly that the head would fly up into the air about thirty feet and then fly out over the water of the lake plopping down into the still water. I had been messing around with my project, trying to achieve the greatest distance into the lake with the biggest ker-splash while William and Great-grandmother were taking the last hundred yards to the cave. As I stepped from my arsenal deployment position on the hill I saw them stepping down onto the first step, I had a feeling in my gut that I was missing something, and I ran as fast as a could to catch up. I almost slid into the turn like a home run.

"Well, young lady, I don't see any point in taking the tom-boy out of you. You are just too good at it. I suppose you are ready for a good swim about now?"

"Yes, mama!" I said. "Can't wait, well, I mean I can hardly wait."

"And that, you shall, my dear."

William set up her wicker chair on the terrace incline as I pulled off my shirt and jeans with my swimming suit under them. Great-grandmothers swimsuit was old fashioned and covered her long garments. She had put it on before we left the house and then covered the swimsuit like I did with her clothes.

I went over and pushed myself off the drop-off into the cool water. When I resurfaced, I saw William holding Great-grandmothers dainty hand as she stepped down onto a set of steps that I hadn't seen or experienced before. She must have been a great swimmer at one time in her life. She sat on the steps watching me and waiting for William to take off his shoes and shirt. He placed his shoes neatly together and set his folded shirt on top of them and then pulled off his overalls, carefully folding them and putting them on top of the others. His long boxer-like shorts were definitely ancient swim trunks; from the olden-days. He then dove into the water and came up on the south side of the pool, slowly moving towards Great-grandmothers side taking her hand again and watching her closely as she submerged into the deep waters. She gracefully swam about ten minutes and then went back to her wicker chair and put the towel I had brought for her, over her wet clothes and rested while I continued to swim.

William sat on the steps and didn't say a word. I was at peace with everything and swimming my own little Olympian marathon. It had been at least thirty minutes I could see that Great-grandmother was napping soundly, and William was basking in the cool of the cavern. As I was returning from the hollow east-side I heard these distinct words, "It is time, you will know soon." Somehow, I knew it was Great-grandfather, and I knew that something was going to be revealed soon. I paused in the depths of the water and wondered what I had been asking about the most. When it occurred to me that he might not be talking to me.

"I think it will be about 106* outside about now, and we shall have our lovely little picnic right here," Great-grandmother said in soft across the water voice. She waited for me to dry my hands and then handed me the little table cover to lay out on the sand. There was just the perfect beach like space for us to have our sandwiches and our tea, and the ginger-snaps she had thrown in at the last minute.

When we came up from the cavern to the open sky and the humming of the crickets and chirping birds, I knew we would be back at the house all too soon. As we reached the flat echoic surface, I remembered the box on the far north wall. I turned on my heel and ran back as fast as I could, grabbing it off its little shelf. Great-grandmother and William hadn't made a pause. When I came up beside her and showed her the box, she smiled at it and rubbed her long delicate fingers across the beautiful V. She had a tear in her eye as she said, "You may bring that to the house, dear."

When we reached the edge of the field and the road in front of the little mansion, there was a crescent shaped moon waiting in the east for the darkness. William helped us in with the basket and chair and then took off in his pearly polished truck, while I was standing in the middle of the road shouting, "Hurry back now!"

Great-grandmother turned slowly in the door frame and went to her room. I was combing her hair when she said, "Upstairs in the extra room is a cedar-chest with a box in it that looks very much like the one in the curio. You may go get it. Hand me the little slate box before you leave."

I handed her the little box and nearly ran upstairs. I could not hold back I had wanted to see this room for two weeks now. I slowly opened the door and to my surprise, it squeaked, and when I stepped onto the floor it squeaked again. It was so strange to me that the craftsmanship of one room in the house should be so much more divine and exotic than the others. The bed was a cedar-pole bed, and there was a hand braided rug on the floor beside the bed. The walls were unfinished cedar planks with beautiful old color, and there was a distinctive smell in the air of pine or cedar. The beautiful stained-glass window drew me in, and as I was looking out it, I realized that the room on the other side would be completely undetectable from this room. I opened the cedar-chest latch, and it opened very gracefully. There in the bottom was a box just like the one downstairs. On the top was a large and elegantly crafted 'W' with blue-lapis, mother-of-pearl, and coral colored tigers-eye stone, inlaid in such mastery that in this room it was completely out of order.

I started down the stairs, and as I took the first step on the landing to shut the door behind me, there was an echo in the stairwell coming off the wall, and I could hear the clock ticking downstairs in the living-room. On the other side of the stairwell against the wall I pressed my ear to listen to the bedchamber on the other side. There was a mysterious amplifier that would allow someone upstairs to hear the sounds coming from the downstairs. So many ways to send messages I thought and to protect the ones you love.

I skipped into Great-grandmothers bedroom and set the box beside her. She put the key that was in the slate box into the cedar-box and it open with the "Skaters Waltz" playing. Great-grandmother put her hand to her lips and breathed in a breath of awe. She started to cry: tears I had seen before that she had a masterful power to suppress were now unleashed. I went to her side and gently caressed her shoulder. Then she took her handkerchief and carefully dabbed her eyes and nose.

"This is the only mystery I have not solved. There were so many little things that John left me to figure out. Your Grandmother Deloris had him make these two boxes while in New York. She was there with him so often. He told me that someday when it was safe I would find the key, and so you have! In New York being a polygamous was not such a dangerous thing as it was in Utah. I had come to believe that I would never know what was in this box and because it was so sacred I chose not to tell your mother or uncle William that these were theirs until the key was found.

Inside the box was a blessing gown worn by Uncle William when he was blessed and given his name. And a picture of him sitting on Grandfather's shoulder with a big grin, he was about ten months old, another one of him in his blessing gown with my grandmother Deloris and my grandfather, John W, another one with Great-grandmother holding baby William; probably taken at the same time. She was standing between to his mother and Grandfather John W. In that picture, it was very clear that Grandmother Delories was pregnant and very close to her delivery. On the back of the picture were their names and the date, taken: October 23, 1904. There was a sealed envelope and pair of women's white leather gloves; also in one of the pictures, worn by Grandmother Delories, and a pair of soft sole shoes also worn by baby William in the same picture.

Great-grandmother slowly and neatly puts the items back in the box and shut the lid carefully. Then she started to push it slowly toward me asking me to take it to her dresser and set it in front of the mirrors. "We will wait until Friday to see what is in your mother's box, and we will call your uncle tomorrow and ask him if he can come over on Friday or Saturday."

The boxes were created so magnificently that to destroy them just to discover the contents would have felt blasphemous.

Great-grandmother and I had said evening prayers almost as soon as we had come in the house. I could tell she was very tired and needed to rest. It had been a long day. When I left her room, I felt the presence of guardians watching over her. As I was going to my room I wished, I could go back to the cavern. In the reflection of the window on the porch was the big crescent moon with a tailing star that looked like it was dangling from the end. It was a happy moment. I was so curious about my mother's box.

CHAPTER 22

The Challenge of Authority

Great-grandmother slept so soundly the next morning that I was worried about her. I thought maybe I should call Brother Kimball. I sat at 9: am wondering quietly if I should try to rouse her. She was definitely dreaming I could hear her muffled expressions.

I decided to go make some eggs and toast with the strawberry and rhubarb jam; her favorite. I basted the eggs in butter with a little water and buttered her toast. She was stirring, finally and I could hear her now. I put a fork on her china plate and grabbed a small glass of milk to take in the room.

When I stepped to the edge of the bed she softly said, "Sometimes my dreams are as real as the daylight. I was swimming and laughing in the cavern with my beloved John, Delories, and Joseph was there with Libby and Sarah. It seems that I can hardly tell who is more blessed. I love them all so much for giving me the life I have." As she turned on her side, she reached for me. I gave her my left hand so she could swing her feet around and onto her prayer stool. "I see that our trip to the swimming hole made it impossible for me to make my morning prayers."

After prayers, she was starting again when I interrupted her somberly with, "Great-grandmother, what causes people to be so afraid that they give up what originally they would have given their life for?"

I had interrupted her before she got a word out with, "How can we make a difference if there is no one who wants to make the change. I'm so curious about the boxes and the amount of passion, sadness as well as anger that would have driven Grandma Delories clear to Mexico instead of staying to fight?"

She went to the 'water closet' to relieve herself and then she started toward the kitchen. I followed her with her plate and said, "These are getting cold. Would you like me to make you some new ones?"

"Oh, no my dear, they don't mind being cold at all. Just give me one minute here." She lifted the phone receiver from the hook and dialed Uncle Williams number. She told him she had a package that he would want to pick up as early as Friday or Saturday and that his sister Vanessa would be here Friday and stay until Saturday evening. She told him she loved him and could hardly wait.

I looked at her like, "Hey!" She laughed and said he would be here Saturday at 10:00 and then she looked at me like, "Hey!"

I shouted, "You heard the voice in the cavern!" she smiled big and said,

"Yes, I did. It was so simple I thought it was William at first, and then I saw them all singing inside the cavern with each other. They were singing, 'When the Light of the Morning.' She ate her breakfast and then went to dress herself.

"Call your mother." She commanded.

"I was just thinking that," I said.

"I know, so was I." She replied.

I went to call my mother and there was no answer. So, I went out and gathered the eggs and watered the chickens and turkeys. The geese were now my friends and the hen would often try to bad mouth me when the gander was coming up for petting. I loved every second with them.

I could feel the time winding down, and I had so many spaces in Great-grandmothers history that were missing. I wanted to stay at her place until she passed. I was creating ways to stay with her; changing school, talking mom and dad into it.

I picked enough asparagus for dinner and some mushrooms that were pleasantly popping their cream-colored heads out of the grass near an elm tree. The apricots were nearly all ripe, and I could see myself climbing the cherry-picker to get the bright red-freckled ones on the top of the tree that were facing the sun.

It was nearly noon when I put the eggs and veggies in the frig. Great-grandmother was sitting on the edge of her bed.

"I think we will sit in the living room until it cools off again. Would you like to make some sassafras tea?" She queried.

"Of course, I would," I said, and I hurried to put the cherry-red teapot on the gas stove to heat up.

"Great-grandmother, how did you fit all those people in this house?" I asked her as I was pulling the sassafras from the pantry shelf.

"It wasn't easy. When we left Orderville to take Jonathan Marmaduke, our little baby that drown in the Sevier river to be buried next to his older brother Alphonso we passed this place and Brother

Joseph pointed it out to the family. At that time, we were three wives and four children strong. With that kind of manpower, there wasn't much we couldn't do. We had several work projects to get the foundation to the house and barn done and then a couple more to set the walls and the roof. We got here the end of June, and before school started on the 5th of September everything was done inside, and the barn was complete. The following year we spent as much time getting the land ready for crops and planting the growth of trees along the south side and the orchards on the east side of the property.

"While we were in the city of Joseph, we established good connections with the Ute tribes and my ability to help extended into Kanab when we went there, and it also helped that I could speak their language. We created powerful support.

"While Brother Joseph was freighting things to us by wagon, young Brother John was causing beauty and cooperation everywhere. Before the first week Brother Joseph and young Brother John had conjured and surveyed the path for the railroad to come from Salt Lake to here.

She seemed so preoccupied by a thought that I waited and waited some more, then asked, "Didn't Grandfather John give you any hints of his affections while he was building your home?"

She came slowly back to me and said, "Even then I never saw young Brother John, as more than my brother. I know now he was very honorable considering his profound affections. He even had long and generous conversations with me about his own courting and the beautiful ladies who were interested in him, after all he was the Prophet's son.

"I know I always loved him. The presence of his vulnerability was obvious when he married his first wife. He married her but was uncertain about ever loving her. He knew he could be faithful, because he loved the Gospel more than Life but her character was a challenge to him. Later I saw how his questions of her character and her belonging were his attempts to get my approval of her. She was a challenge to me as well. I was mostly forthright, but I always felt he was worthy of a virtuous and compassionate woman and that she would be a wonderer, she was and her character rubbed off on their son, Hooper.

"There are two types of converts; those who are looking for the Lord and the values of the people, and those who are looking for a place to hide from something or to get away with something. Even in the Church, there were those who were hiding or withholding the truth about their personal agendas.

"The second type usually stays around long enough to get their fair share of praise and property and then they move on.

'But the first type consistently raised their children to be in service and to be kind to everyone and everything.

"As a people, we had that trait in common with many of the Native tribes. They saw our virtues and respected us. Many of Williams family came to watch and help us build our strange and massive homes.

"Some of the Navaho people also came to help. They were very curious and had been building a more stationary dwelling for hundreds of years. When the railroads came through they were even more curious and wanted to ride the iron-horses…

"You asked about how we fit all of us in here. My room was always my room until I moved to New York to be with my new husband, John W.

"Brother Joseph's room was the pantry. It was set up as an office for him. When it was my night, he would stay in my room. The room you are in was Libby's. Emily had half of the living-room. At that time the big picture window was two windows. Later the smaller windows were removed, and the big picture window was put in. About the time the house was finished the barn was finished. Edward loved the barn and so did Rhea. But they both came inside for the winter. They both moved into the attic, and so did half the surrounding tribes, move in that is. Many nights there would be fifteen or twenty Natives sleeping from the west door to the east door downstairs and some sleeping on the stairwell going up.

"One morning I found six new people living on the porch. I was so grateful for my family and our comfort that commenting on the tight quarters made no sense.

"The men who hunted for the food were very good at it, and we had a variety of venison and goat along with rabbit and fish. The women all fixed the food and always shared it.

"Keeping focused on the work that needed to be done was more about learning how to delegate the chores, and teaching others to give room for some error.

Great-grandmother had come into the kitchen. I could see that she was very tired and that she would soon be taking a nap.

The tea was made, and I took sugar and sweetened it up and then some ice from the icebox and cooled it down. Great-grandmother then followed me into the living room and sat in her big European over-stuffed chair. She looked so peaceful and comfortable. But I needed to know how to prepare for mom.

"How do you want me to set things up for mom and dad," I asked?

"If you turn that knob right there on the side of that cabinet a bed falls out it is quite comfortable. I think Jonathan will want the boy's room upstairs, and your uncle will not be staying the night. If he does, we will move you in here with me.

It was then that I noticed the way the living room was set up, and I could see that the hidden wall doors going from the pantry wall would close off the living room completely. With the pantry door shut and the hall door shut that room would be big enough for an apartment with a shared kitchen and the second bathroom easily accessible.

I let Great-grandmother sleep again and took a trip upstairs to see the beautiful things and to imagine how it would be to have children running up and down the stairs to the hall. The sealed door now made perfect sense to me and I could see how another mother could live up here very comfortably.

I then tiptoed out the back, and I could see how a family of six could close the shutters and lock down the porch like a fort or hut.

I ran to the barn and sped up the ladder to the loft, and I could see how there had been, four rooms up there, along time ago. A very strong old barn I was thinking with lots of memories. Each room had a ramp with a slide going down to the bottom level about 20 feet down and a fireman-pole to slide down. The pole was inside the room, and the ramps were on the outside so that whatever was stored up there could be pushed down easily.

I then wondered how many times my Grandmother, Deloris had slept in the cave, with her brothers and sisters? I knew there was a time when they were all hiding from the law and the Church. I knew from the letters in the attic that they were in constant fear.

I was getting the feeling that a large family had powerful benefits for the mothers, the fathers, and great opportunities for all the siblings. I could see Edward teaching Hyrum how to build chicken coops and how to dig the holes for planting trees. It was like an industry that was run on the power of love. It was so cool.

When I got back to the house, Great-grandmother was still sleeping, so I went to my room to write.

At 2:30 I woke up with a start and tiptoed again quickly to the living room. The sun would be moving to the west side of the sky soon, and I was concerned that Grandmother would roast in that room with the big windows. So, I opened the door and stepped out to the road and checked the mailbox. There was a letter for me from Wendy. In it, she said she had met my boyfriend and that she was going to steal him from me. I could tell she was laughing at her own joke. I decided to go and write her a letter and send it before I forgot or didn't care anymore. I knew as soon as I put the pen on the paper that is the reason she had taunted me. It was to get me to write. So now I was the one laughing at her joke, and I wrote to her that I was glad she wrote and that I would hang out with her when I got home and even go to those funky dances that she said my boyfriend goes too. Then I told her that she could try to steal him it was ok with me. If he preferred her, I would be quite alright with it, but first, she had to figure out who he is. I stuffed the letter in an envelope and stamped it with a .02 stamp and rushed it back to the mailbox.

When I came back inside Great-grandmother had gone to her water closet. As I passed the kitchen, I asked her if she wanted to sit on the porch. She didn't answer me, so I went to check on her. She was standing over Uncle Williams box.

"Will you please put this in the living room with the other one. They will both fit on that shelf if you arrange the items carefully. Then we can sit in the garden. We will only have a few days to see the apricots. Brother Kimball will bring a group of youth over to pick them on Friday evening, Friday afternoon." She corrected herself and then she yawned. "Well, I sure *did* expect to be worn out from the trip to the cavern, but not this beat up. You'd think I was a hundred or something?" She chuckled at her own joke and I was amazed.

I set up the wicker folding chairs in the garden under the apricot tree and was immediately aware of the aroma. Great-grandmother had brought her cane with her, and as she walked, I could tell she was very weak. I helped her get comfortable and then I realized I might not get her back to the house if she was too weak to walk. I cautiously considered stopping her from going on with the tale but then I thought again and knew I would lose.

Then she continued, "In the beginning of our attempt to get statehood the boundaries of Deseret were huge. There were colonies of Saints from Oregon to Mexico and California to Oklahoma. We knew that the Government was pushing the Natives into Canada, so we didn't even push for the Dakotas', but we knew that to bare our righteousness we would need a gathering place. We believe in the literal gathering of Israel. There were colonies in Mexico where your grandmother Delories went which had already been established by Brigham Young and had been given his blessing and approval.

"Your Grandmother Delories had four other children staying with Lucy and Elizabeth Canfield Young in Florence Colorado. There had been so many raids that leaving the children with Brother John's other wives was safer than risking them being recognized and turned in for coming back home. So, that I could deliver her baby she had been staying with me and hiding out. In answer to your question: she could have fought to get them back which would have forced John out of hiding as well and risked getting all of them taken from her. The family that ended up with the two babies were not willing to trade visits with the children unless Delories surrendered Brother John. John hid in the cave, and William Walkara took him his horse. Your Grandfather then left for Colorado. He stayed in Florence for a few days and then moved the children and Lucy to New York. Elizabeth and Hooper would follow later when it was safe for Delories to travel.

"She spent ten years while in New York trying to find William and Vanessa, but they would not let her have her children. She was considered an 'unfit mother.' In the Utah state file, it was recorded that she had abandoned her children in October with freezing weather conditions and should not be allowed to have the older children because she was of 'unfit mind'.

"Utah administrative court issued a warrant that if any of her children were ever in the state of Utah they would immediately become wards of the state. A warrant was sent out for her arrest if she ever returned, with no expiration date on it.

"It didn't matter if she changed her mind the children would never be hers if she came back.

"In 1924 after twenty years of looking for her children and Brother John was dieing of cancer, she came home to see me. By then all of her other children were married. Danny was 34, Connie was 32, Fred was 30 and Alexandria May was 26. They all came here to see her and me before she left for Colonial Juarez. She wrote me all those letters and then five years ago, she came back. She lived thirty days after seeing me again and was buried in Juarez with the other martyred and slain defenders of the faith.

"I can see that you understand your Grandmothers sacrifice in leaving here to protect her other children, but do you see how staying in her belief made her sacrifice worth dying for.

"We were such a beautiful family before the Church decided that it wasn't enough to denounce the Law of Celestial Marriage, but you also had to "get rid of the wives you had."

"Since I'm on this part of the story let me finish something that is also missing in history.

"Brother John Willard Young was ten years old when he was ordained to the apostleship and later reconfirmed when he was twenty-four, in 1879. Many of the apostles had passed who served with his father.

But as the tide of succession was decreasing; a new policy was being created by the Administrative Board of the new Church of Jesus Christ of Latter-day Saints. In their organization, they had caused a political body of interest instead of an institution with religious possibilities. It is easier to understand this if you use a structure of a house to look at. You know what a foundation is?"

I nodded my head, yes.

"You know what footings are?"

I nodded my head again, yes.

"You know what cornerstones are?"

I stopped a half shaking, no.

"In a building, the cornerstones are set as the standard for the rest of the building they are placed on the footings. When you build a family or a business, you also have these structures. Joseph Smiths cornerstone principle of the gospel was Faith, that was placed first but what does it set on? It sets on the defined gospel of Jesus Christ from the beginning of time and all the new and every-lasting covenants of Celestial order. Those were the footings. When Joseph waited four years to receive his, "gift" the book of Mormon plates he had then proved that he had Faith. For four years, he was tested in his faith. He had to prove he could repent, repentance is the second cornerstone, he had to prove he could commit himself so he was baptized, baptism is the third, and he had to be confirmed, the fourth cornerstone is confirmation. The Savior and the Father laid their hands on his head and blessed him.

"These cornerstones are essential to the structure of the church. When they are removed, the footings remain as evidence that the structure existed, but to us, it was evidence that the Church had been changed. The foundation was destroyed when they changed from being"

"Called of God by vision and revelation to: (Policy).

"And from the primitive church to: (Idealism and conformity).

"From the gathering to Israel to: (Conquering all nations). "From the written word and doctrine of God to: (The Voice of the living prophet).

"The walls of our Church represent the privileges we have by living in principles and virtues, not in the standards and ideals of the society that creeps up on us.

"Our species the human has evolved and has been designed to evolve and by virtue of our determination we must have integrity and honor in all our dealings with mankind or we will destroy ourselves. We have conquered not by crowding our theories into other countries but by having an example worthy of following and living. Our ultimate weapon is cooperation and authentic communication, but we yielded to sensationalism and hypocrisy: empty promises and broken covenants.

"This was the order and the measure of the problem for us:

In order of those ordained to keep the original law alive:

1) Joseph Smith was ordained on April 6, 1830 until he passed on June 27, 1844.

2) Brigham Young ordained April 6, 1847 until he passed in 1877.

3) John Taylor ordained in April 6, 1880 until he passed 1887. Only ten years later.

4) Wilford Woodruff ordained April 6, 1889 until he passed in 1898. He died in San Francisco. He was ordained an apostle in 1833 he was the oldest living ordination at that time.

5) Lorenzo Snow ordained an apostle in 1849 and became a prophet by vote but not by ordination on April 6, 1898 until he passed 1901, up to this point all were sustained as Prophet in the April Conference. There were seven men alive at this point who qualified for president of the church, but only one would qualify by virtue of revelation and ordination for: <u>Prophet.</u>

"By ordination: and those still living in 1901: Lorenzo Snow ordained 1849, Franklin D Richards ordained 1849, John W Young ordained 1855, George A. Smith ordained 1855, Albert Carrington ordained 1870, George Q. Cannon ordained 1873, and Joseph F Smith ordained 1879.

"When Lorenzo Snow became Prophet of the Church there was no following of principle just a democratic vote. He was very old and by the time he died only three men John W. Young, Albert Carrington, and George Q. Cannon were left that could qualify for President or Prophet. When Hyrum Smith was the President of the Church, Joseph Smith was the Prophet. The Church changed doctrine to policy on April 1, 1901 and five days later Lorenzo Snow died they say it killed him. In five days, time the church went from a spiritually led institution to a politically governed organization. That's when your Great-grandfather John W. came up with the term "the committee".

"The church excommunicated Albert Carrington. Illiminating one of the qualified, saying he had commit adultery by not giving up his wives as was commanded.

"Then Joseph F. Smith accused John W. Young of financial fraud in 1889, and three different times afterward, and your grandfather was unanimously acquitted each time.

Brother Joseph F. Smith forced your great-grandfather John to resign his position on October 3rd, 1891 because he otherwise would bring further shame to his family by not devoulging the where abouts of his wives and childern. The only apostle left to fill the position of President or Prophet was George Q. Cannon he died April 2ⁿᵈ, 1901 in California before he could take leadership of the Church. It has been speculated that he was killed by these struggles and being forced to give up his beloved Gospel.

"Then the first President to become a prophet by vote and not ordination was Joseph Fielding Smith in October conference 1901.

"For the people who had been driven and persecuted for 70 years, there was now no virtue in suffering. The Church didn't just give up polygamy they gave up their foundation and their cornerstones.

CHAPTER 23

The Little Mansion: in Kaysville

On Wednesday after the trip to the cavern Great-grandmother had been very tired, but the next day Thursday I could hardly get her to respond to anything. She seemed to be processing out of this life and transitioning into the next. While she was resting most of the day I picked as many of the ripe apricots as I could and broke the pits out and laid them on a canvas drop cloth, in the west yard, on the concrete sidewalk. I knew they would dry and I could enjoy them as treats later.

About 3 o'clock Great-grandmother was standing in the doorway of the house watching me lay the fruit out. I asked her if she needed me. She said that she did not need me and that, she was inspired by my ingenuity. I completed the last three dozen halves and went into the house with her. She was using her cane in the house and I was aware that she was dizzy.

In the kitchen, we sat and ate some tuna-salad sandwiches and some cheese slices with cucumber wedges. She was more fragile than I had ever experienced her. I saw the skin around the eyes and her chin shrinking and turning grey.

"Great-grandmother," I whispered, "are you dehydrated?"

Her eyes were shut and her breathing was very labored. I went to the phone and called Uncle Samuel. He said he would be over in about 20 minutes and to not to worry. While I waited for him I started just talking to her.

"You know, Great-grandmother, about four years ago, I was a very happy, little, child, running along the Duchesne river and watching scorpions as they basked in the sun and the sandy benches around our land.

"I loved to watch the hawks and the horses, and I loved climbing trees to watch the world from a higher view.

"I fell in love with someone and I know that it is love because it doesn't change from time to time and I don't need anyone's approval. I feel connected to this love by my relationship to my Heavenly Father. I feel like He is the one who created my love."

I watched her closely as I spoke to her. She was sitting up-right and I was close enough that if she leaned one way or the other, I could catch her.

I continued with, "I know that I am a dreamer and a visionary or maybe ambitious, but my experience is similar to yours. I have never had the desire like other girls to even talk about boys or to carry on about the 'prince charming' and 'knight in shining armor'. What I do have is a desire to have a family and live in a place where our children experience the many challenges and opportunities given to us to grow and expand in the Universe and be very related to Mother Earth.

"I would like to travel someday to the stars or even be transported like Elijah on Ravens wings. I know that's a story but I love to see things from an eagle-eye view.

"And I would like to be loved in this life like you have been, so, I am going to keep my thoughts to myself and wait until the Lord reveals to my beloved one that I even exist."

She reached over and put her hand on my knee and said, "I know. You will be able to secure your love by owning every little bit of it.

"Will you help me get into my room? I would like to lie down. And yes, I am a little dehydrated. Please bring me some tea. And I would like you to tell Uncle Samuel and the doctor when they get here that I said, that I am going to be ok."

After she had comfortably situated herself on her bed, she said, "I would like you to write something down for me." I picked up her writing quill and her stationary and was set to write for her when she said, "Word for word, ok?"

I nodded my yes and we began,

"I, the Lord God of Israel, giveth no commandment unto the children of men, save I prepare a way for them."

She paused and quietly waited for me and then continued.

"In every Word of God there is a Way provided to fulfill on that Word. Seek and ye shall find and in finding ye shall know, in knowing ye shall live abundantly."

She waited for me again and then she very carefully pronounced each word, as if to say, 'get this especially'.

"Prepare every needful thing and establish a house, even a house of faith, a house of worship, a house of God."

She was breathing very slowly and as if she was snoring instead in breathing; it was rough again. I waited and she said, "That is all you need to know about moving forward in your life. It's all there in those few short and easy terms. Each of those houses have specific station and responsibility for growth and happiness. They are one inside the other, the people, then the study and then the ritual. You will understand as you grow and nurture your own Faith."

I heard the gravel stir in the driveway so, I told her they were here and she said that she knew. She asked me if I was afraid and I said, "Only that you leave me before we are complete with our journey together."

She said, "When I leave we will certainly be complete and you will have my spirit with you always."

When Uncle Samuel and the doctor came in I went to my room, shut the door, and knelt to pray. First I cried and then I prayed. In a very few minutes I was revived and went back to her door.

It was 6:15 when they left and I felt like I had worked in the sun all day.

I called my dad and talked to him for about 30 minutes and then to my mom. They both understood that there was no real threat and I was not afraid. But I slept beside her that night on her bed and waited for her to go Home, even though the doctor said her heart was perfect and her lungs sounded great: she was just worn out from the long walk back from the cavern, I felt like she was crossing over. In her dreams that night she talked to her family and mumbled about her boys and her girls. She cried and in the early morning she sat up gingerly and asked me to turn off the lights around the room and to help her into the water-closet. Then she requested some warm milk with honey and went back to sleep.

She woke at 6:00 sharp got up and knelt on her prayer bench. After prayers, we went back to sleep and both of us woke up at 9AM. I was about to make us some eggs and bacon when she asked me if I would make some pancakes. I said I would, and she instructed me as I made them, they were the best pancakes I had ever had, or ever have had since then.

With her appetite renewed I didn't feel worried anymore.

I changed the sheets in my bed and put out the laundry for Aunt Rachel to pick up. We were getting ready for Uncle William and my family to arrive. I was so excited.

I think I had dried about 15 or 20 pounds of dry fruit. Great-grandmother had been resting when Brother Kimball came in and asked if there was anything she needed. He also asked me if I was ok and I told him I could not be better and that I was having the time of my life. He saw the basket of dry apricots and he looked at Great-grandmother and said,

"I see you have great help. Would you like me to bring in some fresh one's for you?" She answered that she would and then we continued preparing for our company.

About 6:PM she was so chipper I thought yesterday wasn't even real. We knew that the families would arrive around 8:00 or 9:00 and we had a whole hour to talk. Aunt Rachel had picked up the laundry and now we only needed to wait.

Occasionally, I would go back through my journal and put words and little notes next to the things she had told me. When I started my

journal, I had the sentences separated by two or three lines; mostly out of habit, but as the days went by the uncalculated loss of words on each line became a blessing. Because I didn't have to rewrite everything or rip pages out I could keep my original manuscript and take it home with me.

I really needed the space after her next story!

She began, "I know you remember me having, confusion and anxiety over Brother Joseph, politely or conveniently forgetting that I purposed to him before he left on his mission to England in 1854, and that when he returned it was earlier then I had anticipated. I had been so grateful for Libby and my new and delighted conversations with Brother Joseph were all centered around the need we had not fulfilled in being sealed in the newly completed Endowment House and my desire to have Libby as a sister-wife.

"His expression was price-less when he heard my request the first time. We had gone on a picnic and I had just announced my up-coming pregnancy and considered that 'she' would be born around the 15th of December. I said that I would love to have Libby as much a part of our family as Sarah had wanted me. He shook his head up and down and then no, and he looked at me and said, 'Am I really, so hard to be with that you are looking for someone to pass me off to?'

"I knocked him over in the tall grass and sat straddled on his lean tummy. I looked in his eyes and asked, 'do you want me to be unfulfilled as a handmaiden in this life?'

"To which he rebutted by throwing me over onto the grass and pinning me down with his leg. 'I think you are a perfect handmaiden just the way you are! No improvement necessary! And I will bring Hannah and Sarah into your rouse.'

"I put my hand on his leg and tucked in tight against my side, which made him very cooperative and it took him off guard when I rolled easily to my right and pulled myself right-back-on-top. He was laughing so hard and said, 'We could do this all the way down the hill, if you want.'

"I told him that Sister Eliza had asked me to help out in the Endowment House for the month of May, he smiled like as if I had just made a joke, and I said, "Listen Mister Fielding you can be charming all day and even all night, but I on the other hand am far too serious for my age."

"Yes, you are my dear!' he replied.

"The Endowment House was beautiful. There were rooms for the ordinances and rooms for meetings. Brother Ward painted the walls to look like the creation of the Earth, and the Garden of Eden. It was the first building to have indoor water-closets.

"We were endowed and sealed on May 28th to Libby, with Myself giving her to Joseph and Sarah and Hannah being my support.

"I gave birth to Rachel Angelina on December 15th in the beautiful Millcreek home. Then we were called to Homestead in Southern Deseret. We had six other families that went down with us and there were already three other families in the area. Young Brother John was called by his Father, too help us establish a county-seat and set up a mayor.

"We started the homestead in March of 1860. Young Brother John was only 15 years old, but not a person who met him considered him under 21 years of age. He was tall, three inches taller than Brother Joseph, and so very handsome. He wasn't boastful or proud, but he was cocky and brave. He was so educated. I never saw him without a book in his pocket or hand. He loved from his birth the law and he was devoted to it like a desert. He was unequivocally trust-worthy. Brother Joseph would leave his entire family with Young Brother John for weeks and expect nothing less than full responsibility in his absence.

"I told you of Libby's first conception and her desire to bring Emily into the family and that after I had studied with the Medicine man, Libby had Victoria, we married Emily Cowdery and we were called to Kanab to start a homestead there. I had your Grandmother Sarah Delories in Kanab and Emily had several miscarriages down there. I told you about Duke's drowning."

I was nodding my head. "Yes."

"I told you how we all fit into this little mansion and how Brother Joseph was injured and died but what I haven't told you yet is how over time; after Sarah, had passed away and Hannah had moved to Ogden with her daughters: both of her sons died with-in 6 months after Brother Joseph passed away: Libby and Emily and I were so spiritually connected and apart of each other's space that we were often mistaken for each other. We could predict at almost the exact same time when Brother Joseph would be returning with a load or if one of the children was about to get hurt. We were very supportive of each other.

"I continued to deliver babies and to attend the sick while teaching in Nephi, in the fall of 1862. Libby was pregnant and delivered her second child Heber Joseph, on April 14th 1863. She stayed at home as I have said, and cared for the children with Rhea. Then we met and married, Rebecca Whitehorse in the Endowment House again in June of 1863. Rebecca stayed in Nephi until August of that year and then came to the Little Mansion to live when I was traveling so often to see Brother Joseph while he was in Salt Lake, from July to September.

"On April 30th Emily gave birth to her first-born Oliver Mangum, in June we married Rebecca Whitehorse, as I said, and on July 3rd Libby delivered Heber right here in this living room. On July 24th Brother Joseph was injured. In August, we found out Rebecca was pregnant.

"Libby got very ill in November, she passed away right here is this room as well, on December 15th and she is buried on the knoll in the East pasture under the one-and-only juniper tree. That was her only request. She did not want to be taken to Salt Lake to be buried she wanted to be near us. She died of a bacterium caused by infection in the breasts, called milk fever. I had not even felt the wound of her passing until I was looking down at her lovely little Heber 4 months old and my little Sarah, just beginning to walk, and Emily nursing Mangum 10 months old, and I knew I was pregnant again. I was 4 months and not showing.

"I went in my room and sat next to Brother Joseph on the bed and combed his hair with my fingers. I asked him if it was okay with him if I took a minute and cried. He smiled at me and nodded, 'Yes, my love, here is my big heart unload right here on me,' he directed my head to his amazing big chest and put his book down. I was sitting on the chair and leaned over and sobbed, while he gently hummed and caressed my back. When his shirt was thoroughly soaked, I got up and removed it along with his long garments and redressed him. He shuttered and shook with pain as I cared for him. Then I took his clothes to the wash room, where I cried further, silently so that he and the others would not hear me.

"We brought him here in September to stay hoping that my immediate attention would help with his recovery. When we had Libby's funeral Brother Joseph, was on a cot carried by the men. Hannah and her daughters and two sons came to the funeral and stayed for a week. During that stay Young Brother John and Brother Joseph toasted and make a sacred pack to love each other for ever and care for each other's children through eternity.

"Young Brother John was married to the Canfield sisters and Elizabeth had come with him for the funeral. They left here on 21ˢᵗ the weather was incredibly warm for December that year and it was likely that getting Hannah home would be eventless. Brother Joseph died 6 days later, on a Saturday night just as the sun was setting, we were celebrating the beginning of the new day. We took his body to Salt Lake and he was buried beside our boys in the City Cemetery.

"I hadn't told him I was pregnant but in the last letter he revealed to me, as you have read, that he knew and that no one could love or cherish me as Young Brother John would. Rebecca was also pregnant. Historically our marriage to Young Brother John was for Time and the people would not experience any resistance to our union until the Edmunds Tucker Law: 1885. When things started to get difficult Young Brother John was more informed than anyone except his Father and John Taylor.

We heard the gravel crunching and knew our first car of family had arrived.

It was my Uncle William. Great-grandmother informed him of his box and as he opened it he cried and handled each item as if it were a new baby bird. He had only known that Great-grandmother was his Grandmother and Mother for seven years. Every moment he spent with her was an unmeasurable gift.

The next set of tires would be my parents I thought, but it wasn't. William Walkara came to stay the night and Saturday to help with anything Great-grandmother could request.

When my dad pulled in, I was so excited. As soon as they stopped the car Mom handed me my new little brother. He was sleeping soundly.

Mom and Great-grandmother spent a few minutes talking. Great-grandmother told her story of her Father (John W. Young's) commitment to the principles of the Gospel and his ever-increasing desire to protect Brother Josephs family and his own.

Great-grandmother told mom how the home in New York had a magnificent wood-shop in the back and how Her Father would spend hours working the wood and the precious metals to craft things no one had ever seen, and how he could cut and shape stones to inlay them perfectly.

Inside mother's box was her mother, Delories, wedding ring: a very expensive set of diamonds with a half karat in the middle surrounded by four other smaller 1/8 karat diamonds, a beautiful diamond, sapphire and ruby hair piece like Great-grandmothers, her first swaddling blanket, and a blessing dress made for her that she never got to wear, a picture of Great-grandfather and her Mother who was obviously ready to deliver her, and little William on her father's shoulders.

My mother cried inconsolably for a while and then went to my room to feed my baby brother. Like Great-grandmother had predicted; Uncle William and his wife stayed in the boy's room upstairs. But mom wanted to see the hidden room.

My mother and father stayed in the sacred room that night. And although things in the world were not as nasty as they were 40 years ago, my family made a promise to not reveal the magic of their find to anyone, until after Great-grandmother had passed into the next life.

Saturday Jonny and I spent the whole day hiking and discovering the world we had found mysteriously tucked away from society. We swam in the cave and I got to tell him everything. After about five hours with him we were heading back to the Little Mansion when he quietly told me that Dad and Mom were looking into the 'Fullness of the Gospel' and that he had been to one of the meetings being held at Brother Jessop's house in Murray.

My family left again at 6PM leaving in time to be home and well rested before church.

CHAPTER 24

The American Road to Suffrage

Sunday, we went to Sunday-school but after the class we came home, and Brother Bensen had the brethren bring sacrament to Great-grandmother. Her fatigue and dizziness had not improved much and her determination to stay up-right until she was 'called' home was almost ridiculous, the ability to have sacrament served to her from home was considered an honor and a privilege. The brethren were kind and generous, asking several times if there was any way they could serve around the property.

Friday when William came by to stay the night he had set up a tipi in the back yard from poles from the barn and a large roll of canvas from the rafters. It had been used for many years previously but not recently.

Great-grandmother asked him to leave it up for a week. She said she would like to rest in it. Saturday afternoon Jonny and I had ventured into it and stood on the soft grass looking up at the star shaped crow's nest at the very top where one pole after another leaned toward the next. There was a long rope hanging down in center of the room making a swirl at the bottom in the grass. We laid down and looked up into the cathedral shaped expanse and started talking about what it was going to be like with Great-grandmother gone, and how we would get along without her deep-rooted history to ground us. We promised each other that we would not stop looking for the truth and that we would always look out for our parents.

Monday when I woke up Great-grandmother was not in her room. So, I pulled the apricots that I had laid out into the canvas cover and tied it up into a big knot, so that I could bring it into the house. She had said her prayers without me and gone back to sleep again, but I was not tired so I went to the cave. It felt like it was already 106* outside even though it was 7am.

It wasn't that she was missing from the bedroom that concerned me and I knew she wouldn't venture up the ladders without me. But that she had gone to the tipi on her own made me feel neglectful.

"Now don't you go chiding me or making yourself wrong, for not being here when I took off to do what I wanted. I'm not surprised that I feel so much better today and I think it will be the hottest day this year." She was so cheerful and radiant. I gave up my need to be scolded and took to helping her lift the sides of the canvas about 6 inches off the grass. She said it would create a draft and keep it cool in there most of the day.

She had set up her wicker chair and asked me to go gather the side-table and some apricots and tea for breakfast. By 10am she was head-long into the tail of her wounded neck. And I felt like I was at the theater.

"We have 23 days left to look all the stories worth the telling. Some of the things that you will sort out, in your life, will come from hours spent with me. And some of the stories we will talk about will cover history that very few have even heard.

"Abreast the long travels to get across the wilderness to the Great Salt Valley were strange encounters with hostile people. The Indians were hostile because they had been encroached upon and greatly lied to and mistreated. But like Red Sleeve and Red Cloud and Chief Joseph there were more red-men that were sensitive to the Mormon plight because they related to being driven from their homes and hunting grounds, they had women and children torn from their arms and they were left to suffer. One of the saddest and longest disputes over hostilities was the Mountain Meadow Massacre; the tragic and mortifying tale of murder and greed. It probably started with the poisoning of the water in Fillmore or Meadow and then continued with the pursuit of the infidels who tried to cause the upset in the first place. In the end the Mormon Militia and John D. Lee their captain was charged with the insight and John was executed in front of a firing squad. Most humans when pressed to that degree; and it doesn't matter their race, will retaliate. The slaughter took all the adult lives and left seventeen children family-less and broken about the wits. The poison was said to have been partly to blame for the story being told a different way by every person who was there and it was thought to have played a part in the tragedy of many Natives having been poisoned also. John Doyle Lee was sentenced to death on March 23, 1877 for the massacre which occurred in 1857

"When we left for the French and Spanish mission, Brother Joseph and I were aware that there were going to be heart aches and troubles for our families left behind. Hostilities occurred nearly every day. I was concerned about the ride from Salt Lake to Saint George, and that trip was taken almost every day by someone in the Church, but the possibility of being attacked was emanate. We had a bodyguard of two and a couple of great scouts that were sympathetic natives and friends.

"My concerns weren't just mine and many similar struggles of the same magnitude were being experienced around the world. There were also struggles in France and Italy. An audacious set of wars was going on with the Persians, in which Britain was trying to be a negotiator, or an ambassador for peace. But they were resented, and the countries were suspicious.

"In America, there was a constant struggle for the government to manage or hang onto the resources that people kept discovering. Bankers and investors had proudly exaggerated the amount of gold, grain and cotton they could produce and sell. Some of the bankers didn't recover the panic of 1857 until after the Civil War. We left for France feeling poorly set financially and yet sure that the Lord would provide.

"It seemed to me that every time a great new valuable resource came into existence there was a side-effect of greed and grandiosity to the point of devastation. In Kansas and Ohio, the iron rails were being set and the future of commerce appeared unstoppable. Terms like 'free soil' and slave trading were being considered for the first time as real and unrighteous dominion. The story of Dred Scott is one story that shook us up. Mr. Scott attempted to sue the supreme court for his freedom but because he was a black man the court ruled that he could not sue the American Supreme Court because he, being black, was not a citizen. This caused outrage not just in Missouri and Kansas but also it seemed to travel into Europe, and France. Everything tied together in a bundle the spot light was taken off the nasty hording of money and bingeing on luxuries that was ruling the upper class and driving a wedge between the struggling pioneers, and frontiersmen. Thousands of properties slipped into tax default and were mortgaging off the antiquities. The tariff imposed by America caused the panic of 1857 in France and though the French Empire was older and more stable it was very much affected as well.

"One of the out bursts and outrages of our stay in France was the beheading of Francis Richeux a robber and a murderer. He was set to a guillotine in the public square with over 12,000 people watching. I was mortified. We were there at that time, but I didn't go to the square nor do I agree with public execution, but the story was wild with noise and the brethren were using the atrocity to calm and gather folks for gospel lessons and encouragement: it gave good reason for people to gather to Zion.

Mademoiselles babies had snuck into the tipi and were playing in the shade with their tails and feet as little distractions and chewing morsels. I was sitting in the grass beside Great-grandmother watching them bounce and tumble about. They would crawl up me and try to get on my head and shoulders. Gently I would put them back in the grass beyond my feet and give them each other to fight and argue with but soon they would be discontent and want to get at my face and head again.

I was in the process of tumbling one down my front when Great-grandmother picked it up from off my shoulder and said, "I think this one is the smartest and most abundantly out spoken." She tipped it up, so she could look into its little eyes and scold it tenderly, when Mademoiselle sauntered in with three other little ones following her. Soon she had gathered them all and had moved to the far corner of the tipi to nurse them and to rest, cleaning her paws and their little faces.

Great-grandmother continued, "As I said there were so many things that could be considered distracting in the history of our Church and our Statehood." She continued as she turned and began her move toward the house.

We went into the kitchen and I set out some banana bread and butter with milk and some fresh baby carrots. We were talking about Mom and Dad's stay and how nice it was to have them in the Little Mansion and how much better I felt knowing that my mother was looking at her history with an open mind and no longer angry at her mother and father for being rebels.

Great-grandmother, started right where she left off,

"By the time, we came back from France the rails had been laid in the East, from the North to the South they called the steam engines "Puffing Billies" and the newer more powerful locomotives were called "iron horses". Heading across the plains in the Northern states was the beginnings of the Transcontinental and in the Southern States was the Southern Pacific, as well. Brother John Young was eager to get the rails laid in Deseret and had lobbied to have the roads improved too. By 1867 we had managed to have the Utah Central Railroad coming into Nephi and passing just to the east of the property here. You could almost set your watch to it: every day at precisely 8:20 AM and 4:35 PM.

"I had much experience with trepidation having traveled so much by the time I was 27 years old. When the opportunity to travel with the woman defending the 'right-to-vote' came I was ready to attend the masses and represent a state of brilliant and well-informed Deseret Queens. Being well spoken in three languages and fluent in Latin and German made me a desirable and valuable resource.

APPENDIX

1. <u>The Leather Wallet Contents</u>

    A. Jonathan William Davis Watch
    B. Tickets from London to Port James N.Y
    C. Train tickets from Port James to Jersey City
    D. Gold Coin minted in 1840

2. <u>The Pink-flower Papered Box</u>

    A. 72 Pictures
    B. 3 patriarchal blessings

3. <u>The Old Blue Denim Box</u>

    A. The key from Gran Hotel Paris
    B. Military papers for John Young Sr. circa 1700
    C. Tickets to King Lear in London
    D. Tickets to the Odeon-de l'Europe Opera in Paris
    E. Certificate of Approval for Science of Botany
    F. Certificate of Approval for Science of Herbs
    G. Tickets to the Ballet on Broadway
    H. Title to Kaysville Property

I. License for Mayor of Juab
J. Gold Bonds for Silver Mine
K. Gold Bonds for Copper Mine
L. Gold Bonds for Granite Quarry
M. Certificate of Graduation from BYU
N. Train Tickets from Washington D.C. to Texas 1879
O. Certificate of Ownership of Union Pacific Railroad partnership with John W Young
P. Will of John W Young
Q. Fathers Seven Wives (playwright)
R. Lullaby: *Primrose and Lavender*, by May Constance Alexandria Young; 1876
S. Song: *Thou Art Worthy*, by May Constance Alexandria Davis; 1942
T. Voters Identification Card 1946
U. Railroad Pass

BIBLIOGRAPHY

100 years of Hollywood: Time Life Magazine, 1999

500 Little-Known Facts in Mormon History: George W. Givens, 2002

A History of Duchesne County: John D Barton; 1998

A History of Uintah County: Doris Karren Burton; 1996

An Enduring Legacy: Daughters of the Utah Pioneers; Vol. 1 thru 11

Blood of the Prophets Brigham Young and the Massacre at Mountain Meadows: Will Bagley; 2002

Building Zion: Thomas Carter; 2015

Discovering America's Past: Reader's Digest

Early Mormon Documents: Dan Vogel, 1996

Essentials in Church History: Joseph Fielding Smith 1922

Gandhi an Autobiography: Sissela Bok; 1957

Gentleman, Scholars, and Scoundrels: Harper's Magazine 1850 to Present; 1915

Hidden History of Utah: Hallet Stone

Historical Atlas of Native American; Dr. Ian Barnes; 2011

Historical Atlas of the United States: National Geographic; 1988

Historical Atlas of the United States: The Centennial Edition

Historical Vignettes: Institute Self-Instruction Course, 1992

History of United States During Joseph Smith's Time;

Indian Depredations in Utah: Peter Gottfredson; Fenestra Books 2002

Los Angeles Times: Front Page; 100 Years 1881-1981, 1980

Mary Queen of Scotland and the Isles: Stefan Zweig; 1937

Millennial Star: Church of Jesus Christ of LDS, Vol.s 1938-1941

The End of Traditional Religion and the Rise of Christianity: Pagans: James J. O'Donnell; Harper Collins 2015

Quest of a Hemisphere: Donzella Cross Boyle

Rough Stone Rolling;

She Walks in Beauty: Siri Mitchell; 2010

Teachings of Presidents of the Church: Church of Jesus Christ of LDS, 2012

The Archos Volume: Dr. McIntosh and Twyman; 1929

The Articles of Faith: James E. Talmage; 1890

The History of the Jews: Paul Johnson; 1987

The Koran: N.J. Dawood; 1919

The LeBaron Story: Verlan M. LeBaron, 1981

The Remarkable Journey of the Mormon Battalion: Michael N. Landon 2011

The Women of Mormondom: Edward W. Tullidge, 1877

The Words of Joseph Smith: Andrew F. Ehat, 1980

Utah Historical Quarterly: Utah Historical Society

Utah the Right Place: Thomas G Alexander: 1999

The New Enchantment of America Utah: 1979

ACKNOWLEDGMENTS

Afton Thomas

Jean Bennion

Belinda Collins

Fern Powell

Kim Singer

Publisher: